THE HARLOW BROTHERS

book two

BRIE PAISLEY

Brie Paisley

This book is a work of fiction. Any names, places, character names, establishments, locations, or incidents are the work of the author's imagination and is used fictitiously. If any resemblance to actual persons, dead or alive, places, locations, establishments, or events are coincidental.

Copyright © 2017 by Brie Paisley

All rights reserved. This book is not to be copied, shared, or produced in any way without the written consent of the author.

Cover art by Rebecca Marie of The Final Wrap

Edited by Karen Mandeville-Steer of Karen's Book Haven Editing Services

Proofread by Nikki Reeves of Saints and Sinners Books

Formatted by Brenda Wright of Formatting Done Wright

Photograph and photography by Christopher Correia of CJC Photography

Cover model: Jonny Sobel

Cover model: Alli Theresa

Other books by Brie Paisley:

Worshipped series

Worshipped-book one

Betrayed-book two

Redeemed-book three

The Harlow Brothers Series

Carter-book one

Caleb-book three (coming soon)

Carter and Shelby: Ever After (coming soon)

Standalone Novels

Temptation

Addiction (coming soon)

Heartless (co-writing with Nikki Reeves-coming soon)

acknowledgements

Okay, I'm going to get a little sappy for a moment. I have so many amazing people to thank, but I don't want to forget anyone. Instead, I'm making this thank you for all of you. Firstly, I would not be here, doing what I love, if it were not for you, the reader. Thank you for taking a chance on me. I honestly don't have enough words to express how grateful I am for you wanting to read my books. I hope you love it as much as I did while writing it and thank you again from the bottom of my heart for reading.

Secondly, to the wonderful ladies in my fan group. Thank you for sticking by me when things weren't going so well. Thank you for keeping me sane, and for all the laughs. Thank you for the naughty posts as they were highly appreciated. You guys are absolutely amazing, and the love and support each, and every one of you show me, is awesome. Ladies, you keep me going, and for that, I cannot thank you enough.

To my beta team, thank you for reading and giving me the wonderful feedback. Thank you for your honesty and wanting to help make Caden the best. To my review team, you ladies rock it. I'm so glad to have such an amazing group willing to read and review for me. It really means the world to me.

I can't forget about my lovely ladies from Saints and Sinners Books. Thank you so much for going above and beyond to make Caden's cover reveal and release day such a success. From all the hard work y'all did, down to tagging me in each post, I can't thank you enough. You ladies are the best.

Thank you to my amazingly talented cover designer. Caden's cover is absolutely stunning, and it's always a pleasure working with you.

A big thank you to Christopher Correia for capturing the perfect photo for the cover. You're so talented, and I cannot express how thankful I am for everything you did to make sure I had the right picture. You're amazing to work with, so kind and sweet, and I can't wait to work with you again. To the models, Jonny Sobel and Alli Theresa, both of you are such an inspiration. I couldn't have picked anyone else to fit the characters so perfectly. It was a pleasure working with both of you, and I can't wait to plan more books with you.

Brie Paisley

To my brilliant and ever patient editor, as always, your suggestions were great. You've helped me with so much, and of course helped me learn what to do and what not to do. It's always a pleasure working with you.

I know I said I wouldn't name anyone, but it's needed with this thank you. Nikki, thank you so very much for supporting me and helping me so much when I needed it. You always cheer me on, giving me the courage to step out of my comfort zone, and I really have no way of thanking you enough. You've been there for me from the very beginning, and I'm so glad I have you on my team. Thank you again for everything you do, no matter how small it may seem.

Last but not least, thank you to my husband. Thank you for your support and telling me more than once how proud of me you are. The support and love you give me every single step of the way means more to me than you know. Thank you for understanding when I disappear for days, and the housework slips. You've always understood me, and I love you for that. Thank you, babe, for being everything I need.

Caden

Water Under the Bridge by Adele

All of Me by John Legend

Mercy by Shawn Mendes

Love On the Brain by Rihanna

Issues by Julia Michaels

Cold by Maroon 5 feat. Future

Influence by Tove Lo feat. Wiz Khalifa

Stay by Zedd & Alessia Cara

Cheap Thrills by Sia

Close by Nick Jonas feat. Tove Lo

Free Bird by Lynyrd Skynyrd

Brie Paisley

Summertime Sadness by Lana Del Rey & Cedric Gervais

Without You by Sixx:A.M.

In the Name of Love by Martin Garrix & Bebe Rexha

Can't Hold us by Macklemore & Ryan Lewis feat Ray Dalton

Don't Leave by Snakeships &MO

The Bliss by Volbeat

Party Monster by The Weeknd

Just Hold On by Steve Aoki & Louis Tomlinson

Lost in You by Three Days Grace

Without You by Three Days Grace

Ship of Fools by Flyleaf

Devotion by Ellie Goulding

Hearts Without Chains by Ellie Goulding

Everything Changes by Staind

M.I.N.E. (End This Way) by Fiver Finger Death Punch

Table of Contents

Prologue: Savannah 13
Chapter One: Savannah 17
Chapter Two: Caden.. 28
Chapter Three: Savannah... 51
Chapter Four: Caden 64
Chapter Five: Savannah 79
Chapter Six: Caden... 111
Chapter Seven: Savannah 129
Chapter Eight: Caden 136
Chapter Nine: Savannah 148
Chapter Ten: Caden 160
Chapter Eleven: Savannah 173
Chapter Twelve: Caden 199
Chapter Thirteen: Savannah 212
Chapter Fourteen: Caden.. 224
Chapter Fifteen: Savannah....................................... 236
Chapter Sixteen: Caden... 257
Chapter Seventeen: Savannah 282
Chapter Eighteen: Caden 290
Chapter Nineteen: Savannah 315
Chapter Twenty: Caden 332
Chapter Twenty-One: Savannah 360
Chapter Twenty-Two: Caden 384

Brie Paisley

Chapter Twenty-Three: Savanah............................... 392
Epilogue: Caden 423

dedication

Thank you J.T. and Nikki for providing me with so many stories and inspiration for Caden's book. I hope I did those funny stories justice, and thank you both for all your support.

Love y'all.

Brie Paisley

Caden

Everything I've ever known has been based off a lie.

I remember the exact moment my entire world changed, and that moment changed everything about my life. I hadn't realized the truth could alter so much that I never thought possible. The people I trusted the most lied to me and now the truth is out, it can't be undone. The truth is much worse than their lies. To be honest, I wish they would have never told me their secret. If they hadn't, I wouldn't be questioning everything about my life, my family, or even myself. I wouldn't have gone so long feeling as if they betrayed me, and I can't lie and say they didn't break my trust. Not a day goes by that I don't wonder what could've been or how my life would've turned out had I never known I was adopted.

I was sixteen when my parents told me the truth. Before the truth came out, I was shy, quiet, and the good girl. But afterward, I changed into someone I didn't recognize. Their news devastated me in ways I never thought possible, and I wasn't the same young woman I thought I was. Drinking and drugs became my means of coping, and I can't even count the times I've been in trouble for it. No amount of talking or counseling helped. After my parents told me, I could see the differences in us. Like how I didn't look anything like my mom who has strawberry blonde hair to my dark brown, or like my dad's brown eyes to my bluish green ones. Both my parents are tall while I'm short. Not to mention, I've never once seen a picture of myself as a newborn. The thing is I was happy with not knowing. I didn't want to know, but I was forced to see what was staring right at me my entire life. After the truth, my once simple life turned into chaos. I didn't know how to deal with it. I didn't understand why my parents lied to me my whole life, and why they finally decided to open up about my birth. The worst part about it is that they had no idea how much the truth would hurt. Not only am I dealing with my parent's lies, but now I have this gaping hole inside of me.

Caden

I don't belong anywhere because no one seems to know where I come from or who my mother is. What's worse is the fact I have so many questions I'm dying to figure out. Questions that plague me every single second of the day. I don't know her name, how old she is, or what she even looks like. Does my biological mother even know my name? Did she just give me away because she didn't want me? Was I a mistake? These questions have been circling around in my head for years. My parents wanted me to wait until my eighteenth birthday, before they would give me anything to go on. I've been so angry with them for dropping a bomb like this on me, but yet they chose to make me wait for the answers I needed. I know my parents love me. They're loving, caring, and they would do anything for me. But at the same time, I have to know why my biological mother gave me up. Why didn't she want me? Why didn't my parents want me to find her until it was the right time for them? I secretly searched for over a year for the answers I so desperately craved, but it seemed at every turn I hit a wall. Every lead I thought would get me closer to the woman that gave me away ended abruptly. Eventually I gave up, thinking I would never find her. I didn't do it willingly. No, it's because I had no hope left in me.

My second year of college, I'd finally got a break in my search. My adoptive father was the one that handed me the key to finding who my biological mother was, and I know he did it so I could move on. At the time, I thought I was hiding the pain of not knowing my birth mother or how I was handling it. But Dad and Mom knew of the downward spiral I was still on, and honestly I don't think I could've stopped myself if he hadn't helped me. The smart thing to do was to finish my college degree, but I was eager to find the truth. At twenty-two, I left behind my friends and family to chase after a woman that probably never wanted to meet me. Mom and Dad both warned and pleaded with me to let it go, but the thing is I couldn't. I love my mom and dad. I'm grateful for everything they've ever done for me, and even though I knew everything I did, I still packed my bags and left for the small town in Mississippi.

I don't know what Columbus, Mississippi has in store for me or if it will have the answers I'm searching for, but I have to try. Dad gave me a copy of her driver's license, and I'm determined to find Tammy Richards and all the answers she knows. It's only a matter of time before I finally know the truth, and then maybe, just maybe, I'll be free.

Caden

one
Savannah

Three weeks have passed since I got to Columbus Mississippi, and I've yet to find any information regarding the mysterious Tammy Richards. It's as if she doesn't exist, and each day that goes by, I find my will to keep looking dwindling. I've Googled her, looked through several newspaper clippings, and I've even thought about putting an ad in the local paper just to help me narrow down my search. It just seems either Tammy doesn't want to be found, or she doesn't live here anymore. And every single day before work, I sit in front of the courthouse. I went inside the huge building on Main Street once, but yet again it was another dead end. It's not easy finding a person that I have no information on, or the fact I can't even prove that I'm her daughter. Although I understand I can't get personal information on her without legal help, it's frustrating that I keep hitting that damn wall I had before I came here. This is why I decided to find a job at the local bar close to the hotel I'm staying at, until I can hopefully find the answers about my birth mother. Staying at The Holiday Inn isn't exactly helping my savings account. I have my adoptive parents to thank for giving me the funds to make this uneventful trip, but I also know it hurt them knowing I wouldn't be happy until I found what I'm looking for.

Looking out the window of the rental car, I let out a deep sigh wishing I knew how to make my parents understand. After they told me about my adoption, it seemed as though everything about myself clicked into place. For as long as I can remember, I always felt … different, but never really understood why. I had friends and loving parents, but I felt as if a part of me was missing. I thought since learning about my birth mother things would change, and I wouldn't feel this gaping hole inside of me. If anything the hole has grown, and the longer I go without finding who Tammy Richards is the bigger the hole will get. It scares me not knowing if I'll ever be complete. If I could just find the ever elusive Tammy, just maybe I can move on with my life.

I will say, Columbus isn't all bad. Glancing around Main Street, I feel a strange sense that I'm where I'm supposed to be. It sounds crazy, and I question this feeling every day, but something deep down is telling me I'm where I need to be. It's partly

Caden

why I sit in the same spot every day for hours just waiting for fate to give me something to go on. Granted it's humid here, but the people I've met are so welcoming. Even now as I have the air conditioner running, I feel the sweat under my armpits. Maybe it wasn't such a great idea to move here at the beginning of May, but I couldn't stop myself from coming once Dad gave me the small shred of information I'd been looking for. Maybe fate or some higher power is in play here. I also like the busy streets of downtown, but yet I like the smallness of it. It's not a huge city by no means, but it's just enough to feel at ease and home. Even if I'm still new to the area, everyone I've met always greets me with a southern twangy hello, and one lady even hugged me once. They're complete and total strangers, but somehow they don't feel like strangers. Growing up in Florida wasn't bad either, but the environment here is so different than I imagined. The air isn't as salty, the people always seem to have a cheerful vibe about them, and the food is unbelievably amazing.

With all the good surrounding me, there's still a deep sense of longing I've yet to fill. It's as if something is missing, or like a part of me isn't whole. It's hard to explain a feeling without knowing the cause, and that just makes the feeling worse. Since finding out I was adopted, thoughts of finding my birth mother have consumed me, and I have high hopes that this part that's missing will be filled once I find her. Huffing out another breath, I glance at the dash clock wondering if I should go back to my hotel room. I've been sitting here for hours, even though I know the answers I seek aren't here and even if they are, I can't get them. My phone begins to ring, and I'm grateful for the distraction. A smile crosses my face as I see my best friend, Kelsey Bennett, calling. "How did you know I needed to hear your voice?" I ask, relaxing back into the seat.

"What can I say? I must be psychic."

Shaking my head, I respond. "That has to be it."

"Are you doubting my mad psychic skills, Savvy?"

I roll my eyes and let out a huff. "No, I'm not doubting you. You're my bestie for a reason." Kelsey and I have been friends since elementary school. She might as well be my sister from another mother because we did everything together. We even went to the same college for our art degree. She went for painting and mine was for photography. Kelsey has always supported me and my search for my birth mother. She and I attended the same college for a while, but once she decided to move to New York to attend a different college, we did lose touch for a year. Once we reconnected, it was as if we never stopped talking. "How are you? Still cooped up in

Caden

that small apartment you call home?" Once Kelsey and I started speaking again, she told me why she closed herself off from the world so much. On her twentieth birthday, she was brutally attacked, and she's never been the same.

"Don't hate on my apartment." She's quiet for a moment, and I wonder if she's really alright. Before I have a chance to ask her, she says, "I'm fine. No need to worry about me. Plus I have Kayleigh if I need anything since you're in the Deep South."

Kayleigh is Kelsey's older sister and recently got married to her high school sweetheart. "I know Kayleigh is watching out for you, but I still worry. I wish you would take me up on my offer and come down to see me."

She huffs and I know she's irritated with me. Kelsey hates when I bring up anything with her leaving New York. Even if I know she hates it there, I also know she's terrified to leave her apartment. Since her attack, she's developed agoraphobia. I hate she's so afraid to literally leave her home, and I wish there was something more I could do for her. "We've talked about this, Savvy. I can't leave."

"But you can, Kel. You're the one that's stopping yourself. If you would just –"

"It's not that I can't." She snaps. "I want to go outside and not have a panic attack. I miss the sun.

I miss feeling the wind on my face, and a million other things. I've tried to get over this fear, but I can't."

"I'm sorry, Kel. I know you want to get over your fear. I just hate knowing you're suffering."

"It's no big deal. Kayleigh and my parents are always on my ass about it."

Feeling guilty, I change the subject hoping to take her mind off me being inconsiderate. "What about your art show? How did it go?" Kelsey's mood immediately changes, and I know it's because of her art. It's her one passion, and she puts her heart and soul into. There's no doubt in my mind that she's still doing something she cares for. It's present in the tone of her voice and the way she describes her most recent painting. It's as if I can see it right in front of me. Even with her agoraphobia hanging over her, Kelsey still manages to deliver every time when she has an art show. Granted it's a bit unconventional how she does it, but with the modern technology, she makes it work. She explained it once to me, and from what I gathered, it's similar to going live on Facebook or like Skype. I'm also glad she has a wonderful agent that cares for her needs and respects her enough to do whatever possible to make Kelsey comfortable.

"I wish you would've been there, Savvy. It was amazing."

Caden

Hearing the happiness in her voice makes me smile, and I know even if I worry a lot about my bestie, she'll be fine. "When is your next one? Maybe I can come up and spend some time with you." It's not like things are going as well as I'd hoped here, but I don't say that to her.

"Are you serious? Savvy, I would love for you to come see me."

I begin to answer her, but I frown as I notice a cop car pulling up behind me. My heart drops when I see the flashing red and blue lights. It's sort of ironic how the colors of our flag, the symbol of our freedom, is the same color as someone who could take that freedom away. Watching the police officer step out of his vehicle, I begin to panic. I haven't had the best past with cops, and my mind begins to race. "Kel, I have to go."

"But wait Savvy. I didn't ask you about your birth mother."

"I'll call you later," I snap and hang up the phone just as the officer reaches my window. Tossing my cell in the passenger seat, I swallow hard as I roll the car window down. "Is there a problem, Officer?" Trying to keep my voice steady, the last thing I want is for him to think I'm nervous. Which I am.

He leans on the car, and I swallow again at his closeness. "License and registration, please."

I scramble to get him everything he needs, and I push my shades up on my head as I hand him my information. "I wasn't doing anything wrong," I say defensively. I can't help myself. With my past, the police and I haven't had the best relationship. As he glances over my license, I look him over. His all black uniform does fit him quite nicely, and it compliments his dark brown hair. It's shaved on the sides but longer on the top. It reminds me of a military cut, but not as short. He's certainly tall as I have to lean my head to the side to get a good look at him, and once I start back down, I notice his name tag reads C. Harlow. He moves back some, and I swear it looked as if he just flexed his arm for me. *Did he know I was checking him out?*

Feeling my face redden, I turn away as he says, "Not from around here I see." Instead of stating the obvious, I stay silent. I've gotten into trouble more than once with my smart ass comments, so it's best to keep my mouth shut. "Well, Savannah Owens of Destin Florida, I've driven by this spot three times today, and you've been here. Planning some kind of heist on the courthouse?"

"What?" Shaking my head, I try to explain. "No, I ... I would never. I'm ... I'm just ..." He begins

Caden

to laugh, and I frown. Is he making fun of me? "This isn't funny."

He lifts his sunglasses on top of his head, handing back my information as he says, "You should've seen your face."

It takes me a second to get my bearings as I take notice of his smile and his bright blue eyes. For a split second, I forget where I am, why I'm here, and the fact he's making fun of me. Shaking myself out of whatever the hell that was, I narrow my eyes at him. "Do you always prank innocent bystanders?"

"Actually, I do. It's part of my southern charm."

More like arrogance. "Am I free to go? Because I have lots to do."

"Are you sure you're not planning anything illegal? Because I'll have to take you downtown if you are."

"What makes you think I'd tell you if I were?"

"Sassy. I like it."

I roll my eyes, but I can't help but grin. "More of your charm?"

"Why, yes. I'm so glad you noticed." He leans his arm on the car, and I have to suck in a breath as his handsome face crowds me. Oh, he smells good too. Our eyes lock, only for a moment, and my stomach flutters with a million butterflies. What the hell is going on? I've seen my fair share of attractive men, but there's something about this one ... I can't put my finger on what, but he's different. "Are you sure you're not from around here? I swear I know you from somewhere."

"Uh, no. I just got here three weeks ago."

His eyes never leave mine, but I look away first. It's too intense with the way his blue eyes penetrate mine. "Newbie for sure then." He starts to say something more, but his radio on his shoulder starts talking. It startles me, and I feel my face flush when I hear him laughing again. I don't catch what I assume is the dispatcher says, but he answers back quickly then turns his attention back to me. "It was nice to meet you, Savannah Owens. I'll see you around."

Watching him slowly back away in my rear view mirror, I stare as he gets inside his squad car. As he drives by, I stupidly watch him more knowing he'll see me. Grinning when he waves at me, I let out a huff as he drives past. My heart is still beating a mile a minute, but I don't understand why. Or why I felt as if he promised me something. Pushing C. Harlow out of my mind, I push my sunglasses down and start the rental. Deciding to chill in my hotel room before work, I make my way there. It's normally a depressing trip back knowing I didn't get any new

Caden

information on my birth mother, but this time it's different.

The way Officer Harlow said my name whispers in the back of my mind. It's like a caress with his deep and husky voice, and the way he said he'll see me later makes me wonder if I really will.

Or if I even want to.

Two

Caden

It's been two days since meeting Savannah Owens, and I can't seem to get her out of my mind. No matter what I do, she's always there. There's just something about her that seems familiar, but I can't put my finger on what it is. If I'm honest with myself, I don't want to admit what I already know. Not to mention, her blue-green eyes seem to call to my very soul. It was weird as fuck, but I brushed it off not thinking much of it. I can't deny she's a mystery. She was evasive and seemed nervous when I approached her. It also put a damper on my ego knowing my charm didn't really seem to faze her. Which I find very attractive. Not tootin' my own horn, but I'm used to the women around here flocking to me. Kind of reminds me of the bug zapper Mama has on her back porch. They fly and attach themselves

Caden

to me knowing I'll zap them. Okay, maybe that's a bad analogy, but it's the only thing I got.

"If you keep frowning like that, your face is going to get stuck that way." I look up across the table and smile at Mama. She knows best, so she could be right.

Just like every morning during the weekday, my brothers and I come over to have breakfast with our parents. It's been this way since we all grew up and moved out, but I don't mind coming here like we all do. It's nice to spend time with my mom and dad. It's also not bad to hassle my brothers. Carter is the oldest and followed in Dad's footsteps with becoming a lawyer. Then it's Cason and me, but I'm the older one. Cason is my identical twin, and he owns his own gym while I work at the police station. Clark is next and is the military because he wants to be a knockoff of Superman. Oh, and I can't forget oops baby. Caleb is the youngest and was literally an oops baby, but he's smarter than anyone I know, and as much as I like to pick on him, I'm ready for him to return home from college. Speaking of my brothers, I have no idea where any of them are. "Where is everyone?" It's not like Carter, Shelby, his long-lost sweetheart, Cason, and Clark not to be here. Clark just got back from a deployment, but he's always around since returning home in March. Caleb, the youngest, actually has a good reason for not being here since he's finishing up his last few weeks at MIT. Mama's face falls, and it makes my stomach churn knowing it upsets her that either my brothers forgot, or they're just being assholes. "How about I call them?"

"It's fine, sweetheart. I'm sure they're just busy."

Watching Dad place a hand on Mama's, I shake my head and stand up. "I'll get them here. It's our tradition." Winking at Mama, I bite my tongue instead of saying what I really want. If I do, Mama will get that stupid wooden spoon out and beat my ass with it. She's done it so many times over the years for my potty mouth, as she likes to call it sometimes. Walking outside, I pull out my phone and decide to start with my twin, Cason.

As the line begins to ring, I see Clark pull up in the driveway. He quickly jumps out of his truck and runs toward the house. I glare at him as he walks past me and says, "Don't start. I'm here, alright."

Shaking my head when I smell the alcohol on his breath, I wonder if he's drinking all hours of the day. Clenching my jaw, I hold back my lecture about him drinking and driving. Deciding to wait and pick my battle with him another time, I stay silent. Something is up with him, and it's beginning to piss me off how he's shutting himself off from me, and the entire family. Hearing the door slam behind me, Cason finally decides to answer. "I'm coming."

Caden

"Well hello to you too, Mr. Cranky Pants."

Laughing as I hear him swear under his breath, Carter and Shelby arrive. "I swear, Caden. For once can you not act like an ass?"

"That really hurts when you call me that."

"I'm beginning to think you like it. I'll be there soon." Letting out an annoying grunt, I stare at my phone realizing he hung up on me. My own twin hung up on me. What. A. Douche.

"It's about time y'all got here," I yell at Carter and Shelby as they get out of Carter's truck. Neither one of them seem to be in a hurry, so I yell out again. "Food is gettin' cold."

"Caden, leave them alone and get back in the house." Hearing Mama's stern tone, I huff wondering why I'm always the one getting in trouble. Pocketing my phone, I do as I'm told like I'm a teenager again.

Walking back to the kitchen table, I take my spot next to where Cason will sit, and across from Clark. Dad is asking Clark what he's going to do about his decision to retire from the military, but Clark doesn't seem to want to talk about it. Typical Clark. I love all my brothers, but for some reason Clark has shut down on all of us. It worries me that I don't know what to do or how to help him. Just as I'm about to comment on something Clark says to Dad, I turn when I hear Mama, Carter, and Shelby walk to the table. Carter tells Mama a lame excuse as to why they were late, but I'm not sure I believe the whole flat tire story. Shelby sits by Mama, and of course Carter takes his usual spot by Shelby. I glance away from the two love birds as they show off some PDA, and my chest constricts knowing I want that. Not with Shelby, that's just ... ew, but I want the love they have. Carter and Shelby have the epic type of love everyone can see and craves to have. Even me. We all grew up around each other, and I knew once Shelby came into our lives that they would end up together. I've never seen Shelby as anything more than a sister, and we all knew her and Carter would never be apart. Granted it happened much later in life due to Shelby's conniving mother, but it all worked out in the end. There was a time I worried a lot about Carter. It was after Shelby ran off to South Carolina once, Carter left for college. It was dark times back then, but once Shelby returned home, I knew they would reconnect. Now I'm just waiting for Carter to pop the question. I know it's going to happen soon, and I couldn't be happier for my oldest brother.

I just want what he and Shelby have.

Epic love.

I'm not jealous by any means, but there comes a time in every man's life that he craves something more, and I'm at that point. It happened

Caden

back in March at Clark's welcome home party. It seems like a lifetime ago, but I remember every detail, every word, and especially how Carter watched Shelby so intently. Seeing how enthralled Carter was and how happy he seemed, something inside of me sort of snapped. It was as if all the puzzle pieces finally fit together, and I just knew what I'd been missing out on. Then meeting Sassy Savannah Owens hasn't helped.

Feeling my twin walking up behind me, I push all these thoughts out of my mind. I always know when Cason is nearby, and sometimes it's like we can read each other's minds. It's strange at times, but I shared a womb with him, so I don't question it. Cason takes his spot by me as he says to everyone, "Sorry I'm late. Flat tire."

"Flat tire, huh? You mean like Carter and Shelby with their flat tire?" I say as I wiggle my eyebrows. Cason shakes his head as I turn and laugh as Shelby's face turns bright red. Yeah, flat tire my ass. I knew Carter was telling a big fat lie with that one.

"Caden, what have I told you about that kind of talk at the table?"

"I'm just kiddin', Mama. Geez can no one take a joke around here?"

"Just keep that mouth of yours shut, Caden," Carter scolds.

"I'm definitely feeling all the love this mornin'," I pipe back sarcastically. Mama gives me a look, and I know she's threatening me silently about her whooping spoon, while Carter goes back to fixing his plate. Dad and Clark say nothing because this is normal for us. Shelby leans over to Carter as she whispers something, and I clench my teeth feeling that same damn pang in my chest. Sensing Cason again, I glance up to his bored stare. "What? Mr. Cranky Pants have something to say?" I can't help but rile him up. He's always so tense, and I know exactly how to push his buttons.

His eyes narrow and fuck. That's not a good sign. He's trying to read me, and I know he'll know I'm hiding something. That and I've confided in him about my feelings. Ugh. Men shouldn't say that word. "Still hung up on that girl you pulled over two days ago?" Damn my twin and our stupid bond.

I don't get a chance to say a word before Mama says, "What girl?"

Then Shelby adds, "When can we meet her?"

Huffing out a breath, I grab a biscuit and toss it at Cason. "Don't throw food at your brother," Dad says sternly.

Caden

Cason takes the biscuit and takes a bite before demanding, "Tell them, Caden. I'm sure they would love to know all about her."

"Well now I have to meet her," Shelby says excitedly.

Clenching my jaw and becoming annoyed with Cason, I wish he would've kept his mouth shut because this is why I haven't said anything. I love my family dearly but damn. Is it so bad I don't want to be picked apart? "It's nothin'. Just some chick I met two days ago." Carter starts to say something, but I beat him to it. "And no. I didn't sleep with her."

"Caden," Mama starts.

"I know. I know. No trash talk at the table."

"Seriously, Caden. Who is she?" Carter asks, and as I glance up, it's as if he and I share a twin bond. It feels eerie that I can see what he's thinking just by the look in his eyes.

"She's just a girl," I state hoping they'll drop it.

"She's not just any girl," Cason says to Carter, and I glare at my twin. I know exactly what he wanted to finish that sentence with. She's *the* girl. I know it, but it's still something I'm working through, and I don't need the third degree about it. Plus who

35

knows if I'll ever see her again. *Wait. That's a lie.* I will see her again once I get my head in the game.

"Well, I'll be damned," Carter says without thinking, and I see the mistake he made written all over his face.

"Carter James Harlow." I snort as Mama finally turns her wrath to the golden child. "I will not tolerate that language at the table."

"You boys are going to give your mother a heart attack." Dad is half right. Mama either worries too much about us, or she's always getting on to us.

Carter mumbles his apology, and all is quickly forgiven. Thankfully nothing else is spoken about my current predicament, but Clark and Cason keep eye-balling me. Choosing to ignore them, we all finish eating and stay at a neutral conversation. Dad and Carter talk about going fishing this weekend as Shelby and Mama plan a shopping trip. Something is said about curtains, and I lose interest. There's not one thing interesting about shopping for curtains. Everyone talks amongst themselves except Cason and I. The pang in my chest is back as I glance to the right, staring at the empty chair beside me. Normally it would be Caleb's spot, but a part of me wishes someone else was here sitting beside me. That someone with shoulder length dark brown hair with natural caramel highlights that shine when the sun hits it just right. That someone with

Caden

bright blue eyes with hints of green swirling around her pupils. The instant connection I felt for her seems unrealistic, but as the tightness in my chest grows, I know it means something. She wasn't just another girl I was trying to charm. No, Savannah is different. It's a feeling, or it's instinct I guess you can call it. It was the way she checked me out because I noticed, and the way her eyes roamed over me like she knew me as well. I won't lie and say my eyes didn't devour her behind my sunglasses because I did. A part of me wishes I had asked her to get out of her vehicle just so I could steal more glimpses of her curvy figure. In the past, most of the women I'd been with have been in tip top shape without an ounce of fat on them, but Savannah has curves that a man craves. She's not big by any means, but I wouldn't say she was skinny. Bootylicious, voluptuous, and all woman describes her better. Either way, I loved what I was looking at.

Feeling a bump against my shoulder, I turn to see my twin staring at me. He leans in close so no one else can hear, but I have a feeling I know what he's about to say. "Day dreaming about the girl?" Raising an eyebrow, I kind of want to punch him in his face when he gives me a smirk. "You know, it's funny to see you so lovesick already."

"Are you jealous?" With his frown, I add, "I know how territorial you can be when I'm not devotin' all my attention to you."

Shaking his head, he sits right in his chair. "Don't forget I know you."

He's right, and I know it, but I can't help but push all those buttons of his. "Awe don't get all sentimental on me now."

"Keep pushin' me," he says with a brooding look.

"Ooh, I'm shakin' in my boots."

"You're not even wearin' boots."

Shrugging a shoulder, I snap back with, "Semantics."

Cason starts to respond back with something I'm sure I can top when Mama interrupts. "Boys, stop arguin'."

"He started it," Cason and I quickly say at the same time.

"One would think y'all were children instead of grown men," Clark states.

Shelby and Carter snicker as I pout. "You wound me."

"I'm sure you'll be fine in about five seconds."

"You're right," I say to Clark as I point my fork at him. "I'm all better and back to my normal awesome self." Clark uses his middle finger to

Caden

scratch his nose to flip me the bird without Mama noticing.

"As much as I love listenin' to you boys bicker, I think y'all should start clearin' the table," Dad tells us and Clark shoots me a dirty look before we do as Dad asks. It's another routine we have every time we come over to our parents for breakfast or dinner. Pretty much anytime there's food, my brothers and I do the cleaning. Sometimes Dad will help, and we all feel it's fair for us to clean up after Mama spends all the time cooking. I mean it can't be an easy task to cook for five grown men. Not to mention, it'll be six when Caleb returns home for good.

Shelby and Mama make their way into the living room as Clark, Cason, and Carter all start grabbing the empty plates. Dad and I take the leftover food into the kitchen and begin to put them away in Tupperware bowls. It's a mindless task, and it leaves me wide open to Dad's question. "Son, what are you goin' to do about your woman problem?"

"I don't know, Pops. What is this problem you speak of?"

The look he's giving me tells me all I need to know. I'm full of shit, and he knows it. "Are you goin' to find her?"

Glancing back into the dining room, I make sure my brothers can't hear me. The last thing I want is for the entire family to bust my balls about a girl again. "It's a small town. Figured I'd leave it up to fate." And I have thought about using my job as a way to find out more about Savannah, but it really didn't sit well with me. I've never been the one to bend the law to my will, and I don't want to start now. Although, it would make things much easier.

"I'm sure you'll find a way to see her again."

Dad's words make me halt all movement, and I frown as I look at him. "Why is everyone suddenly concerned with my love life?"

"Because," Mama says, and I scream making Dad's eyes widen. "What is wrong with you?" She asks.

"Damn, Mama. You scared me half to death." Her eyes narrow at me but before she can scold me I add, "Where did you get those ninja moves from? Cough or somethin' next time."

Dad chuckles, and Mama shakes her head although she's smiling. Carter, Clark, Shelby, and Cason walk into the kitchen with a worried expression. Well except Cason. He just looks bored. "Why are you screamin' like a little girl, Caden?" Shelby asks.

Caden

Pointing a finger at Mama, I explain. "Did you know Mama has ninja moves? She scared me. I might have to check my britches now."

Carter, Clark, Shelby, and Dad laugh, but Cason just glares at me as Mama says, "Now you're just exaggeratin'."

"I am not," I screech. "You can't sneak up on me like that. Dad and I were mindin' our own business, and you come in here creepin'."

Mama walks up to me and places her hand on my cheek. With a sweet voice I've heard all my life, she softly says, "I love you dearly, but you're such a drama queen."

"Tell me how you really feel," I pipe back with a laugh.

"I'm only tellin' you the truth, sweetie. Now take your leftovers and get out of my kitchen. You have a girl to find."

Picking up my bowl of food, I raise it up as I say, "Yes, ma'am." Cason does the same only he kisses Mama on the cheek and says goodbye to Dad before we walk out of the house, and I wonder if maybe if my parents are right. Maybe I don't need to wait for fate to do her job. Maybe I should start controlling my own fate.

Bang.

Bang.

Bang.

Cracking one eye open, I wonder why it sounds like someone is trying to break down my bedroom door.

Bang.

Bang.

What the fuck? Blinking the sleep away, I toss the covers off me and slowly get out of bed. Shuffling carefully in my dark room, I hold my arms out in front of me. I'm not sure what time it is because of my blackout curtains, but this constant banging on the door is sort of freaking me out.

Bang.

Bang.

"Caden!" Jumping at the loud voice, I immediately know who it is. Cason's consistent banging and the tone of his voice lets me know he's in cranky mode. "What are you doin' in there?"

"Hold the fuck on," I grumble loudly. Can't a guy get some sleep around here? Cason and I have lived in the same apartment downtown since we both graduated high school and went out in the big ol' world. There are days I don't mind living with my

Caden

twin, but then days or nights like this that I hate it. I'm certain it's still daytime, possibly in the afternoon, because I have to work the night shift, and I hope I didn't oversleep. Jerking the door open, Cason almost hits me in the face since he was about to bang on my fucking door some more. "What do you want, Cas? What if I was doin' somethin' private?"

Lowering his hand, he glares at me then his eyes widen. "Could you please put on some fuckin' clothes? I don't want to see your junk."

Glancing down, I realize I'm still in the nude. "Huh. Well maybe if you weren't two seconds from bustin' through my room like the Hulk, I could've gotten dressed. You know I sleep in the nude." Flipping on the light, I turn to get some shorts from the dresser on the far side of the room. "Plus it's not like you don't see the same shit every day. Hello," I say as I turn and wave a hand back and forth. "Identical twins remember?"

"You'll never let me forget we shared a womb." As I'm sliding on my shorts, he adds, "And just because we have the same body, it doesn't mean I want to see yours. It's weird."

"You make it weird." With his deadpan look, I shut the dresser with my hip. "What can I do for you, your highness?"

"I can't find my laptop."

"And you thought it was hidin' in here?"

"Cut the shit, Caden. I need it for work. Now hand it over."

Shaking my head, I brush past him and make my way to the small kitchen. The apartment Cason and I share isn't much. It has two bedrooms, one bathroom, a small living room, and kitchen. But it suits us perfectly. "It really disturbs me when you blame me for takin' your things when you know I've never done that."

"Oh, really?"

Putting a K-cup in the Keurig, I press start then turn around. "Yeah, really. You must have misplaced it because I've never taken anythin' of yours."

Cason leans against the kitchen counter as he says, "You stole my G.I. Joe action figure when I was six."

"Blasphemy! I did no such thing." Okay there was that one time when we were kids, Cason had one thing, just one thing back then that Mama and Dad didn't get me, and yeah I took the stupid doll.

"You did so. I also remember you put it on the grill and melted it."

Caden

Crossing my arms and leaning against the counter, I add, "I also remember you cryin' when you found it."

"I never cry."

Grinning widely, I know he's full of shit. "You cried for two days about that stupid doll."

Rolling his eyes, Cason huffs out a long breath. "So you're admittin' you took my G.I. Joe action figure, not a doll, and now you took my laptop." The way he says action makes me chuckle. He's putting way too much emphasis on it, but it's cute he's trying to make it seem like he didn't love playing with dolls. "I need it, Caden. Just hand it over so I can just go back to work."

Grabbing my coffee, I power off the Keurig then face him again. "I seriously didn't take your laptop." We stare at each other, and I know he's trying to read me for any lies. It's our twin bond, and I'm kind of annoyed he wouldn't just believe me. Cason seems to finally believe what I'm saying, and he readjusts his cap then rubs a hand down his face. He seems stressed, and I can sense the uneasiness within him. "I know what you need."

"And I know you'll tell me, even though I don't care to know."

"You're right. I will tell you because I'm your brother, and I know what's best for you." Cason grunts out his disagreement, but I continue anyway. "You need to get laid. How long has it been now?"

"I'm doing just fine, and my sex life isn't any of your business."

"I disagree. You've been on edge and crankier than normal. A night with a fine woman would do you wonders." Setting my coffee mug down, I push off the counter. "I've got someone that would be perfect for you. I'll text her and ask her to come over."

Cason pushes himself off the counter and stops me from going back to my room to grab my phone. "I do not want your nasty sloppy seconds."

"I've never been with a nasty lady, Cas," I say back in a serious tone.

"You know what I mean. I won't stick my dick in anythin' you've been in."

Looking away, I say, "Well, when you put it that way it does sound gross." It was a good idea even if Cason isn't on board. He's never been the one to openly chase after a woman like me, but it's been far too long since he's had a woman's touch. I'm not sure if it's by choice or if he's just not into women. With him, you can never tell. Plus even if I were to hook him up with a lady friend of mine, it's not like they would know the difference between us.

Caden

All Cason would have to do is not talk, and they would think he was me.

"How long has it been for you? Our apartment has been oddly quiet as of late."

Holding up my hands, I try to distract him. "Whoa, whoa, whoa. We're not talkin' about me. We're talkin' about your women problems."

Cason crosses his arms, and I know I can't dodge his question. "How long?"

Grinning at him, I point a finger at him as I say, "You. You're persistent aren't ya?" He doesn't respond, but the look in his eyes lets me know he's not going to drop it. Letting out a deep sigh, I turn to grab my cooling coffee off the counter. "Three months, three days, and some odd minutes and seconds but whose countin'?" I have to admit, I'm a bit surprised Cason seems so shocked by my admission, but it's the truth. I've been given the nickname of a manwhore, but I'm not really. Okay, I like women. I love their soft skin, their sweet lips, and their cries of ecstasy when I make them come. There are plenty of things I love about the women I've been with, but not a single one of them was fulfilling. There was always something missing, and it was just about sex. I'm not man enough to admit since the end of February, I've wanted more than just a roll in the hay with another woman. That and the fact the every woman I've ever been with can't tell the difference

47

between Cason and me. One would think the differences in us would be the first thing they would notice, but I've learned the women I've been with are just as shallow as I've been in the past. I do not take pride in knowing this.

Taking a drink of my coffee, Cason takes his seat at the small dining room table. "No wonder our couch is still intact and the apartment hasn't burnt down."

Swallowing my coffee down quickly, I claim, "Oh my god. That was one time, Cas."

"One time too many. You nearly burnt the entire livin' room."

"You're stretchin' the truth a bit much don't you think?"

Cason shakes his head, but I see the smirk he's trying to hide. "The couch was toast. The rug had to be thrown away. Hell even the coffee table had some smoke damage."

He's never going to let me live this down. Once and only once, I had a girl over, and we were getting a bit frisky on the couch. I knew Cason was out with Carter, so I thought sure why not. The girl I was with was a bit kinky, but I just rolled with it. Things got hot and heavy real fast, and before I knew what was happening, she had my shirt off and a candle in hand. I'm all for trying out new things, so I

Caden

let her light the candle and drip some wax on my chest. Needless to say, when she sneezed, she dumped a shit ton of wax on me, and fuck it hurt. I was so focused on getting the wax to cool, I didn't realize I'd knocked the candle, which didn't go out by the way, out of her hand and it started a small fire. "I don't understand why you keep bringin' this up. I replaced all the furniture." Glancing down at my feet, I add, "Still can't grow any nipple hair back."

"Dude," Cason starts. Looking back up, I hold back a laugh with the disgusted look on his face. He's totally grossed out. "Please don't ever say nipple hair around me again."

"Nipple hair."

"Stop it."

"What's wrong with nipple hair? It's only natural for a man to have nipple hair."

"I'm leavin' before you say nipple hair once more," Cason says and I open my mouth to say it again, but he holds up a hand. Laughing as he glares at me and stands, he walks to the door. Before he opens it, he turns back to me. "Are you workin' night shift?"

"Yep. I'm workin' a double, so I won't be around to smother you with all my love."

"Such a shame." He counters with a deep monotone voice.

"You know," I begin as I make my way over to him. "One day you're going to actually like the things I say."

"I wouldn't hold my breath if I were you," he claims then he walks out the door, shutting it behind him. With Cason gone, the apartment seems too quiet. Huffing out a breath, I head back to my room. I only have a few hours left before I have to go to work, and for some reason that damn pang in my chest is back. My mind instantly goes to Savannah's eyes, and I wonder if I'll ever see her again.

three
Savannah

When I was younger, I desperately wanted to be a photographer. I wanted to be the one to capture all those precious moments from others and create memories that would last forever. Before I left college, I was well on my way to obtaining my dream. Now it seems I should've wished to do something else. Perhaps if I became a private investigator, the path I'm on wouldn't be so disappointing. Day after day, I search for my birth mother, but I'm at my wits end. I'm not sure how much more I can take before I finally accept defeat. It's not in my nature to give up, but what else can I do? Maybe if I had the skills and knowledge to find a person that doesn't want to be found, then perhaps I would've at least gotten something out of moving to Mississippi.

Brie Paisley

Every day I wake up with these same thoughts. It's never ending it seems. Laying back on the hotel room's bed, I wish someone would just give me a sign that I'm in the right place at least. My instincts tell me I am, but then again I'm beginning to doubt them. I'm starting to wonder maybe if my parents never told me I was adopted, then I wouldn't feel the way I do. It's the endless unfilled hole in my heart that stops me from truly living these days, and I fear I'll never be able to find the answers I seek. Closing my eyes, I conjure up bright blue eyes and a drop dead gorgeous smile in my mind. The cop from a week ago seems to be overtaking my brain more and more, but for whatever reason, his eyes and smile make me feel better. I'm not sure why it's him of all people, but I can't seem to stop myself. If I hadn't been so stunned the day he came up to my rental car, maybe I would've remembered to get his name. C. Harlow isn't something I want to call him, but beggars can't be choosers. No matter the reason, when my thoughts go to the handsome and sarcastic cop, a smile forms on my face and my belly flutters. I don't really question why anymore since it happens too often to count, and I can only hope I'll run into him once more. I tell myself if fate is kind to me, and if I see him again, I'll ask him his name. I'll ask him if he loves his job, what his family is like, and what he looks like naked. Wait … No, not that. Moving off the bed, I shake my head. I mean of

Caden

course, it's only natural for me to think of the sexy cop naked, but I can't go there. My reason, and only reason, for being here is to find my birth mother. Not fall into bed with a random guy, let alone a panty melting cop.

Glancing at my phone, I realize I've been wasting the day away in my thoughts. My work shift at Tampico Bay is quickly coming, and although I hate the thought of going into work to deal with drunk customers, I need the job. Being a bartender at the local bar in town isn't exactly what I would call a dream job, but money doesn't just appear out of thin air. Letting out a heavy sigh, I begin to get ready for work. I walk around the small hotel room trying to find some fresh clothes. I really should clean this room up. I've never been the one to be organized, and it shows with the room looking like a bomb went off. The hotel room at The Holiday Inn is smaller than I would've liked to be in for so long, but it has a nice TV and the shower is to die for. While the wallpaper looks outdated and the sheets on the bed are kind of itchy, the room serves its purpose. It's a means to an end, one that I'm hoping actually ends soon. Plus it's convenient my place of work is right next door. Feeling as though I'm wasting my time here, I grab the cleanest looking pair of pants and stop when my stash of weed falls to the ground. Thinking about it only for a few seconds, I pick it up and tell myself one joint before work won't hurt. Another perk of the room I'm in, is that it has a balcony that overlooks the back of the hotel. It's probably not smart to be smoking an illegal drug so openly, but I really don't care. It calms me and lets my mind stop wondering about shit that I can't control.

Opening the sliding door, I step outside and suck in a breath as the humidity hits me. It's almost suffocating, and I'm not sure how the people here can live in this. Florida is humid, but it's different here. Pushing all thoughts of home out of my mind, I pull out a lighter and light the small joint. Taking a deep drag, I let the smoke fill my lungs and slowly let it out instantly feeling the calmness wash through me. Leaning against the brick wall, I tell myself I need this. I need an escape, even if it's only for a small window of time. I'm so sick of worrying about finding a woman that probably never wanted me. I'm sick and tired of looking for her. But as I take another drag, I know I'll never stop looking. I have to know why she gave me away. I need to know if it's because she just didn't want me, or if it's because I can't be loved. A part of me hopes it's because she just wanted a better life for me, but just like all the other times as soon as that thought crosses my mind, my stomach dips and I have a feeling that's not the case at all.

Caden

I fucked up.

Oh God, I fucked up big time.

Why did I think it was a good idea to smoke weed before work? Why oh why did I do it? Swallowing hard, my eyes search for a way out. The cops are all over the place, and paranoia is setting in hard. Everything was going just fine at Tampico Bay until two drunk college students started fighting. They were all but tearing the place down before my boss, Paul, had to call the cops. Now I'm hiding in a fucking corner behind the bar freaking the hell out because cops ... are ... everywhere. One look at me and they'll know I'm high as a fucking kite. An hour into my shift and shit hits the fan.

Unbelievable.

Searching again for a way out, I slowly move out of my hiding spot. If I can just get past the two cops talking to Paul, I can make a break for the back door. Deciding to take a chance, I quickly walk past them hoping and praying no one sees me. I've spent time in a jail cell many times, and I do not wish to do it again. Yes, I made a lot of stupid mistakes in my younger days, okay not that long ago, but I really would rather not risk it again. Making my way around the bar, I look back at the front door then to the two cops seeing they're still talking to Paul. Holding my breath, I sneak past them, and my heart begins to pound as I make my way through the crowd in the small establishment. Normally this wouldn't bother me, but it seems the fight has caused everyone to be on high alert. There are three rooms sectioned off from the front bar, and I have to push my way through the crowd to get to the back door. Thankfully no one pays me any mind as I get closer to the door, but I'm still holding my breath. All it'll take is for one of these drunk fools to ask me what I'm doing, and it'll cause unwanted attention.

I can hear the pounding of my heart in my ears, but freedom is only inches away. Finally reaching the door, I don't think about Paul looking for me once things calm down. I frankly don't care about anything but getting away from the fucking cops. Without a second glance behind me, I jerk open the door and quickly shut it behind me with both hands. My shoulders sag in relief as I feel the night air hitting me, and I close my eyes as I finally let out a deep breath. "Sneakin' out for a break huh?"

My eyes snap open as I hear the deep manly voice with a thick southern accent behind me, and I quickly turn around. "You have got to be shitting me."

His head tilts as a huge grin forms on his face, and dare I say, there's a hint of glee in his bright blue eyes. He walks closer to me, and I lean against the wall for support. This can't be happening. Not while I'm still higher than the freaking clouds. "I never

Caden

thought I would see you again, Sassy Savannah Owens."

"Fate must really love me tonight," I huff out.

He chuckles, and I find I like the sound way more than I should. "Why do I get the feelin' you really don't mean that?"

"Because," I drawl out. "It's the truth."

"Is that why you looked as if you were runnin' away from somethin' chasin' you with a hacksaw?"

"What?" Turning around, I actually check to make sure no one is coming after me.

Mysterious first name laughs once more, before adding, "Or maybe you're tryin' to rob the joint, and I caught you red handed."

Okay, I'm really starting to freak out. In the back of my mind, I know he's joking, but I'm having a bad effect from the weed. In other words, I'm wigging out man. "Oh, please! Don't take me to jail!" Seeing the confusion on his face, I plead some more. "I swear I'll do anything." Unable to stop myself, I grab onto this arms and shake them. "Just don't take me to jail."

His eyebrows furrow as he really looks at me for a moment. I blink away the tears starting to pool in my eyes because I just know he's going to arrest me. But instead of putting me in cuffs, he smiles at me again before asking, "Are you high?"

"Uh … maybe?" I whisper.

"You're so fucked up."

Rolling my eyes, I drop his arms as I confess, "Okay, fine. I'm high as fuck. I did something stupid, and now I'm freaking out. There are cops all over the place, and now I run into you, and you're just you, and I don't want to go to jail." Sucking in a breath, I can't believe I just blurted that out.

"That was quite a mouth full."

Covering my hand over my mouth, I try to hold in a laugh. I end up snorting and the sound alone is so embarrassing, but then again it feels good to laugh. "That's what she said."

We both laugh loudly before his eyes turn serious. At least, I think that look means he's serious. "I won't arrest you," he starts, and I hold in a breath. "On one condition." He adds, and my stomach sinks.

"I don't have to suck your dick do I? Because I know I said I'd do anything, but I don't know. That seems like a bit much."

His eyes widen for a good ten seconds before he smiles again while shaking his head. "I at least would like for you to buy me dinner first. Then

Caden

maybe have a first kiss before we move onto other parts of my body then to yours." I'm speechless as I listen to him. It's as if he already knows how things are going to go between us. It's the strangest conversation I've ever had before. But the more he talks, the more my eyes begin to wander down his face and chest. Then to his bulky arms and manly hands. My eyes get to his crotch, and I imagine what his cock would look like. "My condition," he says loudly, and I meet his eyes again. My face flames with embarrassment knowing he caught me checking him out. God please let this night end already. "One date and I won't arrest you."

"You're serious?" This doesn't seem real. Why would he let me off this easy? But I know he's dead serious about taking me out on a date when he wiggles his eyebrows.

I start to answer him, but a loud banging noise cuts me off. Mystery first name guy turns around, and that's when I notice a man in the back of the cop car. I'm assuming the car belongs to C. Harlow. He signals me to follow him and for a moment I panic. What if all this was just a ruse to get me in his car so he can throw me in jail? Against my better judgment, I follow him anyway, but keep a fair distance in case he tries anything funny. As we get closer to the police cruiser, the guy in the back begins to curse very loudly and bangs his head against the window. "Hey man. Simmer down back there," he yells. The man in the back seat however, either doesn't hear him or doesn't care. "Don't make me pepper spray you." C. Harlow pulls a small can of pepper spray out of his pocket and holds it up. "I will spray you in the eyes. It will hurt like a motherfucker." The man in the back seat instantly calms down, and I snicker. Hearing his southern accent come out so thick is something I'm finding I want to hear more of. "Have you ever been peppered sprayed before?" he asks catching my attention.

"I can't say that I have."

He quickly puts his can of pepper spray away before saying, "I have. Sprayed myself in the face once." His head snaps up to me then he adds, "By accident." He chuckles as I smile and shake my head. "Why would I spray myself in the face with that shit?" Something tells me he might have just been curious, and he did spray himself. There's something in the tone of his voice like he's trying to convince me it was an accident. And the fact he won't look me in the eyes. "Anyway did you ever hear the story about the guy dyin' from shovin' a pepper spray can up his ass?"

Shockingly I know exactly what he's talking about. "You mean the episode on A 1,000 Ways to Die, and the guy is an ex-convict?"

Caden

"And he shoves a can of pepper spray up his b-hole when he gets pulled over so he won't be violatin' his parole?"

Smiling while nodding my head, I add, "But the guy didn't realize in doing so, when the cop pushed him against his car, the can went off inside him."

"I'm sure he had regrets from that," he says while chuckling.

"Well I'm not so sure if he regretted it since he died and all." I deadpan, and when he laughs again, my stomach starts fluttering like crazy. I blame the drugs for the sudden sensation, but I can't help but join him as he continues to laugh.

His laugh slowly dies as he says, "That was my favorite episode."

"No shit. It's mine too."

"Looks like we're made for each other."

Rolling my eyes, I still can't stop a smile from forming. Even if he's full of shit. "Don't get ahead of yourself. I said one date, and that's only because you promised not to arrest me."

My entire body tenses as he steps closer to me. He's so close I can smell him, and my mouth begins to dry up. I'm not sure if he's wearing cologne or not, but he smells divine. It has to be cologne because no man has ever smelled so good around me before. "I know a good thing when I see it," he says huskily and brushes a strand of hair out of my face. It's such a sweet and innocent moment, but tell my heart that. I have to open my mouth to take in more air, and it's as if my mind is trying to play catch up. *It's just the after effects of the joint I smoked.* "Let me see your phone."

"Umm, what now?"

"Phone? Don't you have a phone like every ten-year-old?"

"Okay, Mr. Smart Ass. There's no need to get grumpy on me," I playfully scold. Reaching around to my back pocket, I unlock the phone then hand it to him. Our fingers brush ever so slightly, and I swear I'll never smoke weed again. His touch, no matter how light or innocent it may seem, makes my body react in a way that I've never known before. It's sort of freaking me out.

His bright blue eyes hold mine for a moment more before he starts typing something on my phone. Curiosity nags at me, but I don't have to wait long. "Here," he says as he hands my phone back. "Don't forget about me, Sassy Savannah."

I don't get the chance to respond. He quickly turns around and gets into his police car. Standing in the middle of the back parking lot, I probably seem

Caden

like an idiot as I watch him leave. Shaking myself out of my daze, I glance down at my phone to see what he added. Grinning widely, I read out loud what he put in my contacts. "Caden. The man of your dreams." Well at least I know what his name is now.

four
Caden

"Dude, you seriously need to stop with the grinnin'. You're not supposed to smile so much."

Glancing up at my twin, I flip him the bird. "Why can't you just be happy for me?" He knows I'm joking with my playful tone, but Cason can never take a joke.

"It's not that I'm not happy for you, it's just … weird. You've been walkin' around for three days with your phone attached to your hand, and that stupid shit eatin' grin on your ugly face."

"Hey if my face is ugly, then yours is too. Twins remember?"

"Like I could ever forget," he says in a monotone voice.

Caden

"Lighten up, buttercup." Cason glares at me, and I flash him an even bigger grin. "Come on, Cas. Be happy for once in your life."

He lets out a huff then says, "Yay. Happy."

Bursting out in laughter, I smack him on his shoulder. "Very convincin', bro. I'm sold." I'm really not, but at least he tried. Cason wasn't always this serious, but he sure does make it fun to fuck with him.

"I'm just sayin'. I don't want you getting' your hopes up about this chick because if it doesn't work out, then I'll be the one to pick up the mess."

"Your concern for me is endearin', but I've got this one in the bag." And I do. I just have to figure out a way to keep her. It's only been a few days since I last saw Savannah, but I've been texting her nonstop since that night at Tampico Bay.

Cason sighs deeply as he shakes his head, then gets up from the couch. It's been a rare lazy day for us, but I'm getting antsy just sitting here. "Alright I get it. Get your rocks off then cut her lose like all the others."

"As much as I'm enjoyin' this conversation, I'm goin' to have to stop you, bro." Cason stops before he gets to the front door to give me his full attention. Getting off the couch, I walk over to him and place my hand on his shoulder. He glares at me

65

again, and I think better of it and slowly remove my hand. "She's different, man. I can't really explain how I know. Maybe it's my inner chick comin' out." Shrugging, I add, "Either way. She's not like the others. Just wait until you meet her and then you'll see."

Cason narrows his eyes at me for a moment before he nods. "I just don't want to see you hurt like before."

"Awe my baby bro is lookin' out for me."

"Don't push it, dipshit."

"Come on, say you love me."

"I'm leavin' now. You've ruined the moment."

"Oh come on. Don't be such a wet blanket!" Placing my hands on my hips, I call after him. He flips me the bird over his shoulder, and all I can do is shake my head as he slams the door shut behind him. "What a crybaby." Huffing out a breath, I walk back over to the couch and prop my feet up on the coffee table. Maybe I shouldn't have pushed my twin so far, but his concern isn't needed. I know there's something going on with Savannah, I just haven't figured out what it is yet. *More research is needed.* Okay maybe not so much as research, but I have this need to know more about her. What makes her tick? I wonder what it would take to make her smile again because Lord knows her smile can light up a

Caden

room. It does seem a bit out of character for me to be wondering so much about one woman, but I can't deny what my instincts are telling me. Not to mention, her eyes tell me she's lost. There's a sadness in them, and I'm determined to find out all her deep dark secrets.

Glancing over at the clock, I decide I've waited long enough to text her again. Shifting to my side, I grab my phone out of my pocket and notice my little Sassy Savannah never responded to my last message I'd sent earlier.

Me: What are you wearin'?

Placing my phone face down on my leg, I turn the TV on to catch up on the news. I honestly hate watching the news, but it's something to keep my mind busy while I wait for her to respond. Thankfully she doesn't make me wait very long.

Sassy S: Clothes.

Me: What kind of clothes?

Sassy S: The kind you buy at the store. Duh.

A grin forms as I read her message, and I think once again maybe I have met my match.

Me: What store did you buy them from? Let me guess ... The sexy store?

It takes her a few minutes to respond, and for a moment I'm afraid I pushed her too far. I do have a habit of doing that.

Sassy S: Sexy store? What's that? Another name for Wal-Mart?

Me: How about I take you to the "sexy Wal-Mart" sometime? ;-)

Sassy S: In your dreams maybe.

Me: How about dinner instead?

Smooth Caden. Real smooth. Never in my life have I been so nervous waiting for a chick to respond back to a date request. But in the short amount of time I've gotten to know Savannah, I know she's worth the wait. Even if my balls feel like they're lodged in my throat.

Sassy S: I don't know. You did blackmail me into agreeing. Doesn't seem fair.

Letting out a breath, I realize I can work with this. Yes, I did sort of blackmail her, but I really wanted a chance to get to know her. And mainly to get her phone number.

Me: Don't make me come arrest you. Cause I will.

Sassy S: Why does that sound fun and less of like a threat?

Caden

Me: Oh it'll be fun for the both of us.

Sassy S: You're so full of shit.

Me: Funny. All my brothers say the same thing.

Me: Come on. One date and if you still don't like me then I'll leave you alone.

Not hardly, but one little white lie won't hurt.

Sassy S: I'm not sure I believe that, but fine. What the hell.

Me: It's a done deal. No take backs.

Sassy S: LOL I wouldn't dare be an Indian giver. ;-)

Damn this woman is made for me. Letting out a breath, I try to play it cool. For some reason, she makes me feel like I'm sixteen again.

Me: All-time favorite food?

Sassy S: Pancakes.

Me: I'll pick you up at seven.

Sassy S: Today? I have to work.

Me: Call in sick.

Sassy S: I can't do that!

Me: You can and you will. Come on. Live a little.

Sassy S: Fine, but this date better be worth it.

Me: Oh it will. That I can promise.

I wait a few moments to see if she'll respond, and when she doesn't, I turn off the TV and quickly race to my room. It's only after three in the afternoon, and I know I have a lot of time to kill, but this just gives me more time to plan the perfect date. I'm sure a quick phone call to Mama will help my situation because I'll admit, I might have tooted my own horn a little. But I do want this first date to be epic. I want Savannah to know without a doubt, that after this, there's no stopping me from making her mine.

With having so much time to kill, I decided to forgo calling Mama and instead, I'm parking in my parent's driveway. Quickly turning off the truck, I hop out and make my way to the front door. I don't even bother to knock and walk inside my parent's home as I yell, "Mama, your favorite son is here."

"Well make yourself right at home."

Smiling as I make my way to Mama's voice in the kitchen, I respond back to her. "Now, now. Is that any way to treat your favorite son?"

Caden

Mama smirks as she glances at me from making something that smells divine. "I do not have any favorites. I treat all you boys the same."

Walking over to her, she leans into me as I give her a kiss on her cheek. "It's okay, Mama. I won't tell anyone."

"Won't tell anyone what?"

Jumping away from Mama, I clutch my chest as I let out a breath. "Sweet baby Jesus, Shel. Where did you come from?"

Shelby gives me a sideward glance as she says, "The bathroom. Why are you so jumpy?"

"I'm not jumpy." Dropping my hands, I walk over to the other side of the kitchen bar and pull out a stool. Taking a seat, I add, "I didn't know you were here, and I'm guessin' Mama has been teachin' you some of her ninja moves."

Mama tries to hide her smile before saying, "Maybe I should be chargin' for these ninja lessons."

Shelby snickers as I add, "You should. That's where the money is nowadays."

"As much as I'm enjoyin' this strange conversation, I know there's a reason why you're here, Caden."

Ah and here I thought Mama's sixth sense was gone. "No reason," I quickly respond. There is a reason why I'm here, but now that I realize Shelby is here, I'm not so sure I should delve out all my secrets. She would tell Carter, then Carter would tell everyone. He can't keep a secret for shit. Deciding to switch the topic away from me, I turn to Shelby to ask, "Why are you here? Gettin' tired of the old man already?"

Shelby rolls her eyes because she knows I'm dicking around with her. Everyone knows how much Carter and Shelby love each other. "I'm learnin' if you must know." Turning to Mama, I notice she's getting a whisk out of the drawer. Resting my chin on my hand, I take in a deep breath hoping I'm around long enough to taste test whatever they're making. "I'm goin' to surprise Carter later with a peanut butter cake."

"Homemade of course," Mama adds.

"I figured as much." Mama nods proudly because since I was old enough to talk, Mama always said homemade is the best way to bake. Come to think of it, I've never seen her bake anything from ol' Betty Crocker. "Where's my cake then? I at least get to taste it to make sure there's no poison in it."

"I would never poison Carter," Shelby says loudly as if I'd really thought she would.

"I'm still waitin' for my cake."

Caden

Mama huffs out a long breath, then hands the whisk to Shelby. While Shelby works on the task at hand, Mama walks over to the oven. Angling my head around Shelby, I watch Mama closely because I'm hoping whatever is in the oven is for me. "Here," Mama says as she brings over a batch of freshly made brownies. "Save some for your brother."

I don't even bother waiting for a fork or a knife to cut them with. Diving in with just my fingers, I scoop out a handful of hot brownies and quickly stuff my mouth. "Oaf, ifs wike eaven in my outh," I try to say but damn these brownies are delicious and hot.

"What did you say? I couldn't hear a word you said, and stop talkin' with your mouth full," Mama scolds.

Taking another bite, Mama shakes her head and walks over to the fridge. Shelby is still whisking, but she's laughing at me. Taking one last bite of the best brownie Mama has ever made, I moan loudly when Mama sets a glass of milk in front of me. Gulping the milk down, I swallow a few times before I say, "I was just sayin' that brownie is like heaven in my mouth. Best. Brownie. Ever."

"Sounds like you enjoyed it way too much," Shelby says sarcastically.

"Oh, I enjoyed it. Almost better than se— I mean it was good." Darting my eyes away from

Mama, I begin to whistle hoping she didn't catch my almost slip up.

"I'm goin' to pretend I didn't hear what I thought I did," Mama claims.

"That's probably a good idea, Linda," Shelby tells her.

"Now that y'all have made this visit awkward, I'm going to need three more brownies to make up for it."

"Oh no you don't." Right before my sticky fingers can grab more of the chocolate heaven, Mama quickly takes the pan away. "I said to save some for your brother."

"But ... but ... Mama, those are for me. Cason doesn't even like sweets!" He does, especially brownies, but I want some more. One little white lie never hurt anyone. "This is no way to treat your favorite son."

Mama stares blankly at me because she knows I'm full of shit. "No more brownies for you until you tell me why you're really here."

"Ooh, well played. Well played indeed." Mama grins, and I have to hand it to her. I did play right into that one. "What makes you think I'm here for a reason? Can't I just come chill with my awesome and lovin' Mama?"

Caden

"You forget," Mama starts. "I know you. I raised you too so don't be givin' me any of that crap."

"You should just spill the beans, Caden."

"Thanks, Shel. You're so helpful."

"I'm just sayin'. Whatever the reason, your mom and I will help."

"Yeah, then tell the whole family about it." I deadpan.

"I wouldn't dare," Shelby pipes back with a grin.

"Boy, don't make me get out my whoopin' spoon."

Holding up my hands, I plead, "Please don't. Anythin' but that freakin' spoon." What can I say? That damn thing hurts. When I still don't tell why I'm actually here, Mama moves to the counter by the stove to grab her wooden spoon. "Okay! Alright! I'll tell y'all why I'm here." Mama stops but doesn't move from the counter. Shelby laughs again, and I narrow my eyes at her. "Geez y'all sure know how to get a secret out of me."

"Just spit it out already," Shelby says with a heavy sigh.

"Fine, but y'all have to swear this doesn't leave the room. I do have a reputation to uphold." Mama crosses her arms, and Shelby rolls her eyes as they wait for me to open up. This isn't something I would normally have problems with, but I want everything to be perfect for Savannah. "So there's this woman," I begin.

"Is this is the same girl you met a few weeks ago?"

"Simmer down, Shel. I thought you wanted to know?" When she goes back to making her goodie for Carter, I lean on the counter and let out a sigh. "Anyway I got her to agree to a date."

"By doing what?"

"Jesus H Christ, Shel."

She shrugs as she asks, "What? I'm just askin'."

"Are you done?" Damn, she's very nosey today. "As I was sayin', she agreed to a date, but I sort of promised it would be perfect. Now I'm doubtin' myself." And that's the truth. I want everything to go smoothly and make Savannah want to go on many more dates with me. First dates aren't really my thing because, well, I was a manwhore as my brothers would say. But I've changed in the past few months, and I knew when I met Savannah, she's the only one I want to pursue. "Y'all can understand why I don't want anyone to know. My street cred is solid, and somethin' like this will ruin me."

Caden

"Your street cred?" Shelby asks.

"Yeah, infamous ladies' man remember?"

"In your dreams maybe."

Before I can respond back, Mama cuts in. "What exactly is it you're askin', Caden?"

I was beginning to wonder if Mama would ever say anything, and I know she'll help me once I ask for help. Looking at her, I take a deep breath before saying, "I want tonight to be perfect. I want Savannah Owens to think it's a perfect date." Mama's eyes widen as I continue. "She's unlike any woman I've ever been around, and bein' with her is so easy. She's witty and hilarious. I've seen her twice, but when I think of her and her smile, I know I have to be the one to make her smile and laugh again. She's stunnin' and has a bangin' body," I stop when Shelby snorts, and I cut my eyes to her. "Well I'm just sayin'. She does."

"Everythin' you said up until that was actually very sweet, Caden."

"I only speak the truth, and I'm a very sweet guy. We're getting' off track here."

When I feel a hand on my shoulder, I glance to my right seeing Mama standing by me. She has a wide grin, and I swear her eyes have a twinkle or

77

something in them. Is she about to cry? "You want to know what we think a perfect date is?"

"Well yeah." Mama pats my shoulder before giving me a squeeze. She slowly walks around the kitchen island and takes the bowl of cake batter away from Shelby. She doesn't speak a word as she does so, and Shelby and I watch her closely. My heart begins to pound because when Mama gets this quiet, it could mean two things: One, she's madder than hell, and it would be a good idea to run for cover. Or two, she's about to say something epic and wise as shit.

When she turns back to me, I hold my breath hoping I haven't done something wrong. Because I've been known to put my own foot in my mouth not even realizing it. "Shelby, you might want to go get a pen and paper." My eyes dart from Mama to Shel as she runs off to grab what Mama asked for. "I need you to listen very closely, Caden." Glancing back to Mama, I sit up tall and give her my full attention. "I'm goin' to tell you what to do, and you'll have to follow everythin' to the letter. Are you ready, Caden?"

Shelby walks back into the kitchen as I say without hesitation, "Yes, ma'am. Tell me the ways to woo the woman of my dreams."

Caden

five
Savannah

Shaking out my hands, I question myself yet again as to why I agreed to this date. I'm beyond nervous, and I don't know if it's because I'll be alone with Caden, or if it's because I have no idea what's in store for tonight. I tried to get him to spill, but he wouldn't budge. A part of me is excited, but the other part is freaking out. Of course I've been out on dates before, I'm not a prude by any means. There's just something nerve racking about Caden.

Caden Harlow.

His name always makes me smile. It's nice to finally have a name to the man that makes my stomach fill with butterflies and makes me want things I've never thought of before. He's a distraction, but I have to be careful. If I don't keep my guard up, he's going to turn into something I really don't need. Nodding my head, I tell myself this is just a friendly date, and nothing will come of it. It's just getting my pounding heart and my fluttering stomach to agree. Glancing at the clock on the bedside table, I only have five more minutes until he gets here. Yet another thing he wouldn't budge on. I didn't want him to pick me up because, well, I didn't want him to know what room I'm staying in at the hotel. Caden was very persistent and, of course I caved. Even in a text message, he's very hard to say no to. "Come on, Savvy. It's just another guy, nothing more, nothing less." Why am I so nervous when it comes to Caden Harlow? It can't be because of his looks or smile. It's definitely not his sarcastic charm. Who am I kidding here? It's all the above really. He's the type of guy that women flock to and would love to spend one night with him. He's smooth, but yet I can sense he can be a bit demanding if he needed to be. That could be because he's a cop, and cops have to be a little hard around the edges. Fuck he's dangerous for me. I have a weakness for men that can make me laugh and make me think about them more than once.

The guys I've dated in the past were nothing but a means to an end. I've never really wanted the whole married with two point five kids or the white picket fence. It's not being tied down to someone for the rest of my life that scares me. I'm not exactly sure what it is that turns me away from marriage, but I'm

Caden

not going to lie to myself and claim it doesn't have anything to do with me being adopted. It seems my entire life revolves around it, and I'm not proud of it. But how am I supposed to be committed to one person when I have such a longing for someone who just gave me away? When my parents told me I was adopted, everything I'd known changed. The way I look at the future isn't the same anymore, and until I can get the answers I need, there's no room left for me to give my heart away to someone else.

Which is why I'm very apprehensive about this date with Caden. He already has a hold on me, and while a part of me is attracted to that, I can't fall down that rabbit hole. I fear I'll never be the same if I do. I already have enough to handle, and I really don't need a charming, drop dead gorgeous man to add to my problems. Huffing out a breath, I glance around my messy hotel room and wonder how different my life could've been if I hadn't been adopted. I love my parents more than anything, and I'll always be grateful to them for bringing me into their world of happiness. The thing is there could've been a totally different world for me if they hadn't. I hate wondering about what could've been if my birth mother hadn't given me away. I hate knowing there's really no way to know for sure until I finally find her.

The ringing of my phone pulls me out of my thoughts, and when I see it's my mom calling, my nerves instantly settle. "Hey, Mom."

"There's my sweet bird. How are you?" Smiling, I love hearing Mom call me by my nickname she gave me. "How is Columbus? Have you met any new friends?"

Laughing while shaking my head, it's just like Mom to ask me a million questions. "I'm fine, Mom. Columbus is a nice little town, and I wouldn't say I met friends, but there is someone."

"Oh is it a guy? Is he cute? Tell me all about him."

Sitting on the bed, I clutch my phone tightly. It's good to hear Mom's voice, and I wish we had more time to chat. My stomach knots knowing I've been so absent from my parent's life, but I'm glad she called. I've missed her terribly. "His name is Caden, and he's very attractive." Mom listens as I update her on how I met Caden, and I'm surprised she never interrupts.

Once she's caught up, she says, "He sounds like a very nice young man, sweet bird."

"So far he seems that way." Before Mom can reply back, I hear knocking on the door. "Mom, I have to go. I think he's here for our … date."

"Don't forget to call me and tell me all about it," she rushes out.

Caden

I agree, and hang up the phone as I stand. My stomach clenches with nerves again when I hear more knocking at the door. Sucking in a deep breath, I know it's him. I don't know anyone else since coming to Columbus, and as I glance back to the clock, I see it's seven on the dot. I can add punctual to his list of attractive traits. Holding back a grin, I swallow hard before making my way to the door. With each step bringing me closer, my heart drums in my chest, and it's the only sound I can hear. As I reach for the door, I notice my hand begins to shake. "Get a fucking grip," I say out loud but softly because the last thing I want is for him to hear me and think I'm some nut job. It's just one date. But nothing could prepare me when I open the door.

Shitfire. I'm in deep trouble with this one.

"Sassy Savannah, we meet again." His voice is like warm butter. It's like velvet, silk, and other smooth fabrics I can't seem to think of.

"Uh … hey." Clearing my throat, I shut the door behind me before he can get a look at the disaster my room is in. "Ready?"

"Well hold on now." I stop in my tracks hoping like hell he doesn't want to come inside. Feeling my cheeks flush, I nervously tuck a strand of hair behind my ear. "I have somethin' for you." For a moment, I hold my breath wondering what in the world he means. Watching him carefully, he pulls an arm from behind his back, and my eyes widen. "I wasn't sure what type of flowers you liked, but these reminded me of you."

"You got me flowers?"

"Umm, yeah," he says quickly, and I wonder if he's just as nervous as I am.

"But getting women flowers is sort of pointless don't you think? I mean don't get me wrong," I start as I gaze at the beautiful white lilies. "I appreciate the thought, but they'll just die in a few days."

Caden grins widely as he says, "Which is why I got you this." He pulls something out of his back pocket, and I can't help but laugh when I see what it is. "My mama said this would keep them alive long enough until you can plant them."

"Miracle Grow?" Taking the packet and flowers out of his hand, I gaze into his deep blue eyes. "Thank you. I love them." He starts to say something, but I beat him to it. "How did you know lilies were my favorite?"

"I didn't." He simply states. Our gazes lock, and I swear my heart is fluttering around in my chest. I'd like to say the damn thing is about to beat right out of my chest, but surely that's impossible. I mean that only happens in cartoons. But I can't deny the way he's staring at me like I'm the only woman he's

Caden

ever going to look at again. It makes me feel ... things I don't want to feel. Shaking my head, I tell him to wait for a second while I put the flowers in something. He tries to come in my room, but I shut the door before he can. "I'll just wait here for you."

Giggling as I search for something to place the lilies in, I tell my stupid heart to calm down. "So what. He got me my favorite flower and found a way to keep them alive. It doesn't mean anything." I shake my head at myself because I must be crazy now that I'm having a full blown conversation with myself. Glancing around the room again, I wish I had a vase to put the flowers in, but the water pitcher will have to suffice for now. I'll have to remember to buy a vase later. Satisfied the flowers are fine until I get back, I make my to the door once more feeling the same fluttering of my heart. It has to be the after effects of the joint I smoked a few hours ago. I'm not proud to admit that I did smoke a joint earlier to prepare for this date. I just needed something to calm my nerves, but now it's clearly out of my system, I wonder if maybe it does have a longer after effect.

Because really, it's crazy to have these type of feelings toward a complete stranger.

Even as I think these words, there's a little voice in the back of my mind telling me there's something more going on here than just attraction.

Not to mention, when I open the door again and meet his blue eyes, I have to suck in a breath. "Ready to roll?" I can only nod, as I shut the door behind me and follow him down the hall. "So let me get this straight," he says as we walk out of the hotel. "You like lilies, but you don't like when a guy gives you flowers?"

"Well when you put it that way, it does sound a bit ridiculous. It's not that I don't like getting flowers. It's just sort of pointless because, like I said before, they die too fast." Shrugging, I add, "It's just a waste of money."

He puckers his lips out, and I quickly look away. I can't get caught staring at his lips. Because they're not in any way begging me to kiss them. Just … not going there. "I get what you're sayin', but my mama always said givin' a pretty lady flowers is a way to be a gentleman." We stop now that we've reached what I'm assuming is his truck and he adds, "And my mama raised me to be a fine gentleman." Turning my head to hide my grin, he opens the door for me. Before I climb inside his monster of a truck, he grabs my hand, and his touch alone stops me. "You look very beautiful tonight."

Sucking in a breath, I'm lost for words for a moment. It's his touch alone that makes my whole body warm. What is it about him that makes me feel this way? And damn, he's pulling all the stops out

Caden

with this so called friendly date. "Th … thank you." I bite my lip and hope it's dark enough out that he can't see my blush. He's reduced me to stuttering. I'm grateful no one else is here to witness this. And maybe I did take my time getting ready for him, but I'll never tell him this. I wanted to dress simple yet I also wanted him to notice me. Which is why I struggled for a good ten minutes to fit my ass into my favorite pair of jeans. The only problem with doing so, I hadn't realized how much the washing machine shrunk them so now I'm supporting a muffin top because they're way too small. Thank goodness I just bought a long and flowy tank that worked well with my jeans. It covers up all my frumpy parts. But regardless if he knew or not that I wanted him to notice me, he did and in my eyes that counts.

"You're welcome, Savannah." Oh holy hell. The way my name rolls off his tongue makes my legs feel weak. It should be illegal for him to be able to do that with just my name. All the other times he's said my name, it's always been playful and with sassy in front of it. Now it's just my name. No playfulness, no sassy with it, and damn I like the way it sounds. "Are you alright there, small fry?"

Coming back down to Earth, I frown as I say, "There's nothing small about me." I've never really had a problem with my weight per say, but I know I'm a lot thicker than other women. But I've come to realize my curves are a part of me, and I'm learning to accept them and love them. Caden helps me get inside his truck, and he mumbles something I don't quite catch. It sounded like he said something about liking what I'm putting out, but I can't be sure.

Once he's inside the truck, he starts it up and looks at me with the biggest grin on his face. I can't help but let out a small laugh because he does look so adorable. "Ready?"

"I guess so. No turning back now."

"You're right. You're mine for the night, Savannah."

There he goes again saying my name like that. Why does it sound so good coming from those lips? "You can just call me Savvy. All my friends do." He turns away hearing the word friends, and I quickly add, "It's not like I can get out of this truck by myself anyway. So I'm sort of stuck."

"My truck is a beast. Ol' Betsy is a fine truck."

Letting out a laugh, I ask, "You named your truck?"

"Hell yes, I did. You can't live in the south and not have a name for your truck."

"I'm from Florida, and I've never met anyone that had a name for their vehicle."

"Well," he starts then begins to back out of the parking lot. He pulls onto the main road before

Caden

saying, "You haven't been in Mississippi long enough to learn the ways of real and true southerners." Shaking my head, I turn and stare out the window. Honestly he could be right but then again I don't know much about Mississippians. All the guys I knew back in Florida were the preppy type, and they were way to snobby to have names for their expensive BMWs. Turning my head back to Caden when I feel a warm hand touch mine, I suck in a breath as he says, "Don't worry your pretty little head. I'll teach you everythin' you need to know."

Don't think about his hand on mine. Don't. Dare. Think. About. It. Oh fuck. His hand hasn't moved, and why is it he seems so unaffected by it? That warm sensation I felt before is back in full force, and I swear the air in the truck is getting thicker. Swallowing hard, I try to find something to say, but all the words I've ever learned have suddenly left me. I have to question why his touch or why him? He's a mystery. A dangerous and very attractive mystery. Getting a hold of myself, I pull my hand away from his, and I don't miss the way his smile fades as I do so. "I won't be around long enough to learn much, but I'll take in all I can."

Passing by the Leigh Mall, he stops at a red light as he turns to me. "What do you mean?"

"I'm just passing through," I respond with a shrug. His eyes dart out to his window, and I glance away because for some reason I don't like that he won't meet my eyes anymore. For the rest of the way to wherever we're going, Caden is silent. Not knowing what to say, I don't try to start a conversation either. I feel as though I did something wrong, but I have no idea what it is. Deciding not to dwell on it, I let out a sigh as I take in everything around me as Caden drives. After we pass by Sonic, a little shopping area, and a gas station, I turn to Caden. "Where are we going by the way?"

"It's a surprise."

"I don't really like surprises."

"Aren't you just a bowl of fun," he says sarcastically. "I promise you'll like it."

"I don't know. I hardly know you, and you're a cop. What if this is all just a ploy to take me in or something."

He chuckles softly, and I really wish I suddenly didn't want to hear him laugh like that again. "I must be goin' through an awful lot of trouble to take you to jail."

Oh right. Because of the flowers. "I'm just saying." I huff trying to play it off.

"Are you always this uptight?"

"Do you always call your dates uptight?"

"Only you, small fry."

Caden

Shaking my head, I cross my arms. "Whatever. Don't tell me then."

"Now hold on to your britches." Frowning, I turn to him as he adds, "We're almost there." He takes a right by KFC, and for a moment I think we're going to the movies that's located on the left side of the road. Instead, he keeps going straight but only for a few more seconds.

He turns to the first left, and I sit up straighter in the seat. "Falcon Lair? Are you taking me to your place?"

"The name is lame as fuck. I liked it much better when it was called Northern Heights, but I just live here." Glancing around the area, there are apartments everywhere. They're stacked on top of each other, and the higher ones are connected with a deck attaching more apartments on each side. The apartment's office is on the left, and I notice a gate beside it. I assume it's for a pool, and I like the layout of the apartments. It seems smaller than the others I've seen around town, but it seems homey. "It's not much, but my brother and I like it."

"Oh you live with your brother?" Caden has mentioned having brothers before, but he hasn't given me many details about his family. I haven't asked either.

Caden pulls into a parking spot and cuts the engine as he answers me. "Yeah, but he's not here." Taking the keys out of the ignition, he grins before saying, "I sort of bribed him into givin' me the apartment for tonight."

"You had to bribe him?"

He shrugs as he states, "If you knew my brothers like I do, you'd totally understand."

"I'm almost scared to ask what you told him you'd do," I say while laughing.

"Trust me, you don't want to know."

Laughing some more, Caden turns facing the apartments. He seems lost in thought, and I wonder what he's thinking about. I do like the dynamic he and his brother seem to have, and it does make me curious to know more about him and his family. We sit in silence for a few more moments before I break it. "So uh … are we going to spend our date inside your truck all night or what?"

"We could, but," he stops to glance my way and the way he's looking at me, well, let's just say it's hot. His blue eyes seem to darken, and I lick my lips as I feel the sexual tension thicken. "I should feed you."

"Yeah," I huff out. "I'm starving." He nods and quickly jumps out his truck.

Caden

Before I can open the door myself, Caden appears and does it for me. "Milady," he says as he holds out a hand for me. Smirking, I hold in a giggle as I take his hand. Caden helps me out of his massive truck, and I have to remind myself to breathe. I don't like he has this weird effect on me. I don't like that I want him to keep holding onto my hand. As soon as I'm out of his truck, instead of doing what my body is demanding I do, I take my hand out of his. It's better this way. If I let myself get involved with him, I just know someone will get hurt.

When he grins at me, I feel as if he knows what I'm thinking. Thankfully he doesn't say anything, and I follow him as we make our way inside his apartment. "How long have you lived here?" I ask as we walk upstairs before stopping at the door.

"Since I was nineteen. My brother and I wanted some space from our parents, and we've been here ever since."

"That really doesn't tell me much since I have no idea how old you are," I claim as he unlocks the door and he turns back to me.

His eyes narrow for a moment before he says, "What's with the twenty-one questions?"

"I thought this is what people do on dates. You know? Talk. Get to know one another?" Letting out a nervous laugh, I add, "I mean I know it's been a while since I've been on a date, but I'm sure this is how things go." Damn. Now I'm even second guessing myself.

Caden lets out a loud laugh, and I glance around him wondering what's so funny. "I'm just fuckin' with you. Damn you're gullible. And to answer your question, I'm thirty-one."

Trying not to look shocked at our age difference, I sarcastically say, "I see being a smart ass is just another one of your charming traits."

"You'll learn to love me."

"Doubtful," I mumble, but I'm pretty sure he heard me anyway. He flashes me a cheeky grin before turning to walk inside his apartment. Following behind him, I'm really beginning to think he's not exactly what I thought. It could be just how he is, and he likes to joke around, but I hope he knows I'm going to give it right back. I've never been the type of girl to let shit roll off my shoulders easily. I was taught to stick up for myself, and speak my mind. Honestly I hope Caden knows I'm not a pushover or someone he can play with. He better be glad he has his good looks going for him.

"It's not much," he starts as he turns on the lights. "But it's home."

Looking around his small apartment, I can see why he's stayed here for so long. The living

Caden

room has two couches against the wall. One is in front of the flat screen TV, and the other is on the left side of the wall by the two windows with a coffee table sitting in front of them. To my right, I can see a small dining room with a small round table. The kitchen is also on my right with an open wall theme. I assume the three rooms toward the back of his apartment is the bedrooms and a bathroom. "It's cozy." No doubt two men live here. The place screams man cave. Glancing back to Caden, he stares at me like he's waiting for something. "What's with the tea light candles?" They're sitting on the coffee table, and a few are sitting on the opening in the wall that looks into the kitchen. Walking over to pick one up, it feels warm, as if he left them on for a while.

"Oh those. Funny story, I don't do real candles anymore, but I wanted to do somethin' romantic."

Frowning, I turn around holding the tea light in my hand, I ask, "You don't like candles? Have a bad experience or something?"

"You could say that. Let's just say, candles are so overrated."

Laughing, I can only imagine what happened to him. Setting the light back down on the coffee table, I let out a small laugh as I say, "I agree. Can you imagine the kinky fucks out there that like to be burned by the wax?" His eyes widen as I add, "Don't get me wrong. I'm all for a bit of kink, but getting wax poured on you? That's just ... weird."

Caden begins to rub his chest as he claims, "Fuckin' weirdos out there. Thank sweet baby Jesus you're not one." He winks at me, and I can feel my face flush. "Come on, Sassy Savannah. Let me show you the ways of the cookin' master."

"Now this I have to see," I call after him and quickly follow him into the kitchen. Noticing what all he has laid out on the counter, I snap my head up. "You're making me pancakes?"

Putting his hands together, he says, "Here's the thing, and I'm not proud of this but ..." He looks away for a moment, and I can't help but smile. "I've never cooked pancakes before, and you said they were your favorite, and well I have to give you your favorite food on a first date." He turns to grab something out of the fridge before turning back around. "Just so we're clear, all the other dates we have will include other people cookin' for us."

Admiring his honesty, I smile and shake my head at that last part. "Who said we're going on any more dates?"

"I'm fairly certain after you've had my virgin pancakes, you'll either want to go out again to make

Caden

up for a horrible dinner, or you'll love them so much you'll be beggin' me to cook them again. Win, win."

"You're very confident, aren't you?"

Opening the fridge, Caden pulls out a beer and holds it up asking me if I want one. Nodding, he hands it to me as he says, "You know, I have this thing where shit sounds good in my head, but when it actually comes out, it doesn't sound as good."

"You have that problem too?"

He chuckles, a sound I really enjoy hearing, as he opens a drawer. Handing me a bottle opener, I pop the top off my beer and hand it back to him. "It's good to know I'm not alone in my crazy world I call life."

Jumping on the counter, I realize the kitchen is a lot narrower now that we're both in here. "Look at it this way," I begin then take a sip of the beer. "Life would be very boring without us."

"I'll drink to that." We clink the tips of our beer bottles and our eyes lock for a moment as we both take a drink. Taking a big gulp this time, I glance away as he lowers his bottle from his lips. Snapping my head back up when I hear him clap his hands together, he loudly states, "Alright, let's burn some shit."

"I don't think that's how it goes," I pipe back.

"Oh I know. Okay," he says then gives me his full attention. "I'm goin' to be honest here." Raising my eyebrows, I wait for him to finish. "I might have never used this stove before."

"You're serious?"

"As a cucumber."

"I thought the saying was cool as a cucumber?"

"You say tomato, I say tomahto. Same thing."

Unable to hold back my laughter, I set my beer beside me as I cover my mouth. Caden watches me with a smile, and once I get control over myself, I hop down. "How about this? I'll help you and show you the ropes. Then next time you want to impress a chick, you'll at least know the basics."

"Show me the ways of cookin', small fry."

Shaking my head, I wonder how in the hell he's managed to go for so long without learning how to cook for himself. "I have to ask, how is it you've never learned to cook before?"

"If you must know, I have a secret weapon."

Gazing at him, I think about it for a moment before I ask, "Your brother right?"

"Winner, winner chicken dinner."

"What do I win?"

Caden

Maybe that wasn't the best thing to ask him since now he's looking at my lips, and I'm looking at his. His tongue slowly licks his bottom lip as he sucks in a deep breath, and for a second, I think he's going to kiss me. My stomach flutters thinking of what that kiss would be like, and what it would feel like. But he surprises me when he steps back and raises his pinky finger to his mouth as he says in a high-pitched voice, "One million dollars."

Smiling widely, I snap back with, "Groovy baby." He laughs with me, and for the first time in a very long time, I forgot why I'm really here. I forget what my ultimate goal is, and for once I don't mind forgetting.

Before I realize what's happening, Caden takes my hand in his and twirls me around. He stands close behind me as I face the stove as he whispers in my ear, "I like hearin' you laugh."

The pounding of my heart in my ears makes me think twice about what he said, and when his hands begin to roam down to my waist, my entire body heats up. He's so close all I can feel is him. All I can smell is him. Swallowing hard, I have to open my mouth to take in a deep breath. He's making it so hard to stay calm and act as though he's not affecting me. Warning bells begin to go off in my head, but my heart, the damn traitor, is beating so fast telling me to let go for once. It's tempting to just give into Caden and lean back into his touch, but I can't. Closing my eyes, I clench my jaw for a moment before I take his hands off me. "Alright, Mr. Grabby Hands. We have a meal to cook. You wouldn't like to see me when I'm starving."

Instantly I feel a chill as he moves away, and I'm glad my back is to him. I don't think I could look at him in the eyes. That moment felt way too intimate. It felt way too good to be in his arms. I hear him sigh loudly before he asks, "What about some tunes? Then you tell me what I need to do."

Nodding, I watch him out of the corner of my eye as he leaves the kitchen. Grabbing the box of Bisquick Instant Pancake Mix, I read over the directions just to have something to do. Soon Water Under the Bridge by Adele begins to play, and I glance up seeing Caden staring back at me. He doesn't say a word as he makes his way back into the kitchen, but as I listen to the lyrics of the song, I wonder if he's trying to tell me something. Deciding to let it go, I ask him where his pots and pans are. We work in sync, which is another thing I have to remind myself that doesn't mean anything. I begin to make the pancake batter, and I explain every step to Caden. He never interrupts, only asking a question here and there. What I notice the most is how freaking small his kitchen is yet again. It seems every chance he gets, he touches me. First it was my arm, then a light brush on my hand, and now he's

Caden

moved on to grabbing my hips to scoot me over. And every single time he lays a hand on me, my body reacts. It seems I can't help myself, and by the time we're finished cooking, I'm actually craving his light touches.

Damn him and his addictive touch.

Trying to shake off Caden and his hands, I take a plate from him, and we both fill up on pancakes. He grabs the syrup, and we take a seat at his small table. "This looks really good," Caden says I'm glad he's sitting across from me. I need a break from him, and some distance will be good. At least I think distance is going to be good. Unable to stop myself from watching him take his first bite, I wish I'd actually thought before I let myself do so. My stomach clenches as he moans loudly letting me know he's enjoying that bite way too much. He hasn't noticed me watching him yet, or maybe he has, and he's doing this on purpose. Either way, my lady bits are suddenly on fire as I stare at his lips. My mouth opens as he licks them free of the syrup, and Jesus, I sort of wish I was the one licking the sweetness away. "Are you not goin' to eat?" Shit. Quickly glancing away and hoping he doesn't notice my blush, I fight the urge to look up again when I hear him chuckle. It's official, Caden Harlow is going to be the death of me.

We finish eating our meal in silence, and I don't dare look up from my food. I won't lie, I'm afraid if I do, Caden will catch me in the act again, or I'll end up drooling like some lovesick teen. Taking the last bite and swirling it once more in the syrup, I let out a sigh as I enjoy it. Dropping my fork and wiping my mouth, I lean back in my chair and finally glance up. Noticing Caden is staring at me, I begin to think maybe I have something on my face. "What? Do I have syrup on me or something?"

He smirks before saying, "No. Just watchin' you."

"Well you can stop. It's creepy."

"Maybe I'm a creepy kind of guy."

Rolling my eyes, I take a drink of my beer. Setting it down back on the table, I lean back upright as I ask, "So tell me something about you that no one knows."

His eyes widen as if he's shocked by my randomness, but it only takes him a minute to answer me. "That's sort of a hard question to answer considerin' I don't keep secrets or hide anythin'."

"Come on. There has to be at least one thing."

Taking both of his hands and placing them behind his head, he leans back in his chair. Glancing

Caden

away as I notice his biceps contracting, I bite the inside of my cheek. I swear he's doing this on purpose. "I got it," he says as he drops his hands and lays them on the table. "You have to promise not to laugh."

Shaking my head, I grin. "I don't think I can make that promise."

"At least try to contain yourself then."

"I'm all ears. Spill it."

He lets out a long sigh, and I just know this is going to be hilarious. "Alright so when I was like nine or ten, I had a little incident with my zipper." Frowning, I can only guess where he's going with this. "It was more like a fight gone wrong. Anyway I was at school in the bathroom, and the bell just rang for us to go home. I was so focused on leavin', I wasn't watchin' when I zipped my pants. It was the one time my zipper got stuck, and just so you know, zippin' your britches while walkin' is not a good idea." Oh this is rich. I cover my mouth trying as hard as I can not to laugh. "I'm sure you can imagine how that ended. I was so embarrassed I got my dick caught in my zipper, I didn't tell anyone. Needless to say, I suffered in silence for a few days." I end up losing the battle with my laughing. I can't help myself, especially since I see him visibly shiver as if he's reliving the memory. His eyes cut to me as he deadpans, "Yeah, yeah. Laugh it up. I still have a scar from that, and I've been very careful not to redo that again."

My shoulders begin to shake as my laughter keeps coming. Tears even fill my eyes as I picture what it must have been like for him. "I'm ... sorry ... I just ... can't even."

"I'm sort of disturbed by your lack of sympathy for my penis. It hurt like hell."

Getting some control over myself, I wipe my eyes as I let out a breath. "I'm sure it was, but holy fuck. That was funny."

"Happy to provide you with a good laugh." Caden crosses his arms, but I see his smile. "I could ask you for an embarrassin' story, but I'm a nice guy, so I won't. Instead," he starts, and I hold my breath waiting for what he's about to ask. I have no clue as to why I'm suddenly nervous. Maybe it's the way he's looking at me with those blue eyes of his, or maybe it's the way that grin turns into a cocky smirk. "If you had one wish, what would you use it for and why?"

Oh-kay. That was totally different than I thought he would ask. Caden has surprised me yet again for tonight. "That's an easy one." Using the tip of my finger, I rub around the tip of the beer bottle as I confess, "I'd use it to find my mom." At his confused gaze, I explain. "I was adopted when I was six months old. My adoptive parents told me when I was sixteen, and I don't know. Since then, I feel as if there's a piece of me missing. I've been looking for her for years, and I'd almost given up hope until my dad gave me a vital clue when I was away at college." Taking my finger off the bottle, I lean back in my chair and bring my legs up to my chest. Wrapping my arms around my legs, I glance down at my empty plate. "I had so many plans, and so much I wanted to do with my life." Smiling as I remember my dream, my heart clenches when I realize how I've put my entire life on hold to find the one person that can make me whole again. "I wanted to be a photographer and travel the world with just me, a backpack, and a camera." Looking up, Caden has his chin resting on his hands as he gazes at me. "Do you think it's stupid to give up my dreams for someone who doesn't want to be found?"

"No," he says without hesitation, and for some reason, the confidence in his voice gives me hope. "It's not stupid at all. If findin' your birth mother means this much to you, then you have to keep goin'. Plus it's not like you can't go after your dreams once you find her." I can't seem to find the words I want to say. It's as if he knew I needed strength to continue with my search, and he's given it to me. Our gazes lock and for the first time, I realize there's so much more to him that I thought.

Letting my legs drop, I grin widely as I hear Free Bird by Lynyrd Skynyrd begin to play. "I love this song."

Caden quickly moves out of his chair, and I watch him intently as he walks over to me. Holding out a hand, he moves his fingers back and forth. "Dance with me, Savannah." Without giving it another thought, I place my hand in his. He leads me into the living room and drops my hand for a second to move the coffee table out of the way and to turn the volume up.

Feeling my heart begin to race, I lick my lips as he stands in front of me. Slowly taking my waist, I move forward and place my arms around his neck. Laying my head on his chest, I close my eyes as we sway back and forth like eighth graders at a school dance. But it's everything to me. This song has always been one of my favorites and just knowing Caden wanted to enjoy this moment with me, well that means something right? I don't want to overthink it. I want to live in this moment, just for a second. So instead of pulling away like my head is telling me, I let myself relax. I take in Caden's manly smell mixed with his cologne. I let his warmth flow into me, and when he rests his head on mine, I let out a content sigh. For so long I've forgotten what it was like to let someone touch me, or even hold me like this. It's kind of a big deal I'm doing it now, with a stranger no less.

Caden

As the song picks up the pace, Caden takes my hand and twirls me around. He starts singing the lyrics, and I can't stop myself from joining him. Although we're both off key, it feels good to let loose. Laughing loudly as Caden pretends to play guitar with the solo, I throw my hands up as I let the music and the beat flow through me. We're like two kids again as we dance and sing around his small living room, but I don't care. I'm having a blast watching him, and his grin is infectious. I even cheer him on as he bends down to one knee as he continues to play his fake guitar. "I forgot how long this song was," he yells out.

"I know. Isn't it great?" Spinning around with my hands in the air, I start to remember my once free spirit. My mom always told me I reminded her of a bird. She said if I let my wings spread out wide, I could do anything. Then she would play this song for me, and she and I would dance around the house singing at the top of our lungs.

Which is why when the song begins to end, I feel a deep sadness in my heart. I realize how much I miss my parents, and I think maybe it is okay if I stop this crazy search and go home to the two people that love me unconditionally.

Glancing up as I hear the volume being turned down, I try to control my rapid breathing. I'm out of breath, and I'm sure my cheeks are flushed from dancing. Caden turns around and he of course, doesn't look like he's even broken a sweat. I, on the other hand, probably look as if I've just run five miles. When he stands in front of me, I hope and pray I don't smell like body odor. How embarrassing would that be? His blue eyes meet mine, and I can't seem to look away. He has me entranced in those bright blue eyes. Out of the corner of my eye, I see his hand reaching up, and I suck in a harsh breath as he brushes my hair behind my ear then cups my cheek. I can barely think at this point because I know what's coming. There's no stopping it, and fuck I don't think I want it to. "Do you know you're absolutely stunnin' when you let go, small fry?"

Not dropping my gaze, I let out a small laugh at his ridiculous nickname for me. Why he continues to call me that, I'll never know unless I ask. Even if he's half serious and playful at the same time, I still want him to kiss me. I don't think I've wanted something so much from a guy before. His other hand caresses the other side of my cheek as he leans in. Shit. This is it. There's no going back after this, and I know there's no way in hell I can be friends with him once this is over. I want it too bad, and maybe it's okay to enjoy one kiss for a moment.

Or two.

When his lips meet mine, I know a moment isn't going to be enough.

Caden

Caden takes his time taking my lips, but I don't mind. His kiss is tender and almost too gentle. Maybe he wants to see how I'll react, but when his tongue touches my lips seeking permission, I eagerly open for him. As soon as I do, our kiss changes almost instantly. He groans as the air leaves my lungs, and I grab onto his shirt as I try not to fall into him even more. All I can feel is him, and all I can taste is him. He's everywhere invading all my senses. Caden deepens our kiss when his hand snakes to my neck, and I find myself pulling him closer to me. Tilting my head the way the wants, I let him control our kiss. It's everything I imagined, but at the same time, it's so much more. It feels like sensation overload and desire begins to flow through me. My stomach clenches as he takes my bottom lip and nips at it, and when my hands roam up his back, I realize what I'm doing.

I can't do this with him.

Pulling away, I step back putting some distance between us. His eyes snap to mine, and I try so very hard to control my breathing. Taking my hand and covering my mouth, I relive our first kiss. But I don't want to. I can't let him overtake me like that again. It's pointless to be involved with him knowing why I'm here, and the fact I'm not here to stay. Seeing the hurt in his eyes, I glance down at the floor. "I didn't realize I was so bad at kissin', small fry."

He's trying to lighten the mood, but I can hear how tense his voice is. "No, it's not that." Looking back up, he waits for me to finish, but I don't know how to explain why I can't go there with him. "I ... I think I should go." He only nods then turns to the door. Following him back to his truck, my heart hurts knowing I'm pushing him away. I hate feeling as though I just made a mistake because I could see a life being with Caden. But maybe that's the problem.

I don't want to hand him the power to hurt me.

Six
Caden

Savannah Owens is a fucking mystery.

I'm not sure what I'm doing wrong here. One second she's hotter than the Fourth of July, then with a blink of an eye, she's freezing cold. Like the kind of cold that makes my dick shrink to an embarrassing size and my poor balls suck up into my body. Okay bad image there, but I'm not sure how else to explain it. It's been one day since our date. One that started off epically but ended horribly. Maybe I shouldn't have kissed her, but the moment was too perfect to pass up. Not to mention, I know Savannah wanted me. Her eyes wouldn't leave me all night, and her body language told me she was into it.

What went wrong?

Brie Paisley

I've been going over it since I dropped her off at The Holiday Inn. She wouldn't let me walk her to her room. She didn't even say a word to me after we left my apartment. Running a hand down my face, I feel the frustration building. Before picking up my phone, I turn down my CB radio in the squad car. It's probably not the best idea to be so distracted while on duty, but I really want to figure Savannah out. Plus it's not like there's tons of criminals ripping and roaming the roads this early in the day. I'm so fucking glad I don't have a rookie riding along with me today. It's sad and pathetic at how much I've been checking my phone, but I don't want to miss if Savannah decides to message me. Deciding I should man the fuck up, I send her a message first.

Me: I had this thought.

Staring at the message, I can't help but think how stupid this is. Why when it comes to her, I feel as though all my wit, charm, and everything that makes me who I am fly right out the window? This girl has me all wrapped up in knots, and fuck she doesn't even know it. Setting my phone in my cup holder, I take a deep breath hoping Savannah responds. Deciding to get my head out of my ass, I pull out of the parking lot and begin to patrol around Main Street. It's too early for anything exciting, but maybe I'll get lucky and catch someone speeding. I'll take anything I can get at this point to distract me.

Caden

Just as I'm turning around to do another sweep, my phone pings. I won't lie and say my stomach didn't just drop hearing the sound. Hoping it's Savannah, I pull into an empty parking spot in front of a small bistro.

Sassy S: I'm scared to ask what thought that is.

Thank fuck it's her. Seeing her message gives me a bit of hope that I didn't royally fuck everything up.

Me: You + me and a redo date.

Okay, okay. A bit bold but still. I've never been the one to beat around the bush about what I want, and Savannah is someone I definitely want. Letting the squad car idle while waiting for her response, I wish my heart would stop pounding in my chest. I swear, I'm acting like a lovesick adolescent boy again.

Sassy S: I'm sorry but I can't.

Clenching my jaw, I refuse to take no for an answer.

Me: I promise not to kiss you again.

Sassy S: I can't Caden.

Me: Why not? I'm a nice guy. You're a beautiful woman. I know you enjoyed yourself with me.

Sassy S: It's complicated.

Me: It's only complicated if you make it so.

When she doesn't reply back after ten minutes, I know she won't give me any answers. Tossing my phone in the passenger seat, I quickly back out of the parking spot and continue with my patrolling. I try not to think of Savannah and her vague ass message, but I can't help myself. There's something going on with her, and for once in my life, I'm actually scared to find out what her secrets are. My instincts are going off with full force, but I don't know why. It's just a feeling that something big is coming, and I've learned to trust my instincts. I sort of have to with my line of work.

The thing is no matter how much I try to focus on my job, I still have this burning question that won't go away.

What am I going to do to make Savannah mine?

A few hours have gone by since I've heard from her. I've all but given up and decide maybe it's best she doesn't respond. Lord knows I want her to text me, send a smoke signal, or something to let me know she's still here. The fear she'll up and leave

Caden

without a word bothers me more than I thought it would. I guess now I know how Carter felt when Shelby left him all those years ago. He was a fucking mess, but at the time, I didn't really understand it. My brothers and I have known since the day Carter met Shelby that they would end up together, but now that it's a possibility for me, well it fucking sucks a big donkey dick. Then again, is it crazy how much I already care about Savannah? It seems strange when I think about it because come on, I barely know her. Every time I think of never seeing her again, never hearing her voice, or seeing her smile, my chest begins to constrict.

Which is why when my phone begins to chime back to back with new messages, I raise an eyebrow and pick it up. Knowing I'm parked in a safe area to read them, I unlock it.

Sassy S: I want you to kiss me again.

Sassy S: Do you think my butt looked fat last night?

Sassy S: Seriously still waiting for that kiss.

Confused doesn't even begin to explain what I'm feeling. Reading over her messages again, I have to wonder if she's not under the influence. There's just no way she'd send me mixed signals just because she could. I don't get that kind of vibe from her and highly doubt she's trying to play me.

Me: Are you high?

Sassy S: AF!

Sassy S: LOL you should try it sometime.

Me: Considering my job I probably shouldn't.

Sassy S: YOLO!

Sassy S: Can you come over? I really would like that kiss now.

Me: You're killing me small fry.

Sassy S: What! I don't see any blood.

Laughing out loud, I shake my head. This girl is going to be the death of me. Maybe I should find out who her dealer is because this is twice that, I know of, she's been using drugs. Not wanting to ruin a good thing because this is too good to stop now, I reply back to her.

Me: I didn't mean literally. I thought you had to work tonight?

Sassy S: Oh. Good because I don't want to kiss you.

Sassy S: I meant kill. I do want to kiss you.

Caden

Brushing off the fact she ignored my question, I grin knowing she really must want my lips again. I knew she liked kissing me.

Me: Why do you want a kiss so bad? I thought I was horrible at it.

Sassy S: Oh no. You were amazing and I want more.

Before I can write back, the dispatcher calls a disturbance at a hotel over the CB radio. Thinking nothing of it, I start to ignore it knowing someone else will take it when the dispatcher says the name of the hotel. "Dammit, Savannah." I already know it's her causing the disturbance because my small fry is a total trouble maker. Plus there's never been a call for The Holiday Inn like this before. Taking the call, I forget all about responding to her message. Turning on my siren, I hope I can get there sooner rather than later. Since I'm close by Columbus Air Force Base, it'll take me at least ten to fifteen minutes to get there.

Once I arrive at The Holiday Inn, I quickly jump out of the car and slam the door behind me. Adjusting my holster around my hip, I make my way inside. The smell of burnt popcorn and bleach fill my nose as I step through the door, and I try not to breathe through my nose. Jesus that smell is awful. Turning right, I walk up to the front desk seeing two tiny Chinese workers yelling at each other. Maybe they're the reason for the disturbance? One can hope. "Excuse me. Is there a problem?"

The man, who by the way reminds me of Mr. Miyagi from The Karate Kid, turns to me with a scowl on his face. "You cop?"

"That's why I wear this uniform," I deadpan as I motion up down.

"You come with me." Following the small man, he all but runs to the elevator. "You make her stop. She too loud. Make customers unhappy. We cannot have unhappy people. They leave hotel. Bad for business."

Shaking my head, I will the elevator to hurry up and get to our destination. "Alright just stay calm."

"You make her leave. She pay for all damages. Make customers unhappy."

Sweet baby Jesus, someone help me. "I'll make sure to take care of it." Thankfully the elevator pings and the doors open. Following Mr. Miyagi once again, I already know what room he's going to stop at. That and the fact I can already hear the music playing from her room.

Mr. Miyagi stops at Savannah's room and points while saying, "She too loud. Make her stop. Make customers very unhappy."

Caden

"I know, sir. Please let me do my job now." Letting out a huff as Mr. Miyagi walks away, I hope like hell I don't have to deal with him again. Turning to the door, I run a hand down my face wondering how I'm going to handle this. Maybe I should've let another officer handle this one, but I don't want her to go to jail. Deciding to handle this as professional as I can, I knock loudly on the door. I have to pound on the door more than once before she finally opens it.

"Caden! You're here!" she yells as she flings the door open so hard it bounces off the wall. I wouldn't doubt if there's now a hole in the wall from it, and I'm actually surprised once the door flings back it doesn't knock her ass out.

My eyebrows raise as I look her over and fucking hell. I'm in deep shit here. Her hair is all over the place, which looks so good on her, and her cheeks are a bright rosy red. Her eyes are so dilated I can barely tell what color they are, and I have to swallow hard when I see what she's wearing. Damn. Thank you to whoever invented boy shorts for underwear and skimpy tank tops. She's totally not wearing a bra either since her nipples are straining in that top. Gaining control over myself, I tell my cock to behave. "Savannah Owens. You're in so much trouble."

She frowns but then grins like this is all some sort of joke. "What sort of trouble, Officer? Are you here to take me downtown?"

Don't look at her nipples. Don't you dare look at those hard and perky nipples. Glancing down, I look and fuck me. I wish I hadn't. She raises an arm as she leans on the door frame as her eyes rake over my body. "Let me in, small fry." She willingly complies by pushing the door open with her other hand. Watching her closely as I shut the door behind me once she steps back, she grins widely and makes her way to the dresser in the room. Taking a look at her room, I wonder what the hell happened in here. It's a complete wreck. Her clothes are scattered on every surface, it smells like weed and booze, and I begin to wonder when the last time she had someone clean her room. It freaking reeks in here. Everything she's doing goes against the oath I took, and there's so much more going on here than just her having a good time. Glancing up at Savannah, she dances around the room like she doesn't have a care in the world. As much as I want to watch her like this, I have to at least turn the music down. Star Boy by The Weeknd plays so loudly I hope like hell my eardrums are still intact when I leave. Spotting the source of where the music is coming from, I cross the room in a few steps to turn it off.

Caden

She has her phone hooked up to a playing dock, and as soon I cut the music she says, "Why did you do that? I love that song."

"Can't have you disturbin' the peace, small fry."

She rolls her eyes at me, and I grin at her. I won't lie. I love this sassy side of her. "Is that why you're here then?"

Hearing the hurt in her voice, I make my way over to her. When I reach for her, she turns away and grabs something by her suitcase that's laying in the middle of the room. "I stole this tonight," she says proudly as she holds up a bottle of Tequila. "Want to have a drink with me, Caden?"

Ignoring her comment about the stolen booze, I let out a heavy sigh. "I wish I could, small fry."

She pouts, and I swear she shouldn't look so beautiful while doing it. "What did you tell me?" She uses her index finger to tap on her chin as she adds, "Right. I remember. Live a little? Or something like that."

Shaking my head, I cross my arms as I say, "I'm on duty, Savannah."

Grinning widely, she giggles before saying, "You said duty." Letting out a small sigh as she lets out another round of giggling, I can't help but wonder what I'm going to do about her. "That's such a funny word." She giggles again as she tries to open the bottle of Tequila and just as I'm about to take it from her, she gets it open. "Cheers," she says then turns the bottle up as she takes a drink. Now I'm all for drinking and having a good time, but I have a feeling Savannah has another reason for her wild ways. And I have to give her props. She takes that drink like a champ, only coughing a little as she brings the bottle back down. "We need music," she claims loudly and starts to turn the music back on.

Grabbing her by the waist, I redirect her so her back is to the music now. "No music, small fry."

She narrows her eyes at me as she steps out of my reach again. See what I mean? Even intoxicated she's hot and cold all at the same time. She's so frustratingly beautiful. "You're ruining my fun, Caden."

"I don't think anyone has said that to me before," I say with a frown. Come to think of it, no one has. I'm usually the one letting everyone enjoy themselves, but this is different. She has no idea of the awkward situation she's put me in. Shrugging her shoulders, she takes another drink of the Tequila, and before she can do it again, I take the bottle out of her hand. "I think it's time to put the Tequila down, small fry."

Caden

"Why are you here, Caden? I'm having fun, and you're being ... you. You're acting like a cop ready to arrest me, and I don't like it."

Setting the bottle on the dresser, I try not to let her outburst bother me. But it does. I want her to have fun and enjoy being young, but not at the expense of her freedom. "Savannah, you know why I'm here. The hotel manager called and if I hadn't shown up, what do you think would've happened?"

She blinks a few times as if she can't quite understand what I mean. Surprisingly she takes two steps toward me and wraps both arms around my neck. Smelling the alcohol on her breath, I swallow hard because she still smells divine. "What are you going to do, Officer?" Placing my hands on her hips, she's staring at my lips now, and dammit she wants me to kiss her. I want to kiss her and do many, many, things to her that I know we'll both enjoy. "Are you going to kiss me or arrest me?"

I should arrest her. Yep, just put her fine ass in cuffs and have my wicked way with her. No not that. I should take her clothes off first then cuff her ... fuck. *Contain yourself jackass.* "You're makin' my job a lot harder than it usually is," I breathe out.

"I told you things were complicated."

"I'm startin' to see that, small fry."

"Just shut up and kiss me, Caden."

Lord knows I want to. I knew once I kissed her last night, things wouldn't be the same. I also knew I would want to feel her lips on mine again and again. Preferably for the rest of my life, and I'm not even surprised at the thought of being with her forever. *She's the one.* There's no doubt about it. "I want to believe me, I really want to, but you're totally fucked up. I told you my mama raised a gentleman."

"So?" She presses her body into mine, and she's making my job of being a nice guy a lot harder. Her fingers run through my short hair, and her other hand grips my neck hard as she pulls me closer. "Do you always do what your mama tells you? Break some rules, Caden." We're only inches away from actually touching lips, and my heart is pounding knowing what I want is right here. "Just kiss me," she whispers and fuck.

One kiss and that's it.

One and done.

I can't fight the pull anymore.

Giving in, I take her mouth, and my cock jumps hearing a moan escape from her. My grip on her hips tighten as she opens her mouth to let me in, and one and done is not going to cut it. I have to have more of this from her. The way she tastes, the feel of her in my arms, and everything about this woman is driving me insane with need. Running a

Caden

hand up her back, I press her chest into me as I deepen our kiss. In the back of my mind, I know this isn't something I should be doing while she's under the influence. Gaining control over myself, I begin to pull back knowing if I don't stop this now, I might not be able to later.

But my small fry must know what she wants.

As if she sensed I was about to end our kiss, she breaks away from my lips only for a moment to jump up and wrap her legs around my waist. Groaning as she hurriedly takes my mouth again, I hold her up by her luscious ass and walk forward to the bed. Laying her down not so gracefully on the bed, I hover over her and gaze into her eyes. "Is this what you want, Savannah?" I ask huskily, and I let out a harsh breath as her hips grind against me.

"I want you, Caden." She says, and all the control I have goes into not giving her what she wants.

Leaning down and kissing her sweet lips once more, I commit everything about this moment to memory. If anything, this gives me more reason to claim her as mine, and all I have to do now is wait until she's sober enough to agree. Pulling away once more, I really wish she wasn't high or drunk. This would be much easier. "You're makin' this so hard for me, small fry."

She grins widely before saying, "Well I hope I'm making something hard. Otherwise I'm not doing my job so well."

Knowing what she's referring to, I shake my head and let out a chuckle. "Trust me, my pants are about to explode because of you."

"I can take care of that for you," she sweetly claims and begins to reach down.

Grabbing her wrist, I gently move her hand away from the danger zone because I know if she touches me, I'll end up fucking up all my chances with her. Chicks remember shit like this, and I could never take advantage of her. She watches me with her dilated eyes as I lean down once more and leave a peck on her lips. Moving up to her nose, I do the same before leaving her completely. It's one of the hardest things I've ever had to do, and my cock is really starting to hurt. I'm going to have a serious case of blue balls later. "Time for bed, small fry." She pouts again, but she lazily gets off the bed. She doesn't say a word as she reaches down to pull her top off, and realizing she wants me to see her, I quickly turn around. She giggles loudly, and I can't help but wonder if she's testing me. Feeling something on my shoulder, I glance to the right. Groaning loudly, that little minx threw her panties on me. Which means she's naked. Which means I've got to leave.

Caden

Like five minutes ago.

"I'm ready for my goodnight kiss," she calls out.

Please be under the covers. Please for the love of God, let her be covered up to her neck. Pulling her panties off my shoulder and pushing them into my front pocket, I slowly turn around. Thankfully she is under the covers and smiling at me. Letting out a sigh, I make my way over to her. Leaning down, she watches me with those wide eyes as I brush her hair out of her face and behind her ear. "We're goin' to talk about this tomorrow." Giving her a pointed look, I add, "When you're sober."

"Okay," she breathes out, and I hope she knows I mean it.

"Goodnight, Savannah."

Closing her eyes, she whispers, "Night, handsome cop." Grinning, I kiss her on her forehead then stand upright.

I don't leave right away though. For some reason, my chest begins to ache knowing I have to go, but I stay for a few moments just watching her fall to sleep. Yeah, it might be a little creepy to watch someone sleep, but I don't want to go just yet. She looks so at ease, and I hope I can see her so at peace more. I realize she and I do have a lot to talk about, and she has a lot of explaining to do.

Taking a deep breath, I turn to leave before stopping. She's going to have a wicked hangover so I quickly look around the room hoping she has something she can take in the morning. Once I find some medicine for her, I fill a plastic cup with water and set it on the bedside table. Spotting a notepad and a pen, I quickly write a note just in case fate really wants to fuck with me tomorrow. She needs to remember I was here. Satisfied with my note, I give Savannah one last glance before I walk to the door. Flicking off the lights, I start to open the door but stop when I hear her call out my name in her sleep. "Tomorrow, small fry," I say, but I know she can't hear me.

But even so, it's a promise. Tomorrow she won't be able to hide from me anymore. Tomorrow I'll make it very clear that she's not going to be able to keep me away.

seven
Savannah

Caden's mouth takes mine, and he doesn't even realize he's sucking all the air I have into him. Even if I can't breathe properly, I want him more than I ever have. The burning desire he makes me feel isn't normal. The way he makes my heart pound in my chest isn't normal either. He kisses me ever so passionately, tenderly, and as if he needs me just as much as I need him. Pulling away, I gasp for air before I confess, "I need you, Caden."

He leaves hot and wet kisses on my chin making his way to my neck. Rolling my head to the side, I close my eyes loving the feel of his lips on my skin. "You have me, Savannah," he claims against my neck.

"Then take me." I can't stand it any longer. He needs to put out this fire burning in my stomach.

This need that I have is consuming me slowly, and only he can fulfill it. He pulls away from me, and before I can protest, my shirt is suddenly gone. Standing in front of him showing him some of my intimate parts, his eyes burn brightly. He raises his hand to touch me, and I arch my chest begging him to hurry.

    Bang.

    Bang.

    Bang.

Frowning, I wonder where the banging noise is coming from, but I push it out of my mind as Caden moves closer to my aching breasts.

    Bang.

    Bang.

    Bang.

There's always a moment when you're half in a dream and half awake. Hearing more banging on the door, I snap open my eyes fully coming out of the dream. My face burns hot as I try to shake away the erotic dream I was having about Caden and I. For a moment, I really thought it was happening, and feeling how wet I am, so did my lady parts. I huff out a breath wondering what time it is, and who the hell is at the door, when whoever it is keeps banging annoyingly.

Caden

Pushing the covers off me, I quickly get out of bed. Or I try to anyway. My foot somehow gets twisted inside the covers, and as I stand, I fall hard on the ground. "Son of a bitch," I cry out, and that's when I realize I'm freaking buck ass naked. I never sleep naked, and I vaguely remember drinking and smoking last night. Rubbing my knee for a moment, I grit my teeth at the carpet burn. But the damn banging continues on. "I'm coming! Give it a rest already." Whoever is at the door is really getting on my bad side. Jumping up, I rush to find some clothes and quickly put them on. Once I'm dressed, I don't even think about how else I look. It's probably bad considering I woke up naked in bed and don't really remember how I got that way. Jerking the door open, Mr. Chang the hotel manager, stops midway with his hand. Shit. This can't be good. "What's up, Mr. Chang?"

"You leave hotel. Today," he sternly says in broken English while pointing a finger at me. Clenching my jaw, my stomach drops. Is he really kicking me out? "You too loud. Had customers leave hotel. You leave today."

"Mr. Chang, please," I start, but he cuts me off.

"Leave today!"

He doesn't even bother with letting me explain or at least let me talk my way out of this. He turns his heels and rushes away like there's a fucking fire about to burn his ass. "Dammit." Letting out a heavy sigh, I slam the door shut and wonder what the hell am I going to do now?

Leaning my forehead against the door, I can't believe I did this. I remember very clearly why I came back to my hotel room, got so fucked up, and I just got evicted. Turning around, I let my head fall back to knock it softly on the door. This is all Paul's son's fault. If Mike hadn't tried to get me to suck his dick at work, I wouldn't have walked out of work, stolen some tequila, and came back here to get those images out of my mind. He even had the freaking nerve to whip his little penis out at me. Like that would really change my mind about him harassing me. It does make me feel less like an irresponsible adult knowing I did knee him so hard in his crotch that he's probably still feeling it today. Even so, I can't afford to stay anywhere else considering I don't have a job anymore. My savings is all but gone, and The Holiday Inn was the only hotel in town that gave me the cheapest rate.

Letting my eyes roam around the room, I say a little goodbye to the room and let out another sigh knowing it's going to take me a while to pack up all my clothes. My head begins to pound, and I push myself off the door deciding to take a long and hot shower. My heart literally hurts knowing if I don't have a job or a place to stay, I have to go back home.

Caden

The thought of leaving without finding out who my birth mother is leaves a horrible taste in my mouth. Or that could be from last night's fun gone wrong. My eyes begin to fill with tears, but I blink them away as I turn on the shower. There's no one to blame but me, and I think that's what makes it worse. I did this. I ended this trip with my stupid mistakes.

I just don't know if I can go back home without knowing who Tammy Richards is and why she gave me away. This is probably for the best. Why would Tammy want to see me anyway? I've fallen so far into this hole of despair, and honestly I wouldn't blame her if she didn't ever want to see me. I mean look at me. No job, no money, and I just got evicted. *Way to go, Savannah*.

Pushing my depressing thoughts out of my mind, I quickly shower. Once I'm finished, I step out and dry off. I don't even bother with drying my hair and decide to just pile it on top of my head. After brushing the dirty taste in my mouth away, I find better and less dirty clothes to wear. Mom would be embarrassed if she saw how I've been living. It does make me smile knowing I'll see her again. Even if this trip was pointless, I miss my parents a lot more than I thought I would. "At least I tried," I say to myself as I grab my suitcase. Setting it on the bed, I begin to toss my clothes inside. Ignoring how much my head is pounding, I grab another handful of my things and right before I drop them inside the suitcase, I spot a note under two pills next to a glass of water on the bedside table. Letting the clothes fall out of my grasp, I quickly inspect the note because in a way, I already know who left it. And my stomach drops as I see the messy handwriting, and who signed it at the bottom.

Sassy Savannah,

You're a wild child at heart. As much as I would love to stay all night and watch you sleep, I have a job to return to. Please take the pills. I'm sure you'll have a killer of a hangover.

C.

P.S. We're still havin' that talk whether or not you remember what happened tonight.

Letting my head fall back for a moment, I curse out loud. This can only mean he was in my room last night, and I don't remember what happened. It's just bunch of blurry images and I really, really, really, hope I didn't do something stupid like sleep with him. Having drunk sex with him would so be a bad idea. However sober sex with Caden ... now that I can only dream about.

Wait.

I've already done that. Well sort of anyway.

Trying not to think too much of his promise of talking, I set the note back down and pick up the two

Caden

white pills. Quickly washing them down with the water he left for me, I ignore the fact my stomach feels like it's in knots. The thought of leaving Caden behind bothers me, and it's something I don't want to think about. So I do what I do best and lock it away in a box.

But the thing about boxes, they're not really reliable. All it takes is one little thing, and it's destroyed. Which is exactly what happens when someone knocks on the door again. Thinking it's Mr. Chang again, I don't hesitate to open the door.

When our gazes lock, that stupid box goes up in fucking flames.

eight
Caden

"What are you doing here?" she asks quietly.

"I told you last night, small fry. I'm here to have that talk."

Her eyes dart away as her cheeks turn to crimson. Does she remember how she tried to jump my bones last night? Not that I'm complaining. "I don't think that's a good idea."

"But I come bearin' gifts and the cure for a hangover," I claim before she can shut the door on me. Holding up the bag of greasy fast food and coffee, she glances at it for a moment. Shaking the bag of food, I grin widely. "You know you want this greasy biscuit and warm coffee."

Caden

"Fine. You can come in." Not taking a chance that she'll change her mind, I don't waste a second before getting my ass in her room.

Which by the way, looks a lot cleaner than last night. My eyes spot her suitcase on the bed, and I try to keep my voice neutral as I ask, "Goin' somewhere, small fry?"

Handing her the breakfast I picked up, she takes a drink of the coffee before answering me. "Yeah. I got evicted earlier."

"Mr. Miyagi kicked you out?" Pretending I'm fine isn't as easy as people make it out to be. If she doesn't have anywhere to stay, will she leave?

"Mr. Chang," she clarifies, "stopped by a little while ago saying some bullshit about me making the other customers unhappy. Said I was too loud."

Watching her as she sits down on the bed, she opens the bag of food and begins to eat. "I hate to be the one to tell you this, but you were disturbin' the peace. Which is why I got called to the scene."

She slowly chews then swallows as if she's thinking about what happened last night. "Speaking of that, did we ... um ..." I do find it amusing how her blush returns, and the fact she can't seem to get out what she wants to ask. I could be a nice guy and put her out of her misery, but I'm secretly enjoying this.

She takes a deep breath and glances up at me. "Did we have sex?"

"Define sex." Now I'm just fucking with her.

Her eyes widen as she snaps, "I believe you know what sex means, Caden. Did we or did we not have sex?"

Trying not let my grin show, I wait a few beats before answering her. "Why would you think we had sex?"

"Because I woke up naked and I don't remember, okay? I don't remember." She lets out a long sigh, and I start to feel like a real asshole. "It's just," she starts, and I walk over to her. Bending down in front of her, she says, "I don't let myself get that out of control very often, and I don't like when I can't remember what happened the next day. I know it's not a good idea to smoke weed and drink, but there haven't been many times when I don't remember what happens the next day. It makes me feel uneasy." Her eyes penetrate mine as she adds, "I usually smoke just to relax and when I'm stressed, and I don't do it all the time. Just to take my mind off things."

Shocked she actually opened up so willingly, I place my hand over hers on the bed. Her eyes meet mine, and I decide maybe it wasn't such a good idea to mess with her. "We didn't have sex, Savannah."

Caden

The relief in her eyes hurts my ego more than I thought it would. "It wasn't for your lack of tryin' though."

"You're lying," she quickly says, but I can see the smile trying to show.

"I never lie. Especially not about somethin' like that. You couldn't keep your hands off me. Practically molested me."

"I did not! Now you're just messing with me."

"You did so. I mean who can blame you. I am hot."

She rolls her eyes at me, but I'm glad her smile is back. "You're so full of yourself aren't you?"

"I can't help that you wanted me, small fry."

"Then explain how I ended up naked?"

"Well," I begin as I raise my eyebrows. "You did that all on your own." With her wide eyes staring at me, I quickly add, "I promise I didn't see anything. Don't get me wrong, I wanted to take a peek at those curves, but I couldn't do that to you."

"That's ... kind of sweet of you." Her eyes don't leave mine as we sit in silence for a while, and I'm surprised she hasn't moved away from my touch either. Not that I want her to. But just as soon as I begin to revel in our moment, she shakes her head and pulls away as she stands. "I should finish packing before Mr. Chang comes back and yells at me some more."

"He can be a bit extreme." She nods and goes back to packing, her breakfast long forgotten. The more I watch her pack her things, the more I wonder if she's going to leave for good. The thought of never seeing her again makes my hands begin to sweat, and my heart starts thumping like a freaking jackhammer in my chest. "Are you movin' to another hotel?" I hope my question sounds casual like I'm just making polite conversation, when I really need to know what she plans to do.

She doesn't stop tossing clothes in her overflowing suitcase as she says, "Well considering I don't have a job anymore, I can't exactly pay for a hotel. And there's no reason for me to stay."

Before even giving it a second thought, I blurt out, "Move in with me then."

She snaps her head to me and narrows her eyes. "Move in with you? Why would I do that?"

Because you're my one, and I can't bear to see you leave. "Don't think of it as movin' in that was the wrong word." I'm beginning to panic. Taking a deep breath, I run a hand down my face. "You can stay with me until you can find another job. That way you don't have to worry about it."

"I appreciate the offer, but I don't think so, Caden."

"Why not? I'll let you have my room, and I'll sleep on the couch." I'm grasping at straws here.

"I couldn't put you out like that."

"You wouldn't be." I counter.

She looks away as she sighs and I hope like hell she's at least considering it. "I don't know. This is too weird."

Knowing this is my only chance, I take a step forward and place each hand on her warm cheeks. Hearing her suck in a breath, I know she feels what I am. I can see her pulse beating in her neck, and the way her eyes hungrily glance to my lips lets me know she wants me. "You can't just leave, Savannah."

"Why not?" She whispers.

"Because whether or not you want to admit it yet, there's somethin' goin' on between us, and I'm willin' to do whatever it takes to make you stay."

She tries to pull away, but I hold her still. "Caden, this is crazy. I barely know you."

"Which is why you need to stay. And I don't see you as the type to just give up on findin' your birth mother." It's a low blow, and I know it. But fuck this is a dangerous game she's playing. I'm handing her everything she needs to continue her search. She just needs reminding of it. "You can stay with me until you find somethin' else. I'm not askin' you to marry me. I'm not askin' for anythin' but a chance, Savannah."

"You drive a hard bargain, Caden Harlow."

"So is that a yes?" She slowly nods her head, and I grin widely. "Can I get that in writin'?"

"Don't push your luck."

Unable to resist, I lean in and quickly get a taste of her lips. It's a fast kiss, but it's still just as powerful as the last one we shared. "I promise you won't regret it, small fry."

Dropping my hands from her face, she takes a step back from me, and I know what she's doing. She's still trying to put distance between us. "You better not because I know people."

Chuckling at her serious tone, I turn to pick up her half eaten biscuit and hand it to her. "Now that I don't doubt." She rolls her eyes at me once again, but she does finish her breakfast. "I do have one tiny condition before you actually move in," I say softly. Her eyes lock with mine, and I hope she doesn't take this the wrong way. "I would prefer if you wouldn't use drugs anymore." Her eyebrows raise, but I hold up a hand letting her know I'm not finished. "I know you've been usin', and normally I wouldn't mind.

Caden

However, after what happened last night, I think it'll be better if you just come to me if you're needin' a fix, or somethin' to take your mind off things."

She seems to think about it for a few moments as she glances away. I really hope I didn't just overstep my boundaries, but I can't have her lighting up joints in my apartment. The last thing I need is for one of the neighbors calling the cops. That'll just lead to more problems for the both of us. "Maybe you're right," she finally huffs out, and I relax instantly.

Walking toward her, I lightly run a finger down her arm as I say, "You can trust me, Savannah."

Those blue-green eyes gaze into mine, and I hope she's starting to understand why I'm here, and what my ultimate goal is. "I'll do better. Just because you asked so nicely."

Chuckling once more, she takes a drink of her coffee, and I help her pack up the rest of her things. It doesn't take as long as I thought considering she has more clothes than any woman I've known. "Ready to blow this popsicle?" I ask once we're standing by the door.

"Yeah, I am." She whips her head toward me and adds, "I'm ready to leave. Not actually blow something."

Taking her hand in mine, and I'm surprised yet again that she doesn't pull away, I claim, "The fact you had to clarify that just means you need more lessons on hearin' southern slang."

"And I'm sure you'll be my teacher," she says sarcastically.

"Well who else is goin' to teach you? No one else is qualified."

Savannah pulls the door shut with her free hand, and I feel a surge of pride flow through me knowing she still hasn't let go of my hand. "Are you always like this?"

"What? Charmin'? Awesome? Oh wait, you mean devilishly handsome."

She laughs loudly, and I love the fact I made her do it. The sound alone is unlike anything I've heard before. It's like music to my ears. "You keep telling yourself that."

Pulling her to me, I set her suitcase to the side. Leaning in close, I whisper, "You haven't seen anythin' yet, small fry." It's a promise more than anything. Yes, I'm playful I'm not known to be serious, but with her there's more of me wanting to surface. She might not know it, but she's already changing me in ways I never thought possible, and it's all for the better. Before and I'm not proud of this, I used women and I'm starting to realize, even if I

Caden

had a reason for not opening up more to them, it was wrong. But as I gaze into her blue and green eyes, I know I won't be that guy anymore. Not to her. "Come on, small fry. Let's go home."

"You did what? Because I swear you just said you asked her to move in with us."

"I did say that. I don't remember you bein' deaf, Cas."

"What is wrong with you? Why would you ask her to move in with us when you know nothin' about this girl?"

Okay this wasn't the reaction I was hoping for when I came home to tell Cason the good news. Savannah wanted to take separate vehicles since she said she had some errands to run, and I came straight home to spread the word. "I don't see why you're getting' your panties in a wad. And." I point a finger to him. "She's not just some girl."

Cason blinks a few times and being his twin, I know what he's thinking. "You're actin' like a complete fucktard, you know that right?"

"Well geez, tell me how you really feel." Propping a hand on the counter in the kitchen, I ask, "What's really on our mind, honey?"

"I can't talk to you when you're actin' this way." He turns to walk away but thinks better of it. "There's no way this will end well for either of you. It's too fast and I know I'm bein' a dick about it, but you know why. The last time you went in head first, what happened, Caden?"

Remembering all too well what he's talking about, I can't fault him for being over protective. "That was a long time ago, Cas. Savannah is different. You'll see."

"Yeah, I really hope so. And if not, then she'll just be just like the rest of them."

Watching him walk out of the kitchen, I quickly follow behind him. "Cas." He stands still with his back facing me when I confess, "I need you behind me on this."

He turns back to me, and I can't help but notice the one big difference between us. It's his eyes. While mine are a bright blue, his seem darker. Those dark eyes cut to me, but I know he'll have my back no matter what. He always has. "You're my brother, Caden. I'll always have your back. Even when you're doin' stupid shit."

"See I knew you loved me."

"Don't push it."

Caden

"Can I have a hug before you storm out and slam the door?"

"No." Is all he says, and then he's out the door.

He does slam it behind him too. "Such a drama queen." Turning away from the door, I walk into my room. I wasn't lying to Savannah about staying with me, and I want her to feel at home here. Which is why I begin to move some of my stuff out of my dresser to make some room for her. I even do the same in the closet just in case she needs the extra space.

Am I going overboard?

Probably. But none of it really matters because now I have a chance with her. Now I have something to work for, and I hope Savannah is ready.

I don't back down from something I want.

nine
Savannah

"Am I being crazy for doing this?" I ask Kelsey. The minute Caden and I parted ways, I picked up the phone to call my bestie. "I mean I barely know him. Tell me this is insane."

Kelsey sighs heavily over the line, and for a moment I fear what she'll say. Calling her for advice has never been a bad thing, but for some reason, I want her to like Caden too. Wait … Did I just admit I liked him? "Savvy, I'll be honest with you." Swallowing hard, I wait for the hard truth. "This isn't conventional at all. Like by any means. But." She stops, and I hold onto the phone like a lifeline. "I have to ask. Are there feelings involved? Because I can understand why you would say yes knowing there's something there, and also because I know you don't want to give up on finding your mom."

Caden

"I don't know, Kel. All this is happening way too fast, and I'm not sure what I feel."

"Stop making it so complicated. You always over complicate the simplest things."

Leaning back in the seat of the rental, I know she's right. "I know. It's just … I don't know. There's something different about him that I haven't figured out yet. And yes, he makes me feel things that I haven't thought about in a long time, and things I've never even wanted. It scares me, Kel. Then what happens when I'm done here?"

"What happened to taking it one step at a time? Sounds like you're trying to run before you can walk, Savvy. But I get why you're scared, and it's normal. My advice." She stops again, and I swear she has this whole waiting in suspense thing down. "See where it goes."

"That's it? That's all you're giving me?"

"Didn't you know? I'm charging for advice," she laughs over the phone, and I shake my head. It's good to hear her laughing again, and I hope this means she's slowly beginning to heal. "All joking aside, just stop over thinking it. You don't have to put labels on it. I'm suggesting to go with the flow. You like him, and you know he likes you, so what's really holding you back?"

Honestly I can't answer that because I can't even answer that for myself. "Okay I'll try and see how this plays out."

"Good. I have a feeling this is going to work out for you, Savvy."

"I hope so," I whisper back.

"It'll be fine, I promise." Trying my best to agree with my whole heart, I thank her for listening, and we say our goodbyes.

Feeling better about my decision to stay with Caden, I set my phone in the middle console and pull out of Wal-Mart's parking lot. "No labels. Just go with the flow," I say out loud to myself as I continue to drive to his place. I probably should have this no label conversation with Caden too, just to make sure he doesn't get the wrong idea. I wasn't lying to Kelsey about how he makes me feel. But even coming to terms with it, I'm still scared this will all end very badly. I have to protect my heart first.

Why do I have such strong feelings for him of all people?

What is it about him that makes me want things I never wanted before?

Not able to explain it, even to myself, I push it aside and try not to think about it. For once, I'm really going to take Kelsey's advice to heart. She's

Caden

always been my voice of reason, the one who tells me when I'm over thinking shit, and I know I can always count on her. There's no one else I can rely so much on. Well maybe no one except my parents, but I really didn't want to bother them. Our relationship hasn't been on the best of terms since I left, and it does hurt my heart knowing I'm the reason it's not the same anymore. Promising myself I'll do better, it eases my worries about it some. It also helps knowing Mom called the other day, and I know no matter what, she'll always be there for me.

Hoping once I find my birth mother, things with my parents will be better than they are now I take a deep breath as I wait for the red light to turn. When it finally changes, my stomach dips knowing I'm almost at Caden's apartment. I still have no idea what I was thinking when I agreed to stay with him, but when he brought up giving up on finding my mother, it made the choice easier to make. I'm not known to just give up on something that I know can make a difference, and when I was really faced with stopping my search or take the chance to continue, well I would've been an idiot if I said no. And yeah, maybe Caden's sweet words of giving him a chance too helped. He's really hard to say no to. I haven't really decided if this is a good thing or not.

Knowing it's too late to turn back now since he has my suitcase, I pull into Falcon Lair. Taking another deep breath, I tell my heart to calm down.

Brie Paisley

Why am I still so nervous to be around Caden? He's just a guy. Okay, fine. He's a guy I happen to like and so what if he makes me feel things I haven't in, well, ever. Convincing myself it doesn't mean anything, I park in the visitor's parking and turn off the car. Grabbing the few bags in the back seat I picked up at Wal-Mart, I shut the door and lock it behind me. Making my way to Caden's apartment, I have to take a few extra calming breaths before I stop at the door.

Knocking a few times, it takes only seconds for Caden to answer the door. He smiles brightly when he notices me, and I don't even try to hold back my smile. It really should be illegal for him to be so handsome. "You waitin' for somethin', small fry?"

Shaking my head, I feel my face heat with embarrassment. How is it he always catches me staring? "Are you going to let me in or make me stand out here in his ungodly heat all day?"

He opens the door to allow me inside, and as I begin to step forward, he takes my bags away from me. "Did some shoppin' at the Wally World I see."

Shutting the door behind me, I quickly follow him to the small dining room table. "I mean a girl does have certain needs." Caden places my bags down on the table, and I begin to go through them. He stands close beside me as he watches, and I try to act like it doesn't bother me. Placing a few of the

Caden

items I purchased on the table, I watch him out of the corner of my eye as he picks up the box of tampons. Turning to him, I watch him for a moment as he reads the box. "If you need to borrow some this month, I can totally share."

He immediately drops the box, and I laugh at his shocked expression. "I think I'm good, but thanks."

"You act like you've never seen feminine products before."

"No, I have." Grinning widely as he takes a step back from the table, he glances away from the tampons as he says, "I just didn't know there was a full diagram for how to use them."

Picking up the box, I hold it up. "Relax, Caden. It's just tampons."

"Alright I get it. You got me. Now can you please put them away? Preferably in a place I'll never see them again?"

"Fine," I say as I grab a few more items that need to go into the bathroom. Quickly making my way there, I place them in the cabinet under the sink. Walking out of the bathroom, my face flames as I notice Caden holding up the new bra and panty set I bought. At the way he's staring at it, I can only guess what's going through his mind. "I don't think that color suits you," I say while holding back a laugh as he brings the bra up to his chest.

"I don't know. I'm diggin' this red." He turns toward me to give me a better look. "What do you think? I could totally rock this shit." All I can do is shake my head because I swear, he's so full of it. "I'm not sure about these skimpy things you call underwear though," he says as he inspects them. "I mean not that I'm complain' because you'll look bangin' in this, but I think these will ride up in my ass crack."

Closing my eyes as I suck in a breath, I take a few steps to him and jerk my undergarments away from him. "No offense, but these are mine. Hands off."

He lifts both hands with wide eyes as he says, "Okay ... geez. I thought since we're roomies now we'd share everythin', but I can tell you are an only child."

"You want to share underwear?"

He seems to think about it for a second before saying, "Well now that you put it that way, maybe I didn't think that one through."

"As much as I would enjoy you walking around in sexy lingerie, I think it's best if we keep my underwear off limits."

Caden

Caden raises an eyebrow and smirks then says, "Good point. I wouldn't want to out show you or anythin'."

"You wish," I pipe back and playfully thump his shoulder.

"Ouch!" He yells out and holds his arm. "That hurt. I'm claimin' abuse."

"Seriously? I barely touched you." Trying to hold back a laugh as he pokes out his bottom lip, I ask, "Are you always such a drama queen?"

Dropping his hand, he smirks. "I've been known to over exaggerate things from time to time. Just another one of my amazin' traits."

"How many of these amazing traits to do you have?" I ask sarcastically.

Shrugging his shoulders, he replies, "A lot actually. But I promise you'll love each and every one of them." Rolling my eyes, I have to it hand to him. He's very cocky for someone that practically begged me to stay with him. "Come on. I'll show you where you can put your things." Following him once I grab the rest of my stuff, he leads me to his bedroom. I'm not sure how I feel about being so cramped in such a small room with him, but I manage to hide it. "I cleared out some dresser drawers for you, and if you need extra space, there's some room in the closet."

"I see you went a little overboard."

He chuckles before saying, "Maybe just a little. Then again, you do have a lot of shit." I start to pipe back with something sarcastic, but my stomach grumbles loudly instead. "I should feed you. Chinese alright with you?"

"That sounds great." I hadn't realized how hungry I was until now, but knowing it's well in the afternoon, and I haven't eaten anything since he brought me breakfast.

"Anything in particular you would like?"

I don't even think about it before answering him. "Some Lo Mein would be amazing. Oh and some General Tso's chicken too."

He nods and pulls out his phone and begins typing. "Anythin' else I can get for you, small fry?"

Pursing my lips, I think about it for a second. "Can you get some of those crab rangoon things? You know? The stuff with crab meat and cream cheese?" He glances up at me with humor in his eyes and types again. I'm assuming he's making a list of what to get. "And some brown rice would be great."

"Hungry much, small fry?"

"Famished," I say huskily. Licking my lips as he stops typing and gazes at me, my heart hammers

Caden

hard in my chest seeing the desire in his bright blue eyes. I hadn't meant it so sound erotic or anything like that, but he seems to bring out the lust in me. Shaking my head, I add, "And pretty please don't forget the sweet and sour sauce. Chinese isn't the same without it." He's still gazing at me, and I frown. "Caden? Did you hear me?"

Shaking himself out of whatever had him off in la-la land, he types away as he says, "Yeah, small fry. I got you covered."

Placing my suitcase on the bed, I turn back to him. "Thanks. You're the best."

"Can I also get that in writin'?"

"Really?" Raising an eyebrow, he grins widely as I shake my head. I have a feeling I'll be doing this all the time with him. My stomach grumbles loudly once more, and I ask, "Are you going to get the food or stand here and watch me all day?"

Putting away his phone, he seems to think it over for a moment. "Well you are way better lookin' than Chinese food, but I know my small fry is hungry. So I'll take one for the team and go grab the food." Ignoring the way my stomach dips and how good it sounds he basically claimed me for his, I decide not to respond. He gives me a look I can't really decipher as he makes his way over to me. Which is literally like two steps. Maybe three at the most. His room is so small, but it suits him perfectly. I was lying before when I said it didn't bother me being so cramped with him. It's totally sending sparks of desire through my veins. Reaching me, Caden brushes a strand of hair behind my ear. "I'll be back soon, small fry. Try to stay out of trouble, okay?"

Losing my breath at his closeness, I zone in on his lips. "I'll try my best, but I make no promises."

"Eyes up here, small fry." Blinking rapidly, I glance up seeing humor laced in his eyes. "Caught you starin' again."

Playfully pushing him away, I mutter, "Whatever." He of course, laughs and I turn back to my unpacking.

Feeling him behind me, I stand as still as possible when his breath grazes my skin. Holy shit. *Breathe Savannah.* "I'm leavin' now," he says huskily.

"Okay," I whisper. He doesn't move to touch me or anything, but just knowing he's so close has my entire body on alert. I try not to think about how much I really do want him to touch me, kiss me, or something to make me relax. Suddenly I don't sense him behind me anymore, and I hear him chuckle. Turning my head, I watch his fine ass walking out of the room. "Jackass!" I yell after him, and in return all I get is another laugh.

Jesus, Caden is trouble with a capital T.

ten
Caden

Making my way back to the apartment, my smile widens knowing who's there waiting for me. Who knew having a woman at home would be so fulfilling. Then again, Savannah just isn't some woman. She's special, and I'll admit, I didn't expect her to be my perfect match. It seems crazy, trust me I know, but I have a good feeling about us.

Us. Together.

Cue hammering heart effect.

Yeah, I'm probably acting like a chick with all these feelings, but fuck if I care. Which is why I'm practically speeding to get back home. These few moments we've had, haven't been enough and I have this desperate need to make more memories with her. I've only got one shot to make her need me as much as I need her. So far, I'm slowly working my way to making it happen, but I also get the sense she's holding back. Why I have no idea, but I'll find out.

Pulling into the apartment's parking lot, I quickly find my designated spot. Grabbing the bags of food, I jump out of my truck and all but run upstairs to my apartment. Swinging the door open, I yell, "Honey, I'm home." But it's the loud moans of a woman getting drilled hard that stop me short. It takes me a second to realize what's going on here. Savannah is sitting on the couch with her hands covering her face as the porno plays very loudly on the TV. "Uh, small fry?" It's clear she's embarrassed with her bright red cheeks. "In the mood for some porn?"

Her hands slowly lower and with wide eyes, she explains what's going on. "You're TV is possessed! All I wanted was to watch an episode of Family Guy, and it kept changing it back to this porno." Cue another loud moan and slapping of skin. "Then your remote stopped working and just make it stop."

Calmly setting the food on the coffee table, I hold back a laugh as I reach for the remote. Without saying a word, I point it at the TV and turn it off. Placing the remote back on the coffee table, I say,

"If you wanted to get some pointers for the bedroom, all you had to do was ask."

Her eyes snap to me, and that's when I lose it. "You've got to fucking kidding me. I don't get it. I tried to turn it off multiple times."

Laughing harder at her perplexed expression, I walk over to her. "It's alright, small fry." Grabbing her hands, I pull her up. "The remote hardly works anymore unless you press the buttons hard. I probably should've told you that."

"You think? That might have saved me from utter mortification."

Taking both of her hands, I gaze into her stunning blue-green eyes. "You haven't lived until you get caught watchin' porn."

She rolls her eyes but makes no move to move her hands out of mine. "Haha. Very funny. I didn't exactly want to watch porn but whatever."

"It's okay, small fry. I won't tell anyone. It can be our little secret." At her serious gaze, I let out a chuckle. "How about some food to sooth your embarrassment?"

She shrugs as she says, "I am starving. Plus food cures everything right?"

"That it does." Letting one of her hands go, I grab the food and lead her into the kitchen. We

Caden

quickly fix our plates as I grab us some beers. Shutting the fridge, I set hers on the counter by her. "I have to say, I'm surprised you drink beer."

Smiling, she turns to me as she asks, "What? Didn't see me as the beer drinking type?" Opening our beers, she adds, "Let me guess. You thought I would drink fruity drinks or wine?"

"I'm just sayin'. Most chicks don't like beer."

"I hate to break it to you, but I'm not like most chicks."

That statement couldn't be farther from the truth. I need to stop underestimating her. "I'm beginnin' to see that, small fry." Watching her smile once more, I hope she continues to surprise me. That's what I find most attractive about her. She's different, but not in a bad way. Most women these days are all about themselves, but not Savannah. In the time I've come to know her, although it hasn't been long, she's unlike any woman I've known.

Which means, I'm going to fall hard and fast for her.

"So you never told me why you quit your job," I ask Savannah as we sit on the couch. With our bellies full and beers in hand, I thought it would be a good idea to chill and get to know the ever mysterious Savannah Owens.

She takes a drink of her beer, and I lick my lips wishing I could taste hers. I'm trying to dial back a bit on the affection I've been showing, but it hasn't been easy. Not wanting to scare her away, I sat on the far end of the couch showing I can give her space even though I'm still here. "Oh … that. Well let's see. The hours sucked, I didn't really make that much, and then there's the fact my bosses son whipped out his dick at me."

Choking on my beer, I place my beer on the coffee table as I get a hold of myself. "He did what now?" I'm not sure I really want to hear this.

"Mike is a scumbag. He thinks every woman wants him, but really they don't. And I'll just say this, assuming a chick will want to suck a dick just because it's shown is so not the way to go about it."

Clenching my jaw, I try to remain calm. It's harder than I thought it would be and for the first time ever, I feel a surge of jealousy. I don't like that some asswipe showed my woman his dick. And yeah, I totally just fucking claimed her in my head. "He showed you his dick and wanted you to give him a blow job?"

"Ding, ding. You guessed it."

Caden

Pulling out my phone, I glance to Savannah as I demand, "I need his address, full name, and what he drives."

Savannah sits up tall and tries to grab my phone. "Caden, no. It's not that big of a deal." Giving her a hard look, she adds, "He got what he deserved."

"I hope you mean a good kick in the nuts."

"Again you guessed it. Trust me, he's probably still feeling it."

Even if he got what he deserved, I'm still pissed off he showed his junk to her. Which is why I send a quick message to Cason letting him know Mike is now on our shit list. Poor Mike better watch his back. Taking a deep and soothing breath, I put away my phone. "Remind me to never piss you off or show my junk when you don't want to see it."

She snickers loudly, but I don't miss the flash of desire in her eyes. "Just call me the ball buster."

Chuckling with her, I take another drink of my beer. "It does fit you very nicely."

Watching her as she takes another drink, I still can't believe I convinced her to stay with me, and as she pulls her legs up getting more comfortable, I realize she fits perfectly here. This is where she belongs. My chest tightens as I imagine her being here every single day for the rest of our lives. "Why are you staring at me like that?"

"Like what?" I feign innocence.

"Like ... that," she says as she moves her hand up and down.

"I have no idea what you mean, small fry." She shakes her head, but there's still a smile on her gorgeous face. "Tell me about your family," I say to try and lighten the mood again.

For the next few hours, all we do is talk about our family. She tells me her mother's name is Miranda, and her dad is Phillip. I listen intently as she tells me how they met, what they do, and how much they love living in Florida. She seems to have the perfect family, but I don't miss the faraway look in her eyes when she recalls some of the stories from her childhood. I decide not to ask her about it since she's opening up, and I don't want her to stop. However I do scoot closer beside her, when she talks about her parents not being able to have children of their own. "That's when I came into the picture. They adopted me when I was six months old, and they're the best parents. It's not fair they couldn't give a life to a child of their own, but they never treated me like I was adopted." She uses a finger to rub the top of her now empty beer bottle, and I take her free hand in mine. Using my thumb, I trace circles on the back of her hand as she

Caden

continues to talk. "I guess that's what hit me the hardest when they told me I was adopted. I thought I was theirs you know? I don't know. It's just …" She takes a deep breath as she glances up at me. "I felt like since I wasn't biologically theirs that meant I didn't really belong there. It sounds stupid, but at sixteen everything is already over exaggerated."

"It's not stupid, Savannah. Never discount how you feel, but I will say just from listenin' to you talk about them, it sounds like they love you very much and you them."

"Of course I love them. They're my parents, but things changed after they told me. Our relationship changed and I hate it. Some days I wish I could go back and tell them to never tell me, but then again I've always felt like something was missing. Is that crazy? To know something is not there, but having no clue what it is?"

"No, it's not crazy." It's a simple answer, but it's the truth. I know exactly what she's talking about because I didn't realize what was missing from my life until she came into the picture. Now that I know what it is and what she means to me, I can't just give up on it. Maybe that's why I understand her need to find her birth mother. If finding this woman can help my small fry feel whole again, I'll be there every step of the way with her. "I was thinkin'," I start, and her eyebrows raise. "What if I can help with findin' your birth mother?"

"You would do that?"

"I'd do anythin' for you, Savannah." Our gaze holds, and all I see is her blue eyes searching for something in mine. I'm not sure what she's looking for, but I hope she knows that I would do anything and everything to keep her.

"Okay," is all she says with a heavy breath, and I hope whatever she was looking for, she found it.

"I can ask my brother, Carter, for help too. He's a lawyer so he can check into gettin' your records from the adoption agency your parents used."

My chest swells with pride when she places her legs in my lap. It's the most natural thing she could've done, and she has no idea how much I want to kiss her right now. Laying my free hand on her legs, she asks, "Exactly how many brothers do you have?"

"Well there's Carter, he's the oldest, and then it's me, Cason, Clark, and Caleb."

"How in the world did your mom keep up with five boys?"

Caden

"Honestly," I start and let out a laugh. "I really don't know. But Mama sure does know how to use a wooden spoon."

"Now this you have to elaborate more on." Propping my feet on the coffee table, I tell her all about my crazy family. Talking about how we all are together, she listens only letting out a laugh or showing me that pretty smile I love so much, every time I recall a funny story. "You're family sounds amazing."

"We're a bunch of crazies, but it all works out for us."

"Maybe one day I can meet them?"

Jerking my head in her direction, I smirk seeing the shock in her eyes. "I'd love for you to meet them." That's a very distinctive plan for the future she just let out, and I hope she doesn't regret it slipping out. Because I want her to meet my family. I already know they'll love her, and I know Mama will hound me until I bring her over.

"Yeah well, you make them sound like a super family, so I need to see it for myself." Holding her gaze, I know what she's trying to do. She's trying to downplay what she said as if she really didn't mean for it to come out.

Reaching over, I cup her face and run my thumb across her cheek. "It's alright to want to meet my family, Savannah." Using my thumb, I run it along her bottom lip feeling the urge to kiss her until she begs me to stop. Leaning in, she holds still as I hover inches away from those delicious and soft lips of hers. "It's alright to talk about a future with me," I whisper before gently placing my lips over hers. Trying to take it slow, I tenderly kiss her, but I also want her to know how much I want her in my life. She doesn't fight me and only gives in, kissing me back. My heart drums rapidly in my chest as I deepen the kiss, and I relish in the feel of her lips on mine. When her hands find my hair, I pull her closer so I can feel her more. This doesn't seem real. This woman, this amazing and beautiful woman, is everything I want. She's like a breath of air that I didn't realize I needed, and when my tongue intertwines with hers, all the desire I have for her comes to the surface. It's her taste, the way she caresses me with her tongue, and her fingers pulling me closer that almost send me over the edge. I want her with a force I can't explain. It's not just about the sex with her, no far from it. It's wanting to show her how she makes me feel, and to show her nothing but pleasure.

But I know the moment I lose her.

It happens so suddenly that I get a little light headed.

"Wait, Caden," she says with a firm voice as she pushes me away. Trying to catch my breath, I watch the emotions run wild across her face. Desire, a bit of lust, but what I catch most is her fear. She's scared, but I don't understand why she's afraid. Not making a move to stop her as she gets off the couch, I wait patiently for her to explain what the hell just happened. "I think we need to talk about what this is," she says as she waves a hand back and forth between us. "I don't want a relationship. I don't do them, and I just want that to be clear."

Placing my feet on the floor, I lean down setting my elbows on my knees. "So what is this then?"

She frowns as she says, "I … I don't know. But I don't want any labels on whatever this is."

Standing, I move in front of her. "So you admit it then? You're admittin' there's somethin' here, and you're scared to find out what it is?"

"No," she says way too quickly for my liking. There's no fucking way she doesn't feel what I am. "I'm just saying no labels, no relationship, and whatever happens, happens."

Fuck buddies comes to mind, but I don't say it out loud. "I don't just randomly make out with my friends, Savannah." God just saying the word friends puts a bitter taste in my mouth. I don't want to be just her fucking friend. I want her, all of her, and nothing less. Seeing she's not going to give in, I decide I just have to continue to be patient. She'll eventually come around. I hope. "I get what you're puttin' down, small fry. No labels and no serious relationship. We'll just go with the flow."

All the fear I saw earlier slowly evaporates, and I wish she would just tell me why she's so afraid to just let this happen with us. "Thank you." Nodding, maybe this is what she needs right now. It's hard not to push her for more when she clearly wants more from me, but as I gaze into those blue and green eyes, I have to do what she needs. I can't force this, whatever this is, on her. "I'm ... uh ... I'm going to crash out," she stammers, and I can only watch her as she walks away. Rubbing my chin, I wonder what it'll take to make her realize what we have could be even more amazing if she'd let down those damn walls. Right before she walks into my room, to get in my bed without me, she looks back. "Goodnight, Caden."

"Night, small fry." The sound of her shutting the door echoes through the apartment, and I can't help but think that it also means she just shut me out.

Literally and figuratively.

Caden

eleven
Savannah

Waking up in Caden's bed is unlike anything I've ever felt before. First, his bed must be made of clouds or something super soft. Second, I fell asleep quickly taking in his manly smell, and third, I forgot for a second what I did last night. I'm so conflicted about Caden Harlow. I'm not sure what to think about it. One second everything was going so well, very well actually, then I had to go and fuck it up. When he kissed me, my whole world felt as if it literally stopped. Nothing around me mattered, only his lips on mine. It was only his taste, his tongue against mine, and his hands on me that mattered.

Then my damn head went crazy, and everything turned into shit.

I'll admit, I probably didn't handle things as well as I should've, and I hated to see the disappointment laced in his eyes when I said I didn't want anything serious with him. The thing is that's what scares me the most. I want things with him that I've never wanted before, and when he touches me, kisses me, or fuck just looks at me a certain way I want to give up *everything* for him. That's what freaks me out. How I could go from one extreme to giving it all up for him and not really caring what the outcome will be?

I don't want to lose myself if I do give him a real shot.

I don't want to give him my whole heart only to get burned in the end.

It's ridiculous that I feel this way. Caden hasn't given me any reason at all not to trust him with my heart, but the way he calls out to my entire being is unlike anything I've ever known before. No man has ever made me feel one ounce of what I feel when I'm with Caden. He's utterly consuming. Not to mention, he tends to keep me on my toes and surprises me at every turn. Just when I think I have him figured out, he does something unexpected. Like offering to help find my birth mother and how he really seemed to want to help find her. That soft side of him totally and completely threw me off my game. Maybe that's why when he started talking about his family, I let it slip I wanted to meet them. I do want to

Caden

meet the parents of this amazing and considerate man, but I hadn't exactly wanted to let it be known.

Regardless of how he makes me feel, there's something about him that makes me hold back too. I'm not sure how I feel about him having so much power over me, or how much his kiss makes me want to do things that'll keep us both up all night.

Shaking my head at the predicament I'm in, I toss back the covers and get out of the most comfortable bed I've ever slept in. Putting on some more suitable clothes, I walk out of Caden's room and quickly take care of my bathroom business. As I walk out, I notice him sitting at the dining room table. I won't lie and say my heart didn't just skip a beat.

Because it totally did.

I'm in deep shit here.

Trying to remember Kelsey's advice, I stop over thinking and go with the flow. Slowly releasing a breath, I start to make my way to him. With a stupid smile on my face, I reach a hand out to touch his shoulder when he turns around. Instantly jerking my hand back, I frown. "You're so not Caden."

"You would be correct," mystery man who looks identical to Caden says.

Now I know I didn't wake up into some alternate universe here. This is the same apartment, and I haven't smoked any weed since a few nights ago, so I know nothing weird went down like it sometimes does when I'm fucked up. I also didn't drink that much last night. Searching the room, my eyes land on a body moving around in the kitchen. Not taking my gaze off the Caden look alike, I walk into the kitchen to find the real Caden. "So ... um," I say to grab his attention. He glances up at me taking his eyes off the Keurig as I ask, "Did you know there's a guy sitting at your table who looks exactly like you?"

He smirks as he looks past me. Turning my head, I see identical look alike guy standing in the kitchen now. His arms are crossed, but the vibe I'm getting isn't like the one I have around Caden. Where Caden is warm, fun, and makes my insides do a little dance, the other guy doesn't. He also seems standoffish, a bit cold, and hard around the edges. "That's just Cason. My twin."

"Your twin," I repeat because I should've known this before now. "Wait a second," I begin as the wheels start to turn. Looking back to Caden, I ask, "Did you just pull a Mary-Kate and Ashley Olsen on me?" With Caden's confused expression, I add, "You know the movie when they dress alike to make sure their boyfriends could tell them apart?"

Caden

Caden's eyes widen, as Cason says behind me, "Who the fuck is Mary-Kate and Ashley?"

Frowning, I wonder how in the world does he not know this? "Have you never watched Full House? They played in tons of movies too." Cason just looks confused as he just stands there like a fucking weirdo.

"Cason doesn't watch a lot of TV," Caden answers.

"Clearly he's been living under a rock," I pipe back.

"I'm right here, and I don't appreciate the both of you talkin' about me like I'm not."

Caden turns to me as he says, "Cason also doesn't like it when we talk about him when he's standin' by us."

"Is there anything about Cason I should know about? There isn't a third one of you hiding anywhere right?"

"No," they both reply.

"Oh-kay, this isn't the least bit weird. Like at all."

"Don't blame me. This is all on him," Cason says as he gives his twin a pointed look.

Caden doesn't respond, and I can't help but feel I passed some sort of test. "So what's the verdict? Did I pass or fail?"

"You passed," they say yet again together.

"Could you two not do that? It's sort of freaking me out. Can I just get used to the fact there's two of you first?"

"Cason, can you give Savannah and I a minute?" Watching Cason as he walks out of the kitchen, I feel a little relieved that I don't have to keep whipping my head back and forth between them. Giving all my attention to Caden, I wait for him to explain why he didn't tell me he had a twin. "I'm sorry about that. I was goin' to tell you."

"Really? Apparently after I passed your Olsen twin test."

"Hey," he says softly as he brushes my hair out of my face. "I wanted to tell you, but we just have this thing."

"This thing? Care to elaborate on what exactly this thing is because I seriously don't understand, Caden." I hope he can understand my frustration. We talked about our families last night, and he had every opportunity to tell me he has a twin. Plus he had no reason to hide this from me unless there's a reason.

Caden

Caden rubs his chin as I cross my arms. I'm not budging on this. "Alright I'll be honest here." *You should've been honest from the start.* I want to be reasonable, so I'll let him explain his side for hiding this. "Once upon a time there was this boy," he begins, and I already feel myself relax hearing his voice. "This boy was head over heels in love with this girl, and he tried everythin' he knew to get the girl to notice him. But the boy also had a brother, a twin, and one day the girl began to talk to the boy." I already don't like where this story is going, and judging by the look on Caden's face, it isn't going to end well. "The boy really thought the girl was startin' to like him the way he liked her, but," he stops and glances away. "The girl was just usin' the boy to get closer to the boy's twin. Because she loved the twin, not the boy."

"You were the boy, and Cason was the twin."

"It's a shitty story, but yeah. Her name was Emily Thompson."

Okay I'm not a complete bitch. I do feel bad for Caden and his broken heart over what I assume was his first love, but it still doesn't explain why he didn't tell me he had a twin. "I'm sorry this Emily Thompson was a hoe bag, but that still doesn't explain why you hid it from me."

"Well there's more to the story." Sensing things are about to get heavy, I hop up on the counter. Caden leans his arms down on the counter by me as he finishes telling his story. "So I was heartbroken Emily was usin' me to get to Cason. Of course Cason didn't want anythin' to do with her. He used to say she was too girly for him and was fake. Which isn't far from the truth." He huffs out a deep breath before continuing. "Anyway one day at lunch, Cason and I were sittin' outside on one of the picnic tables. Back in junior high, we didn't have many of the same classes at the same time, so when we had a free moment, we were together." Caden glances up to me, and for the first time, I see hurt in his eyes. "Long story short, Emily walked over by us and the funny thing is she was so hung up on Cason, but yet she couldn't tell us apart when we were together. She ended up talkin' to me instead of Cason and even tried to kiss me."

"What a fucking bitch," I say, and I'm surprised at the anger behind my words.

"Simmer down, small fry."

"I'm just saying. The difference between you two is pretty clear." I noticed it immediately when Cason turned around. It's the eyes that give them away. Any person paying attention would see that. Now that I'm thinking about it more, Cason has a faint scar on his right eyebrow.

He smiles, flashing me his perfect pearly whites, before saying, "Yeah, but you would be surprised at how many women look past those differences. All they see is a hot guy, a good lay, and nothin' else."

Having to glance away at his statement, I try not to let it show how much it really does bother me. How many women has done this to him? It bothers me not only because it's clearly happened more than once, but at how many women has he been with. I may not have a twin or a sibling for that matter, but I imagine it would hurt if people couldn't tell us apart or assumed we were the same person. And I also get everyone has a past, so I try to forget about him admitting he's been with multiple women. Turning back to him, I softly say, "I'm sorry, Caden."

His gaze never leaves mine as he stands tall, and uses his hands to spread my thighs as he steps in between them. "Don't be sorry, small fry." Swallowing hard, I keep my eyes on his and try not to think about his hands on me. On my freaking thighs, and oh so close to the place where I really need him to touch me. "I might not have needed to use the test on you, and believe me it was a complete coincidence it happened because I know you're not like those other chicks. I was goin' to tell you about Cason. Today in fact. You just beat me to it. I actually had a whole day planned out for the three of us."

"So you're saying you didn't plan this? It just happened?" I need him to say it again just to put my mind at ease. I don't think Caden is the type of man to manipulate a situation like this.

"I promise you, Savannah. It just happened." He caresses my face with one hand as the other rests on my waist. "You're the only woman who has ever passed the test. Even when we didn't set it that way. You surprised me yet again, small fry."

"I guess this means I'm pretty special huh?"

Caden moves closer, so he's inches away from my lips as he says huskily, "No. It makes you fuckin' perfect." I don't even get a chance to suck in a breath before he takes my lips. This kiss feels different than our other ones. This kiss isn't tender, sweet, or even gentle. Caden kisses me like he needs me and is trying to show me how much I mean to him. It's passionate, fast, but the intensity of his kiss urges me on. Kissing him back with just as much need, passion, and hunger I wrap my arms around his neck and pull him closer. Wrapping my legs around him, I don't even care that I'm trying to see if he's just as turned on as I am. Caden's kiss always brings my desire for him out more than I thought was there to begin with, and now it's no different. I want him to put out this fire he's started that seems to be consuming my very being.

Caden

His hand moves up from my waist and my stomach quivers feeling his hot palm on my bare skin. He deepens our kiss as his other hand moves to my hair and angles my head just the way he wants me. Moving one hand down from his neck, I run it down and under his arm to hold onto him by his back. Touching the hardness of his back, the feel of his grip on my hair tighten and hearing his groan, I clench my thighs tighter around him seeking the friction I so desperately need. He willingly complies, as if he knows what I want, and grinds his hips forward. His cock hits my clit perfectly, and I roll my hips to meet his again. When he pulls back, I see how much he wants me, and it makes my stomach dip. "I want you, Caden."

He smirks then nips at my bottom lip before sucking the slight sting away. "How bad do you want me, small fry?" He asks as he moves to kiss my neck.

Leaning my head back to give him better access, I close my eyes as I relish in the feel of his lips on my sensitive skin. "I could tell you," I breathe out. "But I want you to feel how much I want you."

My eyes snap open as he leaves my neck, and I hope I didn't go overboard. "That was bold, small fry."

"Yeah, I know. Shit happens when you kiss me so just go with it."

"Shit happens?" he asks as if he doesn't already know.

"Yes, shit. Well not literal shit. You know what I mean."

He grins widely, and I suck in a harsh breath as his hand under my shirt moves right under my bra. "Tell me, Savannah. What's this shit you speak of?"

Arching my back as his thumb rubs across my nipple through my bra, it takes me a minute before I can answer him. I swear I can't decide what I like more. His mouth or his touch. "Let's just say, I'm going to have to change panties if you keep on."

Grabbing onto his arm as he cups my breast in one hand, he kisses my neck again and nips at my earlobe. "That's not good enough, Savannah. Tell me how wet you are for me."

"Caden, please." God, he's making me freaking beg now?

"Please what?"

And he's playing dumb too? "Stop teasing me."

"I like makin' you beg and squirm though," he says huskily, and I really don't know how much more of this I can take. My legs begin to shake with how tightly they are wrapped around him, but I don't dare

Caden

loosen my grip. Moving my hips against him, he pushes into me, and I let out a moan. Deciding I've had enough of this teasing bullshit, I grab his hand in my hair and bring it down to the spot I'm literally aching to be touched at. Caden takes my lips again but, thankfully, doesn't move his hand away. My free hand grips tightly on the counter as he begins to slowly caress me through my shorts, and I rotate my hips up to move with him. When he pulls away, he gazes into my eyes as he takes his hand away from my needy pussy. Before I can protest, he pushes his hand down into the top of my cotton shorts. Grateful I wore clothing that actually works for this, he slips that hand down into my panties, and when those fingers gently slide down in between my lips, I bite the inside of my cheek as I push my hips forward urging him to move faster. His harsh breathing is the only thing I hear until he says, "Goddamn, Savannah. You weren't lyin'. You're fuckin' soaked."

Those skillful fingers begin to move up and down barely putting a damper in my desire. I need so much more than this delicate touching. "Caden, please. I need you."

"I know, small fry." My face flushes as he cups my breast and at the same time, he slowly slides a finger inside me. Letting out a moan, I let my eyes close as I let the pleasure roll through me. Soon one finger isn't cutting it, but he must sense when I'm ready for more. Taking a second finger, he adds it with the first and begins to slowly fuck me with them. I'm already so close the edge from all his fucking teasing, and the lack of sex. All it'll take is a few more deep thrusts, and a touch on my clit before I completely let go.

"Caden? There's a change of plans—"

Hearing Cason's voice, Caden jumps away from me, and I quickly jump off the counter. My face flames with embarrassment, and there's no way I can look up. Glancing down at the floor, I hear Caden say, "Dude, what the fuck? Way to cock-block me."

Unable to stop myself, I laugh loudly as I say, "He totally just cock-blocked you." Feeling eyes on me, I glance up seeing Caden looking at me with a grin on his face. Thinking about it for a second, I ask, "Aren't twins supposed to have this bond thing? Like you know what the other is thinking?"

"This is so fuckin' awkward," Cason says with a monotone voice.

"We do have that bond, but it seems," Caden starts then stares at his twin. "This dick bag never uses it."

Biting my lip to hold back another laugh, Cason deadpans, "Well maybe I didn't want to know you were gettin' freaky on our kitchen counter."

Caden

"Oh and walkin' in without announcin' you were back in the apartment was so much better," Caden snaps back.

They stare each other down before it hits me. "Wait a second. If Cason cock-blocked you, didn't he cock-block me too? Well not that I have a cock. Vagina blocked?"

"I don't think that sounds right," Caden says as he frowns.

"Cunt blocked? Vagina slammed?"

"I like cunt blocked. That's a good one, small fry."

"I would really like it if y'all would stop talkin' about vaginas around me."

Glancing over to Cason, I snort seeing he looks uncomfortable. "What's wrong, Cason? Never talked about vaginas before?"

Cason flips me the bird, but I see the corner of his mouth twitching. "Not that I mind talkin' about vaginas," Caden interrupts. "But I'd like to know what plans you were talkin' about was changed."

Leaning into Caden as he slips an arm around my shoulder, I don't even think anything about it at first. But then I catch Cason's gaze, and something flashes in his deep blue eyes. Glancing away, I reason with myself that it means nothing but my stomach feels like it's in knots now. "Mama called while y'all were … busy. She said Caleb's flight is landin' early, so you need to go get him. I would go, but I have to head to the gym." Hearing the disappointment in Cason's voice, I look up to see him rubbing the back of his neck. "This whole no assistant thing is such a pain in the ass."

"Maybe if you weren't such a grumpy old man they wouldn't keep quittin' on you," Caden claims.

"That last one was not my fault. She had no clue how to file properly."

"Says the guy with a serious case of OCD."

Grinning at their banter, I wish I had something like this growing up. I've often wondered what it would be like to have a sibling. "I'm not arguin' about this with you."

"I'm not arguin' either. Just statin' facts, grumpy."

Cason lets out an exasperated sigh before saying, "Just be at the airport in a few hours." He turns to leave before turning back. "Mama also wants you to bring Clark with you." Something passes between the two, and I think it's their twin bond at work. "She's worried about him."

Caden

Glancing from Cason to Caden, it's clear they're both worried about their brother. "Yeah, we're all worried about him."

Hearing the concern in Caden's voice makes my stomach clench. "Is he alright?"

Caden smiles down at me and places a tender kiss on my forehead. "He will be, small fry. I'll tell you all about it later okay?" Nodding, I think nothing of it when I actually look forward to spending more time with him.

Cason's phone begins to ring, and I look at him as he loudly cusses. "I've got to head out. Catch you later?"

His question is directed to his twin, but when he glances at me, I half wonder if he's asking me the same thing. "We do live together remember, pumpkin?" Cason says nothing as he turns to leave. "Hey, Cas?" Cason stops, and Caden asks, "Do you want a new and improved assistant?"

"Why? Do you know of anyone?"

Caden brings me closer, and I frown wondering what he's up to. "I sure do. Small fry needs a job."

"What?" I ask.

"You told me you quit your other job, and Cason needs help. It's perfect fit."

"Yeah, but I don't want it to be weird or anything. Plus you're already doing enough for me as it is, and I can't keep putting you out."

"Oh hush that pretty mouth," Caden commands. Looking to Cason, he asks, "What do you say, bro? You okay with this?"

Cason and I glance at each other as he thinks it over. "Do you know how to file and be organized?"

Raising an eyebrow, I shrug saying, "Not really, but how hard can it be?"

"Alright then. I'll give it a try, but just so you know, I like shit done a certain way."

"No kidding," I mutter, but I think Caden hears me.

"It'll be fine, small fry. Cason is just all talk. Under that hard exterior, he's just a big and cuddly teddy bear."

Nervously laughing, I somewhat agree. "Yeah. Whatever you say."

"I'll be waitin' in the truck then," Cason calls out as he walks out of the apartment.

"Well that went swell," I say while walking toward Caden's room to quickly change into work appropriate clothes.

Caden

Caden follows behind me, and I turn to him when he claims, "It'll be fine. Cason is just ... how do I put this?" He looks up at the ceiling before adding, "Different. You'll see what I mean."

"I'll take your word for it."

"Hey," he softly says as he pulls me to him. "You'll do great. And when I get back from pickin' up Caleb, you can tell me all about your first day."

Smiling up at him, he's very sweet considering the train wreck I've been lately. "Thank you."

"For what?"

"For the new job. For letting me stay here. For just being ... you."

Using his hand to caress my face, he smiles, and it makes my stomach flutter. "I told you, small fry. I'd do anythin' for you." Before I get a chance to say anything back, he huskily says, "And be ready to finish what we started earlier when I get back."

Sucking in a deep breath, I can't find the words to respond. He takes it as his cue to leave, but not before giving me a quick peck on my lips. Watching him walk out of his room, my heart beats rapidly in my chest thinking about his promise. I won't lie, I'm totally looking forward to finishing what we started.

Turning to Cason, he has a frown on his face, and I wonder if it's always there. Trying to make this car ride less awkward, I attempt to make conversation. "So you own your own gym?"

"Yep."

Oh-kay. That was an epic fail. Trying again, I ask, "Does Caden co-own it with you?"

"No."

"You're not much of a talker are you?"

"Nope."

Huffing out a breath, I pick up my phone to send Caden a text. Plus I need something to distract me from Cason, who by the way, is glaring at me.

Me: So your brother hates me.

I smile when I see Caden's name pop up on my screen. I should probably change it just to Caden, but I actually like the name he added to my phone.

Caden. The man of your dreams: Trust me. Cason hates everyone. Just give him a minute to warm up to you.

Me: If you say so.

Caden

Caden. The man of your dreams: If it helps he has more bite than anythin'. He's really a big softy.

Me: I don't see that but I'll take your word for it.

Caden. The man of your dreams: He likes you small fry.

Me: How do you know?

Caden. The man of your dreams: Twin bond remember? I know things.

Me: Right. That freaky thing you two did? You'll have to explain that one to me.

Caden. The man of your dreams: Later. About to leave to get Caleb. Talk soon.

Me: Drive safe.

Caden. The man of your dreams: Always small fry.

Feeling a bit better about being alone with Cason, I set my phone down and stare out the window. Noticing we're headed north, I wonder if we'll arrive soon. I mean it's not too bad being alone with Cason. It's just the silence is starting to get a bit awkward. I'm not sure what to say to him to break the ice, but I have a feeling he's always like this.

Sitting up straighter when I see the sign to Cason's gym, he slowly pulls into the parking lot in the back. Unbuckling my seatbelt, I reach for the door handle. "It's Savannah right?"

His deep monotone voice stops me from getting out, and I turn towards him. "Yeah, but you can call me Savvy. All my friends do."

"Alright, Savvy," he says with a little bite to his voice. Remembering what Caden said, I try not to let it bother me that he seems to not like me very much. For some reason, I really want him to like me. Not because I have any sort of feelings for him, just because this is Caden's twin. If Cason doesn't come around, well, things are definitely going to be weird. Since I'm staying with him and Caden, not because I have feelings for Caden. *Keep telling yourself that.* "I have to ask. What are your intentions with my twin?"

"My intentions?" I ask slowly to make sure I understand him. When he nods, I ask, "What is this? An interrogation? You know like when dads sit the boyfriend down to ask, 'why are you with my daughter and if you hurt her, I know how to use a shotgun'. Are we really going to have that type of conversation?" Was it such a good idea to be such a smart ass? Probably not, but then again I'm not going to let Cason run all over me. He might be my new boss soon, but I'm not a freaking doormat.

Caden

Holding my breath, I wait for him to respond and I'm nervous of how he will. I don't know Cason at all so his reaction might be bad. When the corner of his mouth twitches, I let go of the breath I was holding. "I can see why he likes you so much."

"We're still talking about Caden right?" At his blank stare, I snort. "I know who you're referring to. I'm not stupid."

"Clearly."

Narrowing my eyes, I ask, "Do you always give women the third degree like this when it comes to him?"

Rubbing his forehead, he lets out a sigh. "Honestly no. But ..." He looks up, and his voice suddenly becomes softer and gentler. "He's different with you."

"Different how?" I'm instantly curious.

"Just ... different."

"Oh-kay. Vague much?"

Rolling his eyes, he takes the key out of the truck before saying, "God you two are so much alike."

Hoping out of the truck, I walk up behind him. "I'll take that as a compliment."

He looks back at me with a blank stare yet again, and I wonder if he ever smiles. "It wasn't meant to be taken that way."

"Holy shit." He frowns at my shocked expression, and I state, "I do believe we just had a conversation. Welcome to the real world, Cason. Where the sky is blue, and people actually say more than one or two words."

"Smart ass," he says, but I see that twitch again.

"Trust me, you haven't seen anything yet." He doesn't respond, but he does shake his head. Following behind him as we walk inside the gym, I get a surge of nervousness. Wondering what my new job will entail, I take a glance around the gym. It's the same as any other gym, but Cason has a nice open layout. Treadmills line the front walls, weights are on the other side in the corner for lifting, and a huge ring is in the middle. I guess it's for training or even boxing. I don't really know much about gyms, but the feel of Cason's gym is definitely laid back. Upon further inspection, I spot a huge blue mat in behind the ring, and I wonder what it's used for. There are some other rooms on the other side of the room that say locker rooms. Stopping to check out the inspirational pictures hanging on the wall, my nerves about starting a new job disappear. Feeling someone beside me, I glance to my right seeing

Caden

Cason. "This place is kick ass. What are the blue mats for?"

"They're for my self-defense classes." He's quiet for a moment then he adds, "It's not much, but I can't complain about business."

"Obviously." Glancing around the room, I take in how many people are actually here. It's packed for only being early afternoon. "This place is banging."

"Glad you approve. Come on, we have work to do."

"Lead the way, boss." That earns me a hard glare, but instead of thinking it means he doesn't care for me, I think he's warming up to me. Following the leader once more, Cason shows me around the gym some more, and we stop the tour in his office. It's a typical office with a desk and computer, but what I notice the most is how Cason has so many filing cabinets. I understand why Caden said Cason has a touch of OCD now. Everything is labeled which shouldn't be too hard to figure out where things go, but I'll admit I'm a tad bit intimated by all the organization. I'm not known to be very organized. To be honest, my head is already starting to hurt realizing how much work is going to go into this. One big plus is how big his office is, and I'm grateful. One could start to feel claustrophobic in here. "Got enough filing cabinets, boss?"

Cason cocks an eyebrow at my comment before he says, "It's not that many."

"You have," I start then take another look around doing a quick count. "Eight cabinets." Turning to him, I ask, "It's a bit much don't you think? Why not just do everything digital?"

"I'm old school."

"Why do I get the feeling I signed up for more than I bargained for?"

Cason shakes his head, but he has to know this is a bit much. "Anyway we have a lot to cover, so let's get to it."

Huffing out a breath, I'm already dreading what all my new duties are going to be. "Rodger that." Taking a seat in the chair in front of Cason's desk, I try to remain positive. Caden wouldn't have offered Cason to take me on if he didn't think I could handle it. Plus I really do need a new job.

It's time to woman up and put my big girl panties on.

twelve
Caden

After picking up Clark from our parent's house, he and I head toward Jackson Airport to get Caleb. So far the ride has been uneventful, and I have a feeling this is how it's going to be the entire way there. Don't get me wrong, I love all my brothers, but since Clark got back from his last deployment, something has been off with him. He's not the same in a lot of ways, and it doesn't help he won't open up to any of us.

Glancing over to my right, I wish he would just tell someone what's going on in that head of his. I'm worried, we all are, and I hope he knows he's not alone. Not caring if I piss him off or not, I ask, "Is today goin' to be the day you tell me what the hell is goin' on with you?"

Looking back to the road, I feel his hard gaze on me. "Mind your fuckin' business, Caden."

"You do know who I am right?" It's never been in my nature to stay out of my brother's business.

"Right. I forgot while I was off fightin' for our country. Please go on and ask me twenty-one questions just like everyone else." He sighs deeply before adding, "I'm fine. I wish everyone would stop askin'. I'm fine."

Clearly he's not. I can hear it in his voice and how defensive he's being. "I get it. I do. You don't want to talk about what went down, and you want to show off how manly you can be." Taking a quick glance at my brother, he stares straight ahead, and I wonder if he's even listening to me. "I just want to make sure you know that you're not alone and if you ever want to talk about it, I'm here. We're all here for you."

Clark is quiet for a long time, and just when I think he's not going to respond, he says, "I know."

It's such a simple response, but at least he knows what I'm putting down. The last thing any of us want is for him to feel like he has no one. That's the worst thing about him going into the military. Every deployment chipped away at him, and the fear he'll take his own life freaks me the fuck out.

Caden

Knowing I can't make him talk, I decide to let things be for now. All I can do is hope that he gets to the place where he's ready to open up. We ride in silence for a while before I get really sick and tired of hearing nothing. Turning on the radio, Cheap Thrills by Sia fills the speakers, and of course I have to sing along.

I don't even get one chorus finished before Clark reaches over and turns off the radio. "Dude, that was my song."

"I am not listenin' to you screech at the top of your lungs all the way to Jackson."

"Why are you bein' such a buzz kill?"

He shoots me a glare as he claims, "I'm not a buzz kill. I just like bein' able to hear. I also like for my ears not to start bleedin'."

"So what you're sayin' is, you don't think I can sing and you hate music?"

"Oh fuck. Really, Caden?"

"I'm just sayin'. You obviously don't like Sia or her cheap thrills."

"She's just fine. It's you that I can't stand to listen to for two and a half hours."

Letting my head fall back against the headrest, I state, "This is goin' to be a long ass trip."

Brie Paisley

It's pitch black by the time I pull up at my apartment. Why I thought it would be a quick and easy trip to pick up my youngest brother is beyond me. Not only was the trip there boring as hell, Clark and I had to wait seven hours before Caleb's plane actually landed. Apparently Caleb missed his flight and Clark was not a happy camper about it. I didn't so much mind having to wait, but it was the fact that Clark was acting stranger than normal that made the waiting deal not so great. I didn't ask knowing he wouldn't tell me anyway, but as I watched him, I think it was the crowded airport that did it to him. And don't even get me started on the trip back home.

There has never been a time where I wanted to murder my brothers until that moment. Like seriously. I am a cop, so I know how to get rid of the bodies. All joking aside, I would never hurt them, even though I really did consider it a few times. Shaking my head, I'm grateful to be home and glad I get a break from Clark and Caleb. Those two have some major issues going on. Opening the door to the apartment, I'm extra careful not to make any noise. Cason texted me earlier when he crashed out, and I assume Savannah has gone to bed too. All the lights are off inside, but the moon is giving me enough light to be able to see where I'm going.

Caden

With only one destination on my mind, I take my shoes off by the door and walk toward my room. I have to see her. I have to make sure she's still here and real. It probably sounds crazy, but I have this fear she'll up and disappear on me. All day I worried she wouldn't be here once I got back, even though she and I talked throughout the day. Slowly opening the door, I quietly walk into the room hoping not to disturb her. Thankful she left the blinds open so I can see, I cross the room over by the bed. My heart thrums in my chest as I see her sleeping peacefully in my bed and damn. The sight of her in *my* bed sends a thrill straight to my cock. *Down boy*. Leaning down to brush her hair out of her face, she moans in her sleep and how I wish I could just climb into bed with her. It's hard to resist the pull I have to just say fuck it and do it. Somehow I fight that pull. Instead of doing what my entire body is wanting, I place a light kiss on her forehead.

She stirs in her sleep, and I hold my breath as she whispers, "Caden?"

"Sorry, small fry. Just tuckin' you in."

"What time is it?"

Feeling like an ass for waking her, I quietly say, "It's late. Go back to sleep, and I'll see you in the mornin'."

I start to turn to leave, but she grabs onto my hand. "No, stay with me." Well I'll be damned. I wasn't expecting her to ask me to stay, but I willingly comply. Quickly getting out of my clothes except for my boxers, I crawl into bed with her. Normally I sleep in the nude, but knowing how rare this moment is, I figure it's best to play it safe. Plus I'm sure Savannah wouldn't like my cock poking her in the butt. Or maybe she would. It's hard to guess what she wants. Staying still as she rolls over on her left side facing me, she asks, "How was the trip?"

"Uneventful. But it's nice to have all my brothers back home."

She's quiet for a few moments, and I begin to think she fell back asleep. "I tried to stay up to make sure you made it back alright."

My heart warms knowing she wanted to make sure I came back home safely. I try not to think too much of her comment or confession, whichever way you want to take it, but it does make me one happy guy knowing she was thinking of me. "Miss me, small fry?"

"Maybe just a little," she says with a lazy sigh.

"Come here, Savannah." Gently pulling her to me, she rests her head on my chest as I wrap my arm around her. Damn it feels good having her in my arms like this, and it gives me hope she's coming

Caden

around with giving me a chance. Running my fingers through her hair, she lets out another sigh as she lays a hand on my stomach. The feel of her so close and knowing she's doing it because she wants to is unlike anything I've ever felt before. She belongs here in my arms, and I know without a doubt I have to keep her by my side. "How did it go today with Cason?"

Knowing my twin, he didn't make it easy on her. He never does with anyone. "It wasn't too bad. I think he's finally warming up to me." Her voice is low I almost miss what she says.

"I told you, small fry. He likes you." Smirking when she hums back a response, I know she's falling back asleep. I can't say I mind because she scoots closer as if she can't get close enough. Pride flows through me knowing even in her sleep, she wants me. Now all I have to do is make it where she wants me when she's coherent. It's going to be difficult no doubt, but she's worth it.

I know she'll be worth everything because of this right here. Because of how my heart won't stop pounding in my chest. But mostly, because I'm already in love with her. I knew she was it the moment I laid eyes on her, and this moment only confirms it.

She's it.

She's the one.

My one.

Kissing her once more on her forehead, I close my eyes as I think of a way to keep her here and in my arms forever.

Want to know what the best feeling in the world is? Not only am I cuddling with the woman I'm falling madly in love with, but she's also squirming that delicious ass of hers against my cock. The two combined? Fucking. Epic. Not sure if she's awake yet, I stay still hoping and dreading that she'll stop moving. Lord knows how much I want her, but then again she's asleep, and I will my cock to behave.

That moment flies right out the window when her small hand grabs me.

Hard.

"Tryin' to cop a feel, small fry?" She gasps loudly and tries to roll away. Catching her before she tumbles to the floor, I chuckle seeing her shocked expression. "Goin' somewhere?"

"What are you doing here?"

She pulls away, and I hate the distance she's putting between us. Going off her cue, I move away and rest my head on my hand as I gaze at her. "I do

Caden

live here, and this is my room and my bed." Lowering my voice, I say, "You asked me to stay remember?"

She frowns as if she doesn't remember and for a moment I fear she'll deny everything. "Oh right." Her face flushes and I wonder what she's thinking. Does she regret asking me to stay? "You can't hold me accountable for anything I do or say if I'm half asleep."

"I don't know, small fry. You were grabbin' on pretty tightly to my Johnson."

When she smiles, I know I've got her. "Your Johnson?"

"Yeah. Otherwise known as, tally wacker, meat stick, one-eyed snake, willy, and a lot of others that I won't name."

She rolls her eyes at me, before she demands, "Tell your Johnson to stay away from my ass."

"Hey now. It's not my fault you were rubbin' against me. I can't help if Johnson likes what you're doin'." The problem is my Johnson *loves* everything Savannah Owens does.

"You're like a horny teenage boy."

Taking a risk, I grab her wrist and pull her to me. Fuck this distance shit she's trying to put between us. She doesn't put up a fight as I pull her back to me, and I hover over her as I gaze into her eyes. "I don't recall you complainin' yesterday about it."

My cock jumps when she sucks in a breath, and her eyes glance down to my lips. Oh yeah. She wants me. "I told you. Shit happens when you kiss me."

"So what you're sayin' is, I should kiss you more often?"

She laughs, a sound I want to hear every day for the rest of my life, as she claims, "Maybe after we brush our teeth."

"Ah. The horrifyin' smell of morning breath." Honestly I hadn't noticed, but mine must be bad if she's hinting about it.

"I didn't want to hurt your feelings but yeah. It's pretty bad."

"Savannah has jokes this mornin'." She laughs again and pushes against my chest. Rolling over, I watch her as she slowly gets out of bed. Gazing at her as she pulls down her top to cover her stomach, I get that warm sensation in my chest again.

"What are you staring at?"

Caden

Her question pulls my gaze away from her, and I grin like a lovesick fool. God I've got it bad. "Just you, small fry."

She tries to hide her smile as she shakes her head, but I see it. I'll take that as a small win. "I've got to get ready. Some of us have to work for a living," she states as she grabs some clothes.

Sitting up in the bed, I glance over at the clock to check the time. Having a few hours to spare before my shift later, I ask, "Want to have breakfast with me and my family?" Okay I'll admit, I whispered that last part about my family because I know she'll freak. It screams relationship, and if I know her, she's going to run away from my offer.

Her eyebrows furrow and I hope she's considering it. How I wish I had mind reading skills. "Thanks for offering, but I told Cason I would get an early start." She glances up then adds, "You know. Since I'm trying to get the hang of things."

It's her cop-out, I know, but it still stings. Playing it off like it's no big deal, I nod. She gives me a small smile the turns to walk out of the room. Suddenly remembering what I promised her I'd do, I toss the covers off me and jump out of bed. She stops as she hears me and her eyes stare at my bare chest. Her lips part as she slowly devours me with those blue-green eyes, and I stand still letting her take her fill. But when her gaze drops to my cock, I can't take it anymore. She's driving me crazy, and since Mama is expecting all of us for breakfast, there's no time to have my fill of Savannah. Who am I kidding here? I'll never get enough of her, and I haven't even had her yet. Snapping my fingers in front of her, I playfully say, "Eyes up here, small fry." Her eyes snap to mine, and I hold back a laugh at her wide eyes. "As much as I enjoy you checkin' me out, Savannah." I stop for a moment, gazing into those eyes of hers. "I have to work tonight, so I wondered if you wouldn't mind givin' me all you have on your birth mother."

I promised her I would help as much as I could and I'll talk to Carter once I see him at Mama's for breakfast. Savannah doesn't waste any time walking past me in a daze, then sets her clothes down on the bed, and my gaze follows her as she walks into the closet. Patiently waiting for her, I hope I can find her the answers she's looking for. I meant it when I said I'll do anything for her. A few moments pass before she reemerges, and I frown seeing the blank look on her face. She slowly walks over to stand in front of me gripping the manila folder with both hands. "This is all I have of her," she says softly, and my heart clenches knowing this folder is all she has of her mother. "I don't have any copies," she glances up at me as she says, "Please don't lose it."

I know how much this means to her and I wouldn't dare dream of losing something so dear to

Caden

her. "I'll guard it with my life." Reaching to cup her cheek, I state, "You can trust me, small fry. I won't let you down." Her eyes search mine for something, and I can only hope she believes me. My thumb rubs her cheek as I plead silently for her to trust me, to have faith in me, and for once lean on me.

I need her to fully let me in and truly believe I care for her, and that I'll do everything in my power to protect her.

thirteen

Savannah

Time seems to stand still as I fight an inner battle whether to trust Caden or not. His words seem true. His actions also make me want to think he only does want to help, but something is holding me back. I don't know what it is, but I've always believed if something is too good to be true, then it probably is. Even as I struggle with my choice, that pull I feel every time I'm near him strengthens. Honestly I'm not sure how I've fought it for so long. His thumb continues to graze my cheek, and I sense he's begging me to lean on him. Maybe it's in his eyes with the way they seem to plead with me for something. It's hard to resist him, especially since he's still shirtless. It's more than just sexual attraction at work here. Even as I stare at him like a juicy steak, like I've been starving for weeks, there's more going on here.

Caden

Maybe that's what's holding me back. Giving myself over to him completely scares me to death, but he's the only man I've ever thought about letting down my walls and opening my heart for. Letting out a long sigh, I decide to take him up on his offer, and I lean into his touch. Even if it's just for a moment, I need his strength to carry me. "Okay," I say so low I barely hear it myself. But Caden must have. He grins widely as if I just gave him everything he's ever wanted. "I'll trust you, Caden." It'll be hard to fully trust him since I don't trust anyone, but I'm willing to try.

Holding out the folder that contains everything I have on Tammy Richards, I hand it to him. He takes it brushing my hand as he does so, and my heart jumps at the small touch. "If there's somethin' to find, I'll make sure to find it, small fry."

Somehow I do believe he will. Am I banking on him actually finding Tammy? Not really, but anything he happens to find will help. "Thank you." His hand drops from my cheek, and I instantly feel the loss of warmth. I know he has things to do, and so do I. Which is why I give him a small smile and turn to pick my clothes back up off the bed.

I know I'm putting more distance between us, but even if I let myself lean on him this one time, I still have my heart to protect. But I have a feeling he's just made a big crack in my walls.

A few days pass before I finally hear something from Caden about Tammy. I won't lie and say I've been waiting for this since I handed over what I had on her, and my nerves are at an all-time high as we make our way to Carter's law firm. In the passing days, I've learned more and more about Caden. Like his dad, Mitchell, started the firm but recently retired leaving it to Carter. Caden also told me a bit about Clark and his struggles with returning home from his last deployment, and how smart his youngest brother Caleb is. It seems the more time I spend with Caden, the more I want to know and meet his family. I haven't let it slip again that I would like to meet them because that just screams serious relationship status. I'm not ready for that just yet. I'm still trying to take it day by day, but it's hard when Caden is constantly there making me smile, and making my stomach dip with every sweet promise he makes.

As if he knows I need him, I glance down when his hand takes mine. He gives me a quick squeeze before he says, "It'll be fine, small fry."

Turning away, I stare out the window as my heart beats frantically in my chest. I've been waiting for the moment for so long, and I just know something is going to go wrong. I feel it deep down,

Caden

and no matter what I tell myself, that feeling won't go away. "I hope so. I wish you would just tell me what you found."

Hearing him sigh, he turns right and pulls into a parking lot. "I just think it'll be better to hear it all at once. I'm not sure what Carter found, but whatever it is I'm here for you, Savannah."

Letting his hand go, I hop out of the truck. Walking over to Caden's side, I let him take my hand again. I know it's selfish to keep pushing him away only to bring him back, but I can't do this alone. I need him too much at this moment. "Can you at least tell me if it's good news or not?" I'm seriously grasping at straws. I don't understand why he just won't tell me what he found.

"I can promise you no matter what I found or what Carter found, you'll get through this."

"Why are you being so vague?" I ask as he leads me down the sidewalk toward the firm.

"You sure are a nosy rosy today."

I know he's trying to lighten my mood, but then again he shouldn't joke around about something like this. "Come on, Caden. Spill it already."

"You'll just have to be patient," he says as he opens the firm's door for me. I want to pipe back that

I've been patient for years, but I keep that comment to myself. Walking inside, my eyes dart around the area. There's a front desk for what I'm assuming is for a secretary, and to my left are some waiting chairs. Beyond the chairs, there's a room with Carter's name on it, and there's another one to my right that says accounting.

Turning to Caden, I ask, "What kind of law firm is this again?"

"Family Law, but I'm in the process of addin' Business Law," says someone to my left and when I turn, I see a tall man that resembles Caden a little walking up to us.

"What's crackin', old man," Caden says as they do some sort of manly hug.

Standing off to the side, I watch them interact, and I'm guessing this is Carter. "Always with the jokes I see," he says as he turns to me. "You must be Savannah. I'm Carter." He holds out a hand, and I take it welcoming the friendly introduction.

"It's nice to meet you," I reply, and I actually mean it. While I've only met Caden's twin, it's nice to finally meet someone else in his family. While Carter and Caden's smiles favor, that's the only thing about them I notice that's similar. Carter is a few inches taller than Caden, and Carter's eyes are a light brown. Even with their apparent differences, Carter

Caden

seems friendly, and from what Caden has told me, I have a feeling I'm going to like him just like Cason.

"Alright now. Stop mackin' on my girl," Caden interrupts and pulls me under his arm. I choose to ignore how my stomach dips with Caden claiming me as his.

Rolling my eyes, I playfully smack Caden's chest. "Stop being so rude."

"I'm never rude," Caden quickly says. Turning to Carter, he asks, "Where's Shelby? I thought she was workin' today?"

"You just missed her. Mama called and needed some help with Caleb's welcome home party."

"Ah. Mama and her wild and crazy parties," Caden mumbles to no one in particular. "Anyway ready to do this shin-dig?" Carter smirks, and I roll my eyes. Caden makes this whole situation seem like it's no big deal, but maybe that's what he's going for. My nerves return with a vengeance when Carter motions us to follow him into his office, and I wish Caden would say something stupid to take my mind off what I'm about to find out.

Unfortunately he doesn't, but he does take my hand again once we're seated in front of Carter's desk in his office. Sucking in a breath, Carter looks through some files while I let my eyes wander around the room. It's smaller than I thought it would be, but it's a nice office. Dark colors make the room seem warm and open at the same time, and the bookshelves on the left side of the room make me curious to know what type of books he has. Most likely lawyer stuff that I have no education on, but Carter seems to know what he's doing. His diplomas hang on the walls, and I recall Caden telling me Carter's been practicing law for a while now.

Letting out a heavy breath, I feel Caden squeeze my hand. Glancing over at him, he grins then leans over. "Breathe, small fry. You're not on trial."

"Obviously," I snap back sarcastically, but all that does is make him smile bigger.

My skin tingles feeling his breath on my neck and ear, and I resist the urge to shiver. Quickly glancing over to Carter, he's not paying us any attention thankfully. I'd hate if he saw how red my face is right now. "You know," he starts, and my stomach clenches hearing how deep and husky his voice sounds. "My hand does need blood flow to survive."

"Oh shit. I'm sorry," I quickly say and let his hand go. I hadn't realized I was clutching onto him so tightly.

Caden

Shaking his hand out, he smirks as he leans back in his chair. "It's cool, small fry. Just ease up on the death grip alright."

"You're such a baby. I wasn't holding on that tight."

"I'll just place my arm here," he says sweetly as he lays his arm around my shoulders. "To prevent any further damage. This is my good hand."

"Your good hand, huh?" I want to say more about his so called good hand, but I don't because we're not alone and I don't want to end up embarrassing myself. However with the way Caden's eyes dilate and when his mouth opens, I know he understands my meaning. I'll never be able to forget what that good hand did to me not that long ago before Cason rudely interrupted us.

"You thinkin' what I'm thinkin'?" Caden asks quietly.

"The kitchen right?"

"That's my girl," he says proudly and I turn away when he adjusts himself in the chair. Smiling while I shake my head, I know what he's doing. He's trying to keep my mind off what I'm about to find out, and knowing he is doing this for me makes my heart clench. Not many people would pick up on how nervous I am about this meeting, but somehow Caden knows me better than anyone.

"Savannah, are you ready to go over what Caden and I found about your birth mother?" Hearing Carter's voice, I snap my head up to him, and even though Caden did distract me for a moment, my nerves are back, and I might throw up. Nodding, he picks up some papers as he begins. "I was able to contact the adoption agency that handled your adoption, and unfortunately they couldn't tell me much." Swallowing hard, I grab onto the chair with my hands until they turn white. My hopes begin to dwindle noticing the sad look in Carter's eyes, and I suck in a deep breathing hoping for some good news. Feeling Caden's fingers caressing my shoulder, I lean back seeking his comfort. "With your adoption being closed, this will make it harder to find the answers you want, but I can promise you there is a way we can track her down." Carter glances to Caden for a second before he says, "The main problem I'm havin' is the agency has no record of your adoption on file."

"I don't understand. I spoke with someone a few years back, and they said everything was there."

Carter regards me with kind eyes, and even though I start to feel my world falling apart, his comforting gaze is holding me together. Honestly if I didn't have Caden beside me, I probably would've already lost my shit. "There was a fire last year. Most of the files were digital, but some didn't make it since the transition was new. You have to understand,

Caden

most of the adoption agencies used over twenty years ago are still trying to play catch up with computerizin' everythin'."

"There has to be a way to find out who my birth mother is," I say mostly to myself.

"I won't lie, Savannah. This won't be easy, but I can start checkin' into hospital records and the surroundin' clinics, but it's going to take time."

Carter glances back to Caden once more, and I frown wondering what's going on between them. "What's up with you two? Is there something else?"

Holding Caden's gaze as he removes his arm from around me, he stands to grab something from Carter then slowly sits back down. Turning his chair toward me, I wish my heart would calm down. The only thing is his sad expression is setting all my instincts off. "There is one more thing I found that's a problem," Caden says, and I sit up straighter in my chair. "The file you gave me, well it's a fake." Shaking my head, I don't understand for a moment until he explains. "Your birth mother's identity is fake, Savannah." He hands me a piece of paper as he says, "This is the real Tammy Richards. She died twenty-three years ago."

"She died a year before I was born," I voice to no one in particular. Clutching the paper with both hands, I stare at the woman in the small photo. This was supposed to be my mother. The woman that holds all the answers that I desperately need. But it's all been a fucking lie. Tammy Richards no longer exists, and the person I need to find has made it nearly impossible to track down. Tears begin to pool in my eyes, and I blink them away as I lift my head. Standing, I feel Caden's gaze on me as I hand Carter the paper back. "Thank you for all your help." Avoiding his concerned glance, I turn to Caden. "Can I have your truck keys?"

Caden frowns as he asks, "What for, small fry?"

I'm about to lose it, and I can't be here when I do. "Please, Caden. Just give them to me." My hands begin to shake as I wait for Caden to pull his keys out of his pocket. He holds them out to me, and I don't say a word as I take them out of his hand. Rushing out the door, my stomach is in knots, and my stupid heart won't stop pounding in my chest and ears. If I can just make it to Caden's truck, I can let myself breakdown. I just have to get there first.

Not caring if anyone sees me, I race to the truck as the tears begin to blur my vision. All this fucking time I've been searching for the wrong person. All this time I've wasted on trying to find the one person that apparently doesn't want to be found.

Caden

Tammy Richards doesn't even exist anymore, and how am I going to find out who my mother is now? Whoever she is, she's just made my search basically impossible. And I don't know how I can live without knowing who she is, or how I'm supposed to move on not knowing the answers to these burning questions.

How am I supposed to handle this period?

fourteen
Caden

Watching with wide eyes as Savannah runs out of Carter's office, I slowly turn around to face my oldest brother. "What the fuck was that?"

Understanding and a hint of sadness in Carter's eyes gives me a shitty feeling. "That was your woman runnin'. Trust me. I've seen that look in Shelby's eyes many times before. She's runnin', Caden."

"Dammit. I've got to stop her." Not caring if he follows, I jump out of my chair and run out the door. I get why she's running, I do, but fuck this isn't how today was supposed to go down. Looking left then right, I try to spot her. She hasn't been gone but maybe two minutes tops, but knowing her, she's long gone. Running a hand down my face, I decide to check and see if she's sitting in the truck. Hearing

Caden

squealing tires makes me stop, and I can only stare. I see Savannah clearly driving away in my truck, I might add, and violating about three different traffic laws.

"Isn't that your truck," I hear behind me and see Carter staring in the same direction.

"Yep. That's ol' Betsy." I've got to hand it to Savannah. When she wants to run, best believe she'll make it happen. Jesus, I've got my work cut out for me.

"So much for stoppin' her."

"No shit, Carter."

"I'm just sayin'. She was haulin' ass."

Placing my hands on my hips, I tilt my head back. "Why me? Sweet baby Jesus, why me?"

Feeling a hand on my shoulder, I huff out a breath as I glance at Carter. "Is she worth it, man?"

"What kind of question is that? Of course she's worth it. Even if she did steal my ride, she's worth everythin'."

"Well then why the fuck are you still standin' here?"

Narrowing my eyes, I ask, "Didn't you just see her speedin' away in my truck? Or was I the only one who saw that?"

Carter chuckles loudly, then looks past me. I already know who he's staring at by the look in his eyes. Nothing but pure love is shining in them. Shelby must be behind me, and my guess is confirmed as I hear her voice. "Wasn't that your truck speedin' away?"

Before I can answer her, Carter says, "Yeah. Caden's woman is runnin'."

Shelby walks up to Carter and places a sweet kiss on his lips. Turning away, I glance in the direction Savannah drove away and give them a moment. Sometimes it's disgustingly beautiful to watch them. They're so in love and all that jazz, but that doesn't mean I like to witness it every single time they're near each other. Looking back at the happy couple, I ask, "Are y'all done with suckin' face? Cause' I might get sick watchin' y'all."

"Shut it, Caden," Carter snaps.

"Tell me more about your girl runnin', Caden," Shelby says as she hands Carter some food.

"Oh you know. I just had to pick the one woman that's making it hard as fuck to be with."

"Look I get it," she starts, and she would know. Poor Carter was a fucking wreck when Shelby ran from him. Multiple times I might add. "It's easier to run away from your problems than face them. But

Caden

I know you, and I also know you won't stop fightin' to make her stay." She's right. Damn she hit it right on the nail, but I have no clue how to get Savannah to accept what she already knows or my help. All of this feels like it's out of my control, and I have no idea how to get Savannah to stay with me. "Come on," Shelby says as she grabs my forearm. "We're goin' after her." She quickly kisses Carter goodbye then takes off toward the back parking lot. Letting her lead me to her car, I can only hope we can actually find Savannah. I have no idea where she would run to, and just thinking I don't know her as well as I want, makes my heart clench. If she tries to skip town without telling me, I'll be pissed as hell. I can't let her slip through my fingers, and I can't even stand the thought of her leaving me. Once we make it to Shelby's vehicle, she whips out of the parking lot like a woman on a mission.

Holding on tightly to the 'oh shit handle', I use my other hand to reach over myself and grab the seatbelt. "Hey, Shel?" She glances at me, and I quickly say, "Watch the road!" She shakes her head, and I'm really starting to reconsider letting her drive. "Would you slow down? You're freakin' me out."

"Stop being such a baby, Caden. I'm not goin' that fast."

Clenching my ass cheeks as she slams on her brakes to not run a red light, I pray she doesn't kill us before we can find Savannah. "I'm goin' to come back and haunt your ass if you kill me."

"Drama queen."

Before I can respond, I hear my phone go off with a text message. Thinking it might be Savannah, I quickly take my phone out of my pocket. But as I read the message, my stomach drops.

Cas: Where are you? Savannah is here packin'.

Me: Things didn't go well. Whatever you do, do not let her leave.

Cas: I think she's cryin'.

Me: Are you sure she's packin'?

Cas: I don't know for sure. She ran inside the apartment and then went into your room. She slammed the door in my face too.

Me: Well what do you expect? She's upset. Don't be butt hurt about it.

Cas: I'm not. Just hurry the fuck up.

Me: Shel is drivin'.

Cas: Oh fuck. Don't die first.

Me: I'm prayin' I don't. Be there soon.

"Was that her?" Shelby asks as I put my phone away.

Caden

"No. It was Cas. He said she's at our place and he thinks she's packin' her things."

Gripping onto the door handle as Shelby guns it, she says, "I won't ask how you got her to move in with you already, but you can't let her leave."

My entire body is ridged as Shelby whips in and out of traffic, and I hope she doesn't get pulled over. If she happens to get a speeding ticket, I'll be able to get her out of it, but I'm still scared for my life. "Not that I'm complainin' or anythin', but why are you in such a rush to get me there?"

It takes her a bit to answer me as she concentrates on getting me home. Right before she pulls into Flacon Lair, she says, "You've been different since you met her. I have to think she means somethin' to you, otherwise you wouldn't be helpin' her find her birth mother. Plus the way you talk about her lets me know you care for her a lot more than you're lettin' on."

When she finally parks, I relax and let out a breath. Unbuckling my seatbelt, I turn to her. "I know she's the one, Shel. It sounds crazy as fuck, but the moment our eyes locked, somethin' just clicked inside of me."

Her eyes soften, and she grins from ear to ear. "She's your soulmate then. Now go get em', tiger."

"Thanks, Shel." Opening the door, I place one leg out then turn back to her. "Also thanks for not killin' me. I really do appreciate that." I hear her laugh as I shut the door, but it's nice to know she understands where I'm coming from when it comes to Savannah. Racing up the stairs to my place, I make it there in record time. Jerking open the door, the first thing I notice is Cason standing in front of the door leading to my bedroom. When he notices me, I can already tell what he's thinking. It's a big benefit of having a twin. Sometimes I can't tell what anyone is thinking, but with Cason, it's like we share a brain. Right now, he's thinking, *"Dude, get your fuckin' ass in there and get your woman."* Nodding, he steps away from the door as I approach. Taking a deep breath, I slowly lift my hand to the door handle. I won't lie. I'm fucking terrified of what I'm walking into. *Time to man the fuck up, Caden.*

Opening the door, the first thing I notice is her suitcase on the bed. Well that just won't fucking do here. The second thing I see is all the drawers are open. That won't work for me either. Then lastly, I watch Savannah walk out of the closet with a handful of her clothes. Keeping my voice as calm as possible, I ask, "Goin' somewhere, small fry?"

She startles when she notices me, and I swallow seeing the tears falling freely down her cheeks. "I can't do this anymore. It's just too hard."

Caden

Alright fuck this shit. Taking a step to her, I grab the clothes out of her hand and toss them on the floor. I'm done playing this hot and cold game. "You're not goin' anywhere." Wiping a tear away as it falls down her cheek, she stares at me, and I hope she knows I mean it. I'll be damned if she walks out of here. "So what if this is hard? Life is hard, small fry. But the thing is when shit gets rough, you don't give up. You keep fuckin' fightin' and pushin' back. That's why I'm here." Using my finger, I point it to my chest. "I'm here to help you carry this, Savannah. Not anyone else. Me."

"You think this is easy for me? You think it's just a fucking walk in the park? Because it's not. Not by a long shot. You have no idea what I'm going through or what I'm dealing with."

In a way she's right, but I want to know everything there is to know about her. "I never said it was easy for you. I know it's not since it's written all over your face. But you can't up and leave when shit hits the fan."

Shaking her head, she steps back putting distance between us. I fucking hate it. "I have to go, Caden. There's nothing here for me anymore." Damn she knows just what to say to drive a stake right through my heart. Clenching my jaw, she takes a deep breath. "The only reason why I came here was to find my mother, and knowing now she created a fake identity to keep my adoption a secret kills me. I can't deal with this. I'm tired of looking for a person that obviously doesn't want to be found."

"So that's it? Just give up and run away?"

"What other option do I have?"

Closing the distance between us, I grab both sides of her face. "Let me in, Savannah. Stop pushin' me away and let me help you. You don't have to face this alone." More tears fall, and it kills me seeing her so hurt. Knowing this is my one and only chance to convince her to stay, I gaze into her eyes as I say, "You can't leave me, small fry. And I know it's insane, but I can't stand the thought of you leavin' me behind. There's somethin' between us, and I know you feel it. I promise you, I'll find out who your mother is if you'll just stay. With me." She searches my eyes for something, and I hope to God she knows how serious I am. "Please, Savannah. Don't fuckin' leave me." This is a new low for me. Fucking begging the one woman I'm falling for to stay with me, and I've never wanted someone to stay so bad before.

Holding a breath as she seems to decide what to do, I swear my heart is about to beat right out of my chest. If she leaves, it'll ruin me. If she leaves, it'll fucking kill me. There's not a chance I can live without her. "Okay," she breathes out, and I sigh in relief.

Caden

Unable to help myself, I lean in and steal a quick kiss. Pulling back, I whisper, "Thank you."

"You have to swear you'll find her, and tell me as soon as you do."

"I swear," I say without a bit of hesitation. Dropping my hands, I pull her to me and wrap my arms around her. That was close, too close for comfort. "You have got to stop tryin' to give me a heart attack, small fry. I'm too young to die." Hearing her let out a small laugh, I grin knowing I did that. I put that smile back on her face, and I'm the one to give her the one thing she needs.

Hope.

Eventually I'll give her all the love I have.

But not just yet. She's still a flight risk, and I have a feeling if I professed how deeply I care for her, she'll probably run right out the damn door screaming.

Pulling her back, I brush her hair out of her face and wipe the rest of her tears away. She sniffs as she glances up at me and says, "I'm sorry for snotting on your shirt."

Grinning, I glance down at the big snot spot on my shirt. Shrugging, I claim, "I don't care. If you need me to be your snot rag, then I'll be there every single time."

She frowns and I wish I could read her mind. I'd give anything to know what's going through her brain. "Should we talk about what this means?"

"About what, small fry?"

"Us," she huffs out.

Knowing she's been through a lot today, I decide to give her an out. "Not unless you really want to." I do want to. I want to make damn sure she knows how I feel, and that I'll never let her go but I can't. Not yet anyway. She already has a lot on her plate, and a part of me thinks if I do confess my feelings, she'll reject me and leave anyway.

"Thank you," she says after a few minutes pass.

"For what?"

"For convincing me to stay. For promising you'll find my mother, and for just being you. Don't ever change, Caden."

"I told you before, small fry. I'll do anythin' for you. There's no need to thank me."

She nods then glances around the room. "I should clean up your room."

"Nah. It's cool. How about we climb into bed and have a Netflix and chill day?"

Caden

"That sounds amazing." Before stepping away, I caress her face once more. Trying not to overcrowd her while she's vulnerable, I walk over to the bed and toss her suitcase on the floor. Her clothes fly everywhere, but I don't care. It's actually welcoming to see her things scattered all over my room instead packed away.

It means she's not going anywhere.

It means she's going to stay right here with me where she belongs.

And knowing she's here, well it gives me hope that she'll let me in and just maybe one day soon, she'll accept what all I have to offer her. Realizing I almost lost her today makes me want to hold onto her tightly, and never let her go. I may never be able to control everything about Savannah, but I do know I can fight like hell to keep her. I don't care what it takes, what I have to do, or what lengths I might have to go through.

I will make her see that I'm everything she needs.

fifteen
Savannah

Climbing in the bed with Caden, I push away the overwhelming thoughts running wild in my mind. There's just too much for me to process at once, and even though I told Caden I'd stay, the feeling of getting away from all of it is still present. It's like my entire body knows I can't deal with this, and I honestly have no idea how I'm going to get past it. Finding out my birth mother had a fake identity wasn't something I'd ever expected. It hurts deeply knowing she went through so much trouble to keep my birth a secret when it's supposed to be celebrated. I wonder if my parents even knew her identity was a secret, but then again how could they have known? This news is like an endless track running around in my head, and I wish it would just stop for a while. I'm still shocked that Caden got through to me when no one else has before. I won't even let myself think of what all he said, how he said it, or what it all means. Deep down I know it's big, but I'm putting it away in my 'to deal with later box' and calling it a day.

Getting comfortable on the bed, I glance at Caden. He seems happier now that I've decided to stay, and I find I like those blue eyes shining back at me with nothing but excitement. He opens his arms, and I don't even hesitate to move over and let him embrace me. Is it selfish I'm using him like this? Probably, but I need his strength. I need his comforting arms around me to remind me I'm not alone. Just like he said. Sometimes I forget there are people willing to help me, but it's easier to push people away when you have such deep insecurities like mine. I could blame it all on me being adopted, but I can't. I've always felt out of place, as if I was an outsider looking in. Even at the happiest times of my life, I've always felt something was missing.

But with Caden, that whole in my heart starts to fill a bit more each day.

That's why I lean on him now, and why when he reminds me he's here, I'll continue to lean on him. I know it seems like I'm headed down that road of serious relationship land, but I'm not ready just yet to admit it. Being with Caden is easy, and if I'm not careful, I might find myself falling for him.

Placing my head on his chest, I glance to the TV that's mounted on his wall as he scrolls through Netflix. "What are we going to watch?"

"Well," he sighs out, and I feel content hearing the strong beat of his heart. "I was thinkin' we could watch Supernatural. Supernatural is really good, and oh yeah, have you watched Supernatural before?"

Chuckling, I lift my gaze to him. "Do you want to watch Supernatural?"

"Only if you do," he says in a serious voice.

"I'm okay with watching Sam and Dean. They're the best. And Dean isn't so bad looking either."

I'm totally fucking with him, but I think he takes me seriously. His eyes widen, and I bite my bottom lip to stop myself from smiling. "Do you have a crush on Dean Winchester?"

"Well I mean look at him. He's sex on a stick."

His eyes narrow as he gazes into my eyes, and it takes him a moment to respond. "I'm just goin' to pretend you didn't say that so I can enjoy the show. Because you'll totally ruin it if you tell me you love Dean Winchester."

Letting my arm rest on his stomach, I ask, "Are you jealous of a celebrity?"

Caden

"What? No," he scoffs too quickly. "I mean why would I be? I'm way hotter than Dean Winchester."

"You keep telling yourself that." Looking away when he pulls me in tighter, I let out a sigh loving how his arm feels around me. I feel safe, warm, and yet again Caden shows me he there is so much more to learn about him.

Caden hits play and shifts down to get more comfortable. As the show plays on, Caden's hand never once stops rubbing up and down my shoulder. My skin prickles at the soft touch, and the longer he continues to lightly touch me, the more my heart pounds in my chest. I can't even focus on the show with him being so close, and my face warms feeling the desire start to flow through me. What is it about him that makes me go crazy with need? He's hardly doing anything, and I feel as if the room just spiked ten degrees. Trying to ignore his touch and how I'm reacting, I move a pillow between my legs to try and put out the slow building fire he's created. But when that doesn't seem to help, I begin to fidget. Huffing out a loud sigh, I jerk the pillow out from between my legs and toss it on the floor. I'm not comfortable, and it's all Caden's fault. All I can think about is how close he is, and how much I like him touching me. Then I begin to think about how he made me feel a few days ago in the kitchen when Cason rudely interrupted us.

Feeling Caden's eyes on me, I turn to him. He's grinning widely, and I'm sure he's just loving this. "You okay there, small fry?"

I give him a pointed look because he knows what he's doing. "I'm fine," I snap with more crass than intended.

He raises an eyebrow then smirks. "Someone is cranky." My breath catches in my throat when he reaches over to caress my cheek. Leaning in, my gaze never leaves his lips as he stops inches from mine. *Just kiss me already.* "Want to mess around?"

Letting out a small laugh, I ask, "What's that? Southern slang for want to have sex?"

Caden moves his hand down to my neck as he huskily says, "It is. So what's it goin' to be, small fry?" I don't even let myself think about if this is such a good or idea or not. Closing the small distance between us, I place my lips on his and wrap my arm around his waist. Caden quickly responds by deepening the kiss, and I already feel desire flowing through me. It's worse than ever as his grip on the back of my neck tightens. Everything about him sets me on fire, and I've never wanted someone so much before. How can he do that? How is it he's the only man to make me experience something so intense? Before I know what's happening, I'm on my back, and Caden is hovering over me. "I take that as a yes to messin' around," he says with a playful tone in his voice.

"Shut up and kiss me, Caden."

"Yes, ma'am."

And boy does he kiss me. Jesus, this man knows exactly what he's doing. His tongue intertwines with mine, and I let out a moan as his taste fills my senses. Running a hand under his shirt, I pull him closer. Even though it's physically impossible for him to be any closer, I still try anyway. Spreading my legs wider to accommodate him, I run my other hand through his hair. My hips rotate when he starts to kiss his way down to my neck, and my eyes close as he presses his hips into me hitting my sweet spot. Wrapping a leg around his waist, I keep moving my hips loving the feel of his hard cock against me. I need more than just this dry humping shit he's doing. "Caden, please."

Hissing in a breath when he nips at my earlobe, he whispers, "What do you want, Savannah?"

"You. I just want you." Can't he tell how much I need him? I'm about to burst into flames if he doesn't do something to relieve this ache and hunger that's growing.

He kisses me hard as his hips grind into mine, and I use my nails to keep him there. He lets me up for air, and all I can hear for a moment is my breath coming out in pants. Opening my eyes as his fingers lightly trace down my cheek, his blue eyes gaze into mine. Swallowing at seeing his pupils dilate and how his breath catches, my stomach clenches with need. "Are you sure about this? I know you've been through a lot today, and I'll stop right this second if you're not okay with this."

Frowning, I cup his cheek as I honestly say, "If you stop right now, I might kill you." He grins widely then takes my mouth again. This time it's not sweet or gentle. Caden kisses me like he needs me to breathe and with so much passion. A wave of lust rushes through my veins as one of his hands moves down to one of my breasts and cups it with the palm of his hand. Arching my chest, he chuckles at what I assume is my eagerness. I wasn't joking around when I said if he stopped I might kill him. He's driving me mad with his teasing. Taking matters into my own hands, I reach down and pull at his shirt. "This has got to go," I claim as I take it off and throw it to the side. And let it be known that I've never once ogled a man like I am now. Holy fuck. Caden is beautiful shirtless, and even though I saw him shirtless once before, it's as if I'm looking at him for the first time. Not caring if he sees me staring, I take my fill. Using my hand to run down his abs, his stomach jumps at my touch. He has a light tan, and it compliments his rock hard abs and chest perfectly. Moving my eyes

Caden

and hands to his arms, I glance up when he visibly flexes. "Did you just do that on purpose?"

"I have no idea what you're talkin' about," he says sweetly as he leans down to kiss me once more. Running my hands up his back, I relish in the feeling of his warm skin. When he pulls away, I want to protest. I'm enjoying his tender kisses more than I thought. "It's my turn, small fry."

Leaning up as he takes my shirt off, I lay back down as he tosses it on the floor. "You're prettier than I am," I say softly.

Now I've never really had insecurities about my body. I know I'm a bit heavy, my boobs are huge, and not to mention I do have belly rolls but even if I did have any insecurities, they would be completely washed away with the way Caden's eyes roam over me. "You're fuckin' stunnin', Savannah. Never forget that." I can't help but believe him. The tone of his voice tells me all I need to know, and I won't ever question it. His hands run up the middle of my breasts, and I know he can feel how hard my heart is pounding.

His eyes never leave mine as he does so, and I begin to feel something more than just lust. I'll admit it scares me. Which is why I lean up once more and take off my bra. Now that Caden is focused on my naked breasts, the desire I have for him hits me with full force and the warm feeling I felt in my heart slowly dissipates. "Are you just going to stare at me or what?"

"Yeah. I could stare at you all fuckin' day, small fry."

Pushing my chest up when both of his hands caress me gently, I breathe out, "Stare all you want, just not right now."

His hands run down to my stomach and stop at my shorts as he asks, "Impatient are we?"

Lifting my hips to find some sort of friction, I hiss out, "Yes. Please hurry up." He's killing me, and he knows it. Watching him with wide eyes, he quickly unbuttons my shorts and pulls them down my legs. Tossing them away, those blue eyes seem to darken as he gazes into mine, and I swallow when he reaches up to take off my panties. Raising my hips to help him take them off, I suck in a breath as the cool air hits my core.

"Goddamn, Savannah." Looking up, he's staring at me like a man dying of thirst. As if I'm the only one he needs to survive. It's intense, and the desire in his blue eyes make my stomach clench with a hunger I've never felt before. His cock is straining in his khaki shorts, and it sends a thrill through me knowing I'm turning him on so much. "Last chance to tell me to stop, small fry."

Caden

I don't even hesitate as I answer him. "Don't stop." Using both hands, he spreads my legs wider, and I hold my breath as he crawls back on the bed and places each hand behind my thighs. Watching him as he slowly moves closer to my aching pussy, I begin to panic knowing where he's headed. Clamping my thighs against his head to stop him, I ask, "What are you doing?"

"I was goin' to taste you. Would you mind easin' up a bit? You're hurtin' my face."

Opening my legs just a little, I feel my face flame with embarrassment. "I'm sorry. I just … I've never …"

"No one has ever gone down on you before?" Shaking my head, he asks, "You're not a virgin are you?"

"Oh God, no. I've had sex before but never … what you want to do." Maybe I've been with all the wrong guys because I've never had one want to go down on me. I've always wondered what it would feel like, but it's a little intimidating at the same time. And very intimate.

"Just relax, small fry," he says as he runs a hand up and down my thigh. He places a kiss on my knee as he huskily says, "I promise you'll love it." Trying to do what he says, I let out a long sigh. Unable to leave his eyes, my heart begins to race as

Brie Paisley

I wait for him to do what he wants. Caden kisses my inner thigh as he slowly makes his way down to my aching core, and I swallow hard as he hovers over me. Feeling his breath lightly touching me, my skin breaks out in goosebumps as I wait for him to taste me. He's only inches away, and the anticipation is beginning to get the best of me. Seeing his tongue dipping out of his mouth to lick his lips, I move my hips away. This is so unreal, and I'm not sure if I'm going to like this. "Relax, Savannah." At his demand, I try to stay still but it's hard though, and I hold my breath as he starts to kiss my inner thigh again. Caden sure knows how to get me riled up, and I almost beg him to just fuck me already. But then I see then feel him lick me from top to bottom, and I let out a loud moan as my head falls back. He wasn't lying when he said I would like this. I freaking love it. He licks my pussy slow as if he doesn't want to go too fast, and when he groans my stomach dips.

Letting the pleasure of his mouth take over my erratic thoughts, I rotate my hips up as he starts to suck on my sensitive clit. "Oh, God." How in the hell have I missed out on this? His fingers begin to dig into my hips, but I don't care. All I want is for him to make me come while using his tongue. "Caden," I moan out and raise my head to see him staring back at me with those intense blue eyes. Watching as one of his hands move, I wonder what he's going to do next. Feeling him at my entrance, I lick my lips, and

Caden

my head falls back on the bed. Clutching tightly onto the sheets, my mouth falls open as a ripple of intense pleasure hits me when he pushes a finger inside of me. It's the perfect combination, and I'm already feeling the sensation of an orgasm coming on.

The strokes of his finger match the pace of his tongue, and just as I'm about to ask for more, he adds another finger inside of me. Caden sucks on my clit, and I can't decide if I like that best or just him using his tongue. I can feel myself getting ready to fall into the abyss of euphoria, but the sound of someone knocking on the door makes me snap my head up. Caden stops all movement, and doesn't bother taking his fingers out of me as Cason says, "If y'all are hungry, I ordered pizza."

Caden glances to me with my essence on his face, and I'm panting heavily hating we were interrupted. Again. "We'll be there in a minute," Caden calls out, and I frown.

"A minute?" I practically yell. "We need more than a fucking minute."

"Good point," he says then turns toward the door to yell, "We need more than a minute."

Oh my God. Feeling my face warm, I just know Cason knows what we're doing. "Uh alright. I'm just ... I'll be at work."

"Why did you do that? Now he knows what we're doing," I whisper yell at Caden.

He grins widely as he says, "He left, didn't he? Now we don't have to worry about bein' interrupted again." Caden places an open mouth wet kiss on my pussy, and I let out a rush of air as I feel his fingers curl inside of me. "I'm goin' to have my wicked way with you now." I can't even find the words to respond. His mouth is suddenly back on me, and those fingers inside me work overtime. My entire body warms feeling the instant sensation of my pending orgasm, and I know it's not going to take him long to make me come. God do I want him to. All this pent up sexual tension hasn't been easy to ignore, and I can tell how much I need this.

My stomach begins to clench and my heart rate spikes knowing I'm right on the edge. Caden must know I'm right there because right as I'm about to let go, he sucks hard on my clit, and those fingers of his thrust hard inside me. "Fuck, Caden." A wave of intense pleasure rushes through me, and I don't care if the whole town can hear me. He lets me ride out my orgasm, one that I don't think will ever end.

When I finally come down, Caden places one last kiss on me before standing at the edge of the bed. He uses the back of his hand to wipe my essence off his chin, and I swallow hard knowing I want more of him. "Damn, small fry. You're fuckin' beautiful as hell when you come for me." Moving up to my knees, I make my way to him. Eagerness has me rushing to get him naked, and he smirks as I quickly try to unbutton his shorts. Before I can get them undone and pull down his shorts and boxers, he takes hold of my wrist stopping me. Glancing up at him, I think for a split second that he doesn't want this. "What's the rush?"

Wrapping my arms around his neck, I kiss him to show how much I need him. Pulling away, I claim, "I need more, Caden." Moving my hands down his stomach, I whisper in his ear. "I want you inside of me." His breath hitches and I smirk knowing I'm affecting him. Kissing the side of his neck, my hands continue to roam down until I reach his cock. Cupping him in my hand, he groans loudly and grips my hips. "Don't you want me?" Caden moves so quickly I don't realize what's going on until I'm lying on my back once more with him between my legs. He grinds his hips into me and uses a hand to grab my ass. Lifting my hips to meet his, he takes my mouth and kisses me roughly. When he starts to pull away, I grab him and bring him back. It seems we can't get enough of each other, and I'm ready to beg for him to take me already.

He caresses my face as he breaks our kiss, and my breath catches in my throat seeing his eyes gazing into mine. God he's utterly breathtaking. "I want you so fuckin' bad, Savannah."

"Then what are you waiting for?"

"I don't want to embarrass myself," he says with a wide grin, and I frown. "You're drivin' me insane and fuck. I might just come in my pants if you keep on."

Rotating my hips up, his jaw clenches as his eyes close. "Condom, now," I demand, and his eyes snap open. He takes a deep breath before moving off the bed leaving me feeling needy, and my pussy throbs watching his abs contract.

My erratic panting fills the room as I stare at him. "Is this what you want, small fry?" He asks as he unbuttons his shorts. Only able to nod, he smirks knowing he's driving me crazy. Slowly taking off his shorts, I swallow and suck in a breath seeing how hard his cock is through his boxers. I start to move to help rid of him of his clothes, but he shakes his head, and I poke out my bottom lip. "Patience, Savannah." I don't want to be patient any longer, and this teasing game he's playing is making this ache I have for him worsen. Those blue eyes never leave mine as he slips his boxers off his hips, and I break contact to see all of him. My face flames seeing him completely naked for the first time, and my mouth suddenly dries when his cock jumps at my attention. Caden is utterly breathtaking, and I lick my lips wondering what he would taste like. That desire I feel? It's multiplied by a hundred now. I have to have

Caden

him. My gaze snaps up when I see him moving toward me, and he reaches down to his bedside table to pull open a drawer. Never in my life have I been so ready for a man to take me before, and my heart races wildly in my chest when Caden pulls out a condom.

Spreading my legs as wide as they can go, he moves back in between them, and I feel a piece of my walls crumble. It's the look he's giving me that threatens to knock my walls completely down, and realizing there's more to this than just lust, well it changes things. Doing what I do best, I ignore it and take the condom out of his hand. Quickly opening it, Caden chuckles as I move as fast as I can to put it on him. He hisses loudly when I grab his cock with my hand, and slowly slide on the condom for him. My pussy throbs once more knowing what's about to happen, and I know it's been a long time coming for us because the sexual tension has always been there. It's just surreal knowing this beautiful, charming, and utterly delicious man wants me.

Me. Of all people.

Trying not to think about it, I finish rolling the condom on him and wrap my legs around his. One of his hands brushes my hair out of my face as the other takes my right leg behind my thigh. He's opening me up further than I was before, and I raise my hips sensing he's right at my entrance. "Caden, please," I beg hoping he'll hurry up. Why he continues to make me wait, I have no idea.

"I don't want to hurt you," he says against my lips, and my heart clenches knowing he's so concerned about me.

Running a hand down his back and the other caresses his face, I give him a sweet peck on his lips. "You won't break me. I promise."

He nods and huskily says, "I'll go slow." As soon as slow comes out of his mouth, I feel him pushing his way inside. Letting my eyes close and my head falls back, I rotate my hips up to help him more. His pace is so slow, I fear I might explode with sensation after sensation. With his slow pace, I can feel myself stretching for him. It's the most consuming and intense pleasure I've ever felt before. Is this how it'll be with him every time? I can't help but wonder why things feel different with Caden, and why my body is reacting to him so much differently than with anyone else. It's like I can't get enough of him. Choosing to push it out of my mind, I focus on his cock inside me and how good it fucking feels. Right before he's all the way in, Caden touches my lips and demands, "Open your eyes, Savannah." Quickly doing just that, I gaze into his eyes and my heart does a little flip. The way he's looking back at me, well it looks a lot like love shining in those blue eyes. But that can't be right. We've only just met a few weeks ago, and there's no way he can love me.

Rising to take his mouth, I kiss him with a fervor I hadn't known I could feel for him. Running my hand down to his ass, I pull him to me as I raise my hips. The movement makes him push deeper inside of me, and I break the kiss to call out his name. God he feels amazing, and I have no idea if I'll be able to get enough of him. His pace is slow, but his thrusts are deep. Caden hits the spot I love the most each time, and I'm even surprised that I begin to feel another impending orgasm. My grip on his ass cheek tightens, and it's only my moans and his heavy breathing that fills the room. Everything about this moment is intense, sensual, and it's so freaking consuming. Caden doesn't seem to be in a hurry, and neither am I. Wanting this to last as long as possible, I hold off on letting go. My free hand moves to his bicep and feeling how hard it is makes this need grow stronger than before. Loving how his muscles contract with every thrust, I let out a loud moan. Caden's fingers around my thigh grip me harder, and he groans when I clench around him. "Damn you feel so fuckin' good," he huskily claims and moves to my neck. Tilting my head to give him more room, I grip his arm hard willing him to stay right where he is.

My skin starts to warm with our combined body heat, but I don't care. He feels too good to worry about overheating. All I can think about, feel, and want is for him to keep going. My orgasm continues to build, and I know once I let go, I won't ever be the same. That's how powerful this is between us. Caden kisses and nips at my neck as he moves the hand on my thigh to my breasts. While he caresses my right one lovingly, his leg moves under mine, opening me up more than before. His pace begins to quicken, and I can't hold off any longer. "Tell me you're close," he asks with a grunt in my ear. Only able to answer with another loud moan, he demands, "Come with me, Savannah." Turning my head to him, he takes my mouth and kisses me deeply.

That kiss is everything.

That kiss is my undoing.

Breaking away to cry out, my orgasm hits me with such a force I lose my breath. My entire body tingles as it ripples through me, and an intense wave of pleasure rushes through my veins. Hearing Caden's loud groan as he lets go with me, I relish in knowing I made him feel this way. It's a powerful feeling knowing I can make him experience something like this. He doesn't bother rolling off me once he's spent, and his body sags on top of mine. Running my hands up and down his back, I kiss his shoulder and neck. Feeling his racing heart and hearing his rapid breaths, I smile sensing pride. Closing my eyes, I let his warmth surround me.

We lay like this for a while, forever it seems, before he uses his arms to prop himself up. "I'm not hurtin' you am I?" There's so much concern in his voice, and I grin as I shake my head. Technically, I can't breathe very well with his weight, but I'm starting to get used to him stealing my breath away. "You okay? I don't think you've ever been so quiet before."

Grinning widely, I sigh deeply in content. "I'm perfect. Just enjoying the after effects."

"Good because I plan on makin' you look this fuckin' happy all the time, small fry."

"Cocky much?" I ask playfully.

He raises an eyebrow as he claims, "You know you loved it." Narrowing my eyes, I try to pretend I didn't, but it doesn't last long. Letting out a laugh at his serious expression, he smiles down at me. "I'm goin' to get rid of this condom. Don't move." Sucking in a breath as he moves out of me, I roll to my side so I can get the perfect view of him hopping off the bed. He flashes me a cheeky grin, before turning around. Shaking my head seeing him flex that perfect ass of his, I quickly crawl under the covers as he leaves the room.

Glancing at the door as I wait for him to return, something begins to happen to me. I'm not sure how to explain it, but it feels a lot like happiness. My chest warms, and I can't stop smiling. Every time I think of what we did and what we shared together, my stomach dips and flutters. When Caden comes back into the room, my gaze locks with his and once again, my breath hitches. Swallowing hard, I know what this feeling is, and I won't lie it scares me.

Because this feeling I have, this feeling that's beginning to spread throughout my entire body, seems a lot like love.

Shit. *I'm falling in love with him.*

And that's something I swore to myself I wouldn't do.

Caden

sixteen
Caden

Gazing into Savannah's eyes, I see the emotions playing across her beautiful face. She's working through something, and I hope she's beginning to realize what this is between us. Because I won't sit here and claim I don't want anything more from her. *I want everything from her.* I want her heart, her soul, and I want to make her mine forever. In the past, the thought of marriage used to freak me the fuck out because I couldn't understand why a guy would only want to be with one woman for the rest of his life. But seeing Savannah laying in my bed, and with that relaxed expression on her face, well now I totally fucking get it. Granted she looks confused and a bit scared, but I can work with that.

Walking over to the bed, I crawl over her and get underneath the covers. Pulling her to me, she rolls over so she's facing me. Whatever is going through her mind, she must have worked through it because now she's smiling at me again. And damn, that smile makes my heart stop for a few seconds. That smile is just for me and only me. "You looked thoroughly fucked, small fry."

She snorts at my bluntness, but she does. I take pride in knowing I made her look this way and knowing she's so content. "Do you say that to all the girls you've been with?"

Frowning, I wonder why she's bringing up my past. Granted we haven't really talked about it, but I'm sure she's guessed I've been around the block a time or two. I'm not proud of the amount of women I've been with. Especially now that I have Savannah. If I could go back and erase every single woman I've been with, I would. I only want her, and I wish I'd met her sooner in life. "Actually no. You're the only one, Savannah." And it's true. I've never really cared enough about my previous lays to ask. That makes me sound like an asshole, but like I said once before, Savannah is different.

She glances away when she whispers, "Can I ask you something?"

Placing a finger under her chin, I move her to look at me. "Why are you whisperin'?"

Caden

Shrugging, she says, "I don't know."

I have a feeling she does know but doesn't want to tell me. "We're the only ones here, small fry. You can ask me anythin'."

Savannah looks away again, and her cheeks turn bright red. Whatever she wants to know is apparently embarrassing her. I'm curious to know what she's thinking, and I wait patiently for her to ask me her question. "Exactly how many women have you been with?" Ah the dreaded question I was hoping to avoid. It's my turn to look away now as she says, "That many huh?"

Glancing back to her, I place my hand on her hip and take a deep breath. "Here's the thing," I start. Everything I'm about to say is going to make me seem like a dick bag that uses women. I guess that's true to a point. "I don't know how many exactly. It's not like I kept a little black book of all my sexual partners." She smirks with my joke, and I'm glad. I'm worried telling her this will make her want to leave. But I want to be honest with her. "It's no secret I got around before, and yeah my brothers gave me the nickname of manwhore, but ..." I stop to pull her closer, and I begin to rub circles on her hip. "I hadn't been with anyone in a long time. Not until you showed up that is, and now." I gaze into her eyes as I truthfully say, "Now I wish I could forget all about my past and all the women I've been with. None of them really gave a shit about me, and yeah it makes me seem like an ass for usin' them, but I never mistreated them or made any promises. They all knew what they were gettin' themselves into when they were with me. You're the only one I've chased, small fry. You're the only one I want to be with."

She's silent for a while and, damn it worries me. I hope she doesn't judge me for my past because everyone has one. But I did tell her how I felt, and everything I've said is nothing but the truth. When she takes a deep breath, I fear the worst and hold mine as she says, "You're just saying that because you just had a good lay."

Pushing out a breath, I know what she's doing. I laid some relationship type words on her and now she's trying to play the denial game. Moving my hand off her hip, I caress her face and stare into those blue-green eyes of hers. The hints of green in her eyes seem to flare at me and fuck she's got to understand she's it for me. "Just because you're the best woman I've had doesn't mean everythin' I said wasn't the truth." She sucks in a breath as I continue and I hope this means she's starting to understand. "There's no one else I would rather be with, and there's no fuckin' way I can compare you to any woman of my past. You're so different than anyone I've ever met, Savannah. I know you're scared and you don't want any labels, but I want you to know that what this is between us is way more than just

Caden

sex." God I want to confess how much I want to be with her, and how I'm falling for her. "Just so you know, there's so much I want to say right now, but I won't because I know you're not ready to hear it." I know I'm right by the way her eyes shine back at me. She's still fighting her feelings for me, and that's okay. "I'm a very patient man, Savannah. So whenever you're ready, you let me know and I promise you I'll be everythin' you need and more."

Her eyes search mine, and her chest quickly rises and falls. I wonder if she's thinking about denying what we have again, or if she's going to try and give me the slip. But she surprises me when she softly says, "I'm not sure what to say to that."

Smirking, I rub my thumb across her cheek. "You don't have to say anythin'. Just remember this conversation, okay?"

Nodding, she lets out a small, "Okay."

Feeling better about my confessions, I place a tender kiss on her lips before laying back down on my back. Holding my arm out for her, my chest warms as she doesn't hesitate to move closer to me. Having her in my arms is so surreal. I still half wonder if it was a mistake to make it known how I feel about her, but I have to take a risk. I can't keep going on this path without her at least knowing some of how I feel. Yeah, I held back because it's clear she's not ready to hear it all. But soon she will. Soon there won't be any reason to hold back, and she will know that there's no running from this. Moving my hand up and down her shoulder, she lets out a sigh, and I grin knowing she's so relaxed in my arms. Glancing up, I realize we both completely forgot about our Netflix and chill day. An episode of Supernatural is ending, and I feel around in the bed for the remote. Finding it under my pillow, I place a kiss on Savannah's forehead. "Back to Netflix and chill?" She hums out her yes, and I figure she'll be asleep soon which is okay with me. I'm perfectly content just holding her in my arms for the rest of the day. I'm totally fine with listening to her deep breaths letting me know she's close to sleep. Continuing to rub her arm, I turn the TV down so not to disturb her and my chest constricts knowing this is the best day of my life. Well so far that is, and it's all because of her.

The next day rolls around and I have to admit, I'm proud of Savannah. After confessing how I felt about her, well technically not everything, she hasn't tried to put distance between us or even hinted she was going to disappear on me. But that doesn't mean I'm still not worried. Which is why I didn't tell her we're going to my parents today to attend Caleb's welcome home party. Knowing how she reacted the last time I invited her to meet my family, I thought it was best to surprise her.

In fact, we're on our way there now. She looks gorgeous in her casual attire, but then again she could wear a paper sack, and I would still think she's beautiful. Reaching over, I take her hand in mine. She turns to look at me with that smile I love seeing, and I swear my heart skips a beat. I've got it bad for her. "Are you going to tell me where we're going?"

Placing a kiss on the back of her hand, I smirk before I answer her. She narrows her eyes at me, and I'm sure she knows I'm up to something. "It's a surprise."

"Don't you remember me telling you that I don't like surprises?"

Of course I remember. It was our first date, and yeah, it might not have ended how I wanted, but I still consider it a great night. "I remember everythin' you tell me, small fry."

"Then why are you trying to surprise me again?"

Shaking my head, I've never met anyone that didn't like being surprised. But Savannah is unlike anyone I've met before. "I promise it'll be a good surprise."

She huffs out a breath and glances out the window. We're only a few minutes from reaching my parent's house when she turns back to me. "Can I at least get a hint?"

Chuckling at her impatience, I state, "I don't want to ruin it."

"Caden, come on. Just tell me."

"If you'll just hold onto your britches for five more minutes, you'll see."

"But I want to know now."

"You're killin' me, small fry." Seeing her unbuckle her seatbelt out of the corner of my eye, she lifts the middle console and scoots by me. Wondering what she's up to, I look at her. "You're goin' to get me in trouble."

"I somehow doubt that," she says sweetly.

"At least put the middle seatbelt on."

Glancing to the road then back to her, I feel relief she actually listens to me. "Happy now?"

"Yes, ma'am. I'm only lookin' out for your safety."

"But wearing seatbelts makes it hard to do this," she whispers in my ear as she reaches over and grabs my cock. Hard I might add. Clenching my jaw, this little minx is going to be the death of me.

Caden

Her hand starts to rub my cock and of course, my dick has to go and get hard for her. This isn't going to work out so well since I'm literally about to pull up at my parents. "Tell me where we're going, Caden."

Groaning as she caresses me, I wish I could skip out on this party and take her right here, right now. "We're here," I breathe out. Parking the truck in my parent's driveway, I grab her wrist and take her mouth. Kissing her deeply and a bit rough, I want her to know how fucking turned on I am. And yeah, I kind of want her to want me as much as I want her knowing there's nothing either of us can do about it until we get back to my place. Pulling away, I grin seeing her cheeks flushed and her lips are a bit swollen from my kiss. "Do you want me, Savannah?"

Her eyes slowly open to meet my gaze, and my cock jumps as she licks her lips. "Yes," she says in a raspy voice.

"Good because that's how I feel." Leaning over, I whisper, "I want you wet, needy, and practically beggin' me later to fuck you."

Sitting back in the seat, I watch as her eyes dilate and I know she's thinking about me taking her again. "Why are we still parked? Let's go now."

Chuckling at her eagerness, I take a deep breath. "I would love nothin' more than to be inside you right now, small fry." Glancing toward my parent's house, I know if I miss this Mama will kill me. "The thing is we kind of have to go inside."

Savannah starts to say something, but we both turn when someone begins to knock on my window. Rolling my eyes as I see Clark, I wish he would've waited just a few more minutes before interrupting us. It seems to be an ongoing theme with Savannah and I. Adjusting myself before opening the door, I hop out as Clark asks, "Y'all coming in or y'all going to stay out here all day makin' out?"

Resisting the urge to punch him in the arm, I sarcastically claim, "Not like I could make out with my girl anyway. Between you and Cason, I'll never get past first base without gettin' rudely interrupted."

"Maybe you shouldn't be tryin' to get to first base in our parent's driveway."

"We're at your parents?" Savannah asks, and I turn around to help her out of the truck. Once she's on her feet, I shut the door and take her hand. "Caden?"

Clark pretends to look away, but I see that stupid smirk. "Don't freak out," I begin because I'm worried she might freak the fuck out. "Today is Caleb's welcome home party, and I wanted you to meet everyone." Turning to Clark, I say, "This is my douche brother Clark."

Caden

Savannah's eyes widen, and I hold my breath waiting for what she's going to do. She takes a deep breath and looks away from me before turning to Clark. "It's nice to meet you, and thank you for your service."

Pushing out a breath, I'm grateful she isn't making a big deal out of this. Not yet at least. But Clark, on the other hand, must be in a shit mood. The smirk he had suddenly disappears, and it's not hard to miss the ghosts of his past playing across his face. "Thanks," he snaps, and I start to step in when he adds, "I'm goin' inside."

What the fuck? Shaking my head at my brother's rudeness, Savannah asks, "Was it something I said?"

"Honestly there's no tellin'. Just ignore him." I know Clark has been through a lot recently, but he and I are going to have words later about this. "Ready, small fry?" I ask nodding toward my parent's house.

Savannah glances past me, and then back to me as she says, "I don't know, Caden. I wish you would've told me so I could've been prepared."

Frowning, I pull her to me. "Why would you need preparin'?"

She stares at my chest as she softly says, "I ... I don't know." Taking my finger, I lift her chin to look at me. She sighs deeply as she rushes out, "What if they don't like me? Clark clearly didn't seem too impressed."

I see what's going on here. She's nervous, but she has no reason to be. "I know for a fact they're goin' to love you, and you can't let Clark make you think any different. He's an ass so he doesn't count."

Those blue-green eyes stare into mine as she asks, "How do you know?"

Using my free hand, I take a deep breath as I brush her hair out of her face. "Because, small fry. I lo— I mean … I like you, so I know they will." My heart pounds in my chest knowing I almost slipped out the L-word. But it is true. I do love her, but I don't think she's ready to hear that just yet.

Her eyebrows furrow and I think she did hear me for a second until she states, "Well if you're so confident they will, then I guess we should go inside."

"That's my girl," I say with a grin. She rolls her eyes, but she comes willingly when I start to make my way toward the house.

She holds onto my hand tightly as we walk up the steps of the front porch, and right as I'm about to open the door she pulls back, and I turn to her. "Are you sure about this?" With my frown, she says, "I don't know why I'm so nervous."

Caden

I'm not sure why she's so nervous either, but I have a feeling it has something to do with the fact this is kind of a big deal for me. I've never once brought a woman home before. So yeah, maybe she knows how much this means for us. Deciding to keep that tidbit to myself, I grin widely as I claim, "Just be yourself, small fry."

One eyebrow raises as she sarcastically asks, "So what you're saying is, I should be a smart ass?"

Chuckling, I shake my head. "Come on, small fry." She takes a deep breath, and I lean in to leave a sweet kiss on her lips. "It's going to be fine. I promise." When she nods, I squeeze her hand and turn back to the door. Once we're inside, I smile hearing my family hanging out in the kitchen. Making my way there, I glance back to Savannah seeing she's looking around the house. It does send a thrill through me knowing she's here with me and about to meet my family. Reaching the kitchen, Cason and Mama are standing by the kitchen island, and I announce loudly, "The party can start now that we're here." Dad and Clark walk back inside as soon as the words leave my mouth, and they shake their heads. Cason doesn't look the least bit amused by me, but Mama laughs. "What? No cheers of glee?"

"The last time I checked," Cason starts. "This party isn't for you."

"That's a shame. I'm the life of the party."

"Boys, I don't want any fightin', you hear me?" Mama scolds. Cason and I glare at each other, but we silently call a truce. It's always like this with us, but I find it hilarious how I can get him so worked up over nothing. "Who do you have hidin' behind you, Caden?"

Ah small fry is hiding now. Pulling her from behind me, I watch Mama's eyes and smile widen as she sees Savannah. "This is Savannah." I want to say more, but seeing how red her cheeks are, I hold back.

Placing my arm around her, she leans into me as Mama dries off her hands and walks over to us. Mama winks at me before she says, "It's nice to finally meet you, Savannah."

Savannah's head snaps to me and asks, "You talked about me?"

"Only good things, I swear."

She's quiet as she turns back to Mama, but I don't miss the small smile on her face. "I was wonderin' when Caden was goin' to bring you over." Mama gushes, and I shake my head. The way Mama is acting one would think Savannah was a rare jewel or something.

"It's nice to meet you too, Mrs. Harlow."

Caden

"Oh hush now. You can call me Linda."

Noticing everyone is staring at Savannah and the room suddenly is quiet, I ask, "Where's Carter and Shelby?" Feeling Savannah's shoulders sag, I know I made the right call.

"They should be here any minute," Dad answers.

"Why are they always late?" I ask no one in particular.

Mama shoots me a sideward glance, and I grin widely. "I don't know why you're always givin' Carter and Shelby a hard time."

Not thinking before I speak, I claim proudly, "I just like bustin' their balls."

"Caden," Mama warns as Savannah snickers beside me. "Don't make me get out my whoopin' spoon."

Knowing she would in a heartbeat, I quickly say, "Don't embarrass me, Mama."

"You do that all on your own," Cason pipes back.

Sighing loudly, I glance down to Savannah. "You're seein' this right? My whole family is against me."

She steps away from me as she states, "Don't drag me into this. I'm Switzerland."

"Oh I like her," Mama announces as she takes Savannah by the arm. Savannah winks at me as Mama leads her to the kitchen island, and I follow behind them feeling the warmth spreading through my chest. I take pride in knowing Savannah fits in perfectly already with my family. I can't keep my eyes off Savannah as Mama literally takes her under her wing, but I don't mind. Dad and Clark take a seat at the kitchen island, and I glance to Cason when everyone begins to talk amongst themselves. He nods his head to me, and I know he approves. I'm not even surprised when Cason joins in the conversation flowing. They all seem very interested in my small fry, but I expected it. No one would've guessed she was so nervous right before we walked inside the house. Now it seems she belongs here, and all those nerves have all but vanished. Which can only mean one thing. She does belong here with me, and I hope one day soon she realizes this too. My eyes lock with hers as she laughs at something Mama says, and her face blushes with my intense gaze. I've never seen her so open and free. Except like that that one time in my apartment when she was dancing around as we listened to her favorite song. I'm not sure how to explain it, but in my heart I know this is where she's supposed to be.

Caden

Seeing Savannah will be alright for a moment, I walk over to Cason. "Is Caleb in his room?" I'd forgotten to ask Mama, but I assume he's hiding out until the party starts. I never really quite understood why Caleb was so shy.

"Yeah. I think he's gettin' ready."

Wiggling my eyebrows, I playfully say, "Or he's gettin' off."

Cason glares at me, which isn't anything new. "That's disgustin'."

"I'm just sayin'. Never know. Plus you have to watch out for the quiet ones." Cason shakes his head, but he knows I'm right. Catching Savannah's gaze again, I motion for her to come stand by me. Her grin lets me know she's enjoying herself and once she reaches me, I brush her hair behind her ear. "I'm goin' to find Caleb. Will you be alright for a bit?" I'm not worried about leaving her alone with my family, but I want to make sure *she's* alright with it. The last thing I want is to overwhelm her.

"I'll be fine, Caden. No need to worry that pretty little head of yours," she sweetly says. "Plus I have Cason here to help me if I put my foot in my mouth."

Cason grunts in response then seems to think better of it. "You do realize there are some things even I can't help."

"Don't be a buzzkill, Cason," Savannah pipes back.

Covering my mouth, I try to hold back a laugh with Cason's blank expression. "You're startin' to freak me out with how much you're like this one," he says as he points to me. "And the last thing we need is another Caden."

"Hey! That hurts me deep, man." I snap as I smack his arm.

"And what's wrong with Caden?" Savannah starts. She glances at me with those wide eyes and softly says, "I think he's perfect the way he is."

Turning back to Cason, I state, "See. She thinks I'm perfect."

"I won't even comment back to that."

"Oh lighten up, buttercup." Cason huffs out a breath in annoyance, but it's so much fun riling him up. Taking Savannah by her hand, I pull her to me and wrap my arm around her. "It's good to know you think I'm perfect."

Shaking her head, she claims, "Don't let it go to your head. Your ego is big enough as it is already."

I can't help but smirk at her witty response. It's just like her to give it right back to me. "I promise not to let my ego explode with awesomeness." She

Caden

laughs lightly as she gazes up at me, and I can't resist those lips of hers. Leaning down, I place a gentle and tender kiss on her lips that have seemed to become like a drug to me. Pulling away before things get too crazy and knowing we have an audience, I use my thumb to caress her cheek. "Don't get into any trouble while I'm talkin' to Caleb."

She sucks in a breath and swallows before saying, "I make no promises." Giving her one last kiss, I step away and glance to Cason. He nods, and I know that's his way of letting me know he'll stick by her side.

Because honestly, I never know what to expect from Savannah. Who knows what my small fry will do while I'm away.

That in itself is a little scary.

But I wouldn't have it any other way. She makes life interesting and fun. Damn she really is my perfect match. Watching her as I walk away, it's harder than I thought to leave her side. Although I could've stuck to her like glue, I need to talk to Caleb. Leaving the kitchen and opening the door to the basement, I make my steps as loud as possible and yell out, "Caleb! Please cover up anythin' you don't want me to see." Thinking better of it, I call out, "I do not want to see you jerkin' the chain alright." Making it to the bottom of the stairs, I quickly use my hand to cover my eyes. "Caleb? Are you even down here?" I know this is his new and improved room. He claimed when he returned home that he needed more space. For what, I have no idea. My brothers and I helped him move into the basement even though he could've done it all himself.

"What the fuck is wrong with you? Why are you coverin' your eyes and yellin' like a crazy person?"

"Is it safe to look? Please don't let me see you naked, oops baby."

He huffs out loudly as he says, "I'm not naked. And stop callin' me that. You know how much I freakin' hate it."

Not fully trusting him, I take a peek through my fingers. Seeing he is indeed not naked, I drop my hand. He is however, shirtless and that's pretty close to being naked. Deciding not to dwell on it, I ask, "Why aren't you upstairs?"

Taking the towel from around his shoulders, he dries his hair as he says, "Didn't realize you were Dad now. And the party doesn't start for another hour."

"Yeah," I start and give him a pointed look. "But you know the family is goin' to show up at least an hour early. You know? Just in time for the craziness to happen."

Caden

Caleb tosses the towel in a hamper by a dresser then turns back to me. "Yeah. Should've known that."

Narrowing my eyes, I have a feeling he wants to say more. When he doesn't, I glance around his room. It's a nice set up he has going. It kind of reminds me of a studio apartment with its open layout. Granted he's still crashing with Mama and Dad, but it suits him. I mean it's nothing spectacular by any means, but it's homey. "Place is lookin' good," I say to fill the silence. Honestly I'm not sure how to go about asking him what I need him to do.

Caleb walks over to his closet and pulls out a shirt and puts on his glasses before turning back to me. "Did you come down here just to bust my balls about stayin' with Mama and Dad? Because I know you didn't come down here just to compliment my room."

Placing a hand on my hip, I chuckle then say, "Alright you got me." Sucking in a breath, I hold it in making my cheeks puff out before letting it go. Caleb watches me carefully because I'll admit, this is way out of character for me.

"Dude, what's with you?"

I've never had a problem asking any of my brothers for anything because I know no matter what, they'll be there and do whatever they can for me. The problem is what I'm about to ask Caleb, goes against everything I stand for. Because it's fucking illegal. "I sort of need a favor."

Caleb shrugs his shoulders as he says, "Okay. Whatever it is, I'm here for you. I don't get why you're freakin' out about it."

"It's not your typical favor," I state vaguely.

"Just spit it out already, Caden."

Running a hand down my face, I pull out the paper from my back pocket. Savannah has no idea I still have the proof of her mother's fake identity, but it's needed at a time like this. I also promised her I'd find out who her birth mother is, and if I have to go beyond the law to do so, I will. Savannah means the world to me, and if finding this woman will help her heal, then I'll do whatever I can do make it happen. "You still in the business of hackin' shit?"

"Uh yeah. I guess so."

"Good." Handing him the piece of paper, I add, "Can you find out who made this fake ID and who bought it?"

Caleb stares at the paper for a while then adjusts his glasses before he looks back up. "Maybe. You have somethin' more for me to go on?"

Caden

Shaking my head, I say, "If that trail is cold, I would start with hospitals in Florida or even adoption agencies."

"Is there any reason in particular you want me to hack a hospital's database? Or possibly end up in jail for this shit?"

I was afraid he would need some convincing, but I know he'll do it just because we're family. "It's for someone I care for. You're actually goin' to meet her soon." With his raised eyebrows, I add, "She's here."

Watching him as he folds the paper and walks over to his desk, he lays it down and moves back in front of me. "I thought I'd never see the day when Caden, the manwhore of Columbus, had a serious girlfriend."

"Well technically she's not my girlfriend." Another eyebrow raises from him, and I explain. "It's complicated. So can you do it or not?"

"Yeah. You could've at least given me a challenge."

Chuckling, I shake my head. Of course he would be a smart ass. Apparently it runs in the family. "Thanks, man. I owe you one."

"Yeah, you will. Especially if I get caught. Which I won't, but it's good to know you'll bail me out."

"My advice," I say calmly because this shit cannot go beyond this room. "Don't get busted. I mean yeah. I'll get you out of a pickle if I have to, but this doesn't need to leave this room."

"No, I understand. I won't say anythin'."

Walking over to him, I place my hand on his shoulder. "Thank you. I really do appreciate your help on this. And for not blabbin'." I don't need to get Savannah's hopes up for nothing. Who knows if Caleb will find anything? For all I know, there's nothing to find anyway.

Caleb nods as he says, "Give me a week or two. If there's anythin' to go on, I'll find it."

"Thanks, man. That's all I need to hear." Feeling better about this whole situation, Caleb follows me back upstairs. The need to see Savannah again makes me take the steps two at a time. It's like a force pulling me to her. Craziest shit I've ever felt, but once I make it back to the kitchen and she turns to look at me, nothing as ever felt more right.

And I swear that smile is going to give me a heart attack one day from it making my heart continuously skip a beat. But if I were to die seeing

Caden

that smile from her, that smile that's only for me, then fuck it. I'll die a blissfully happy man.

seventeen

Savannah

I feel him before I see him.

It's like a sixth sense or something, but I swear it's like an invisible force that wants me to turn around. So I do, and come face to face with those intense blue eyes gazing at me. My breath catches as if that force just knocked the wind out of me. Caden walks right over to me, completely ignoring the looks his family is giving him, and he kisses me. Those hands cup each side of my face as mine land on his waist. The kiss doesn't last too long, but it's still just as powerful.

When he pulls away, I'm stuck in a daze for a second. Getting my bearings back, I glance up to ask, "What was that for?"

Caden

"Just needed some sugar, small fry," he explains with a wide grin.

"I vote to never witness that shit again," Cason deadpans.

"Cason, leave them alone." Mrs. Harlow tells him, and I bite my lip to hold back a grin. Caden's family is so much more than I thought. Granted I was a ball of nerves before, but now I shouldn't have been. From the moment Caden's mom saw me, I instantly felt as if I belonged here. The Harlow family is loving, caring, and they do make great company. They make me feel as if I'm a part of their family, and for the first time in a long time, I welcomed the feeling.

"Don't worry about him, Mama," Caden says as he pulls me under his arm. "Cas is just being a Debbie Downer."

"I am not," Cason snaps back. "I'm sorry I don't want to see any of your PDA all up in my face."

Shaking my head, I wonder if Cason is always like this. I've seen two sides to him. One is just like this, kind of cold and bitter. Then that other side can be very sweet and caring. There's just more to him than he lets on, and it makes me curious to know more. "You do realize once Carter and Shelby get here, they're goin' to be ten times worse right?"

"You don't have to remind me, Caden."

"How about we move this outside," Caden's dad cuts in. Caden and Cason glare at each other for a few more moments before they concede.

Cason is the first to leave, and I glance up hearing Caden's loud sigh. "Everything okay?"

The rest of the Harlow family follow behind Cason, and Caden rubs my shoulder. Once everyone but us is outside, he finally answers me. "I'm good, small fry. Cason just irritates me sometimes."

"Isn't that what brothers are there for?"

Grinning, Caden says, "I reckon so. Come on, small fry. I want you to meet Caleb." Nodding, I follow him outside to the back porch. Cason stares at us, but at least now it seems as though he's not as grumpy. Mr. and Mrs. Harlow stand by the grill, and Clark sits off to the side drinking a beer. The one brother I haven't met yet is pulling out a cooler and sets it close by Caden and me. "Caleb, I want you to meet my small fry."

Caleb snaps his gaze to me, and I hold out my hand. "I'm Savannah, or you can call me Savvy."

Caleb takes my hand, and I don't miss his quick glance to Caden. "Nice to meet you."

He and Caden share another look, and I ask, "What gives with you two?"

Caden

Before Caden can answer, Caleb says, "Oh it's nothin'. Just shocked Caden finally brought a girl home."

Frowning, I turn to Caden. "You've never let anyone meet any of your previous girlfriends before?"

"I told you, small fry," he begins as he turns to me. "You're different from anyone else. You're perfect." Not knowing what to say, I stare at him in amazement. Now in the back of my mind, I know this is more than us being fuck buddies. I also know it means there are strong feelings here, but for once it doesn't really scare me. It seems at every turn, Caden continues to break down the walls around my heart, and the warming sensation in the pit of my stomach tells me all I need to know.

I'm falling for him.

Standing by Caden's mom, I let out a laugh as she tells me more stories about Caden as a kid. Feeling his gaze on me, I look across the porch seeing him smiling. I'll admit, being here most of the day has been wonderful. I've met so many of the Harlow family's friends, and even though I can't remember most of their names, it's been a great day. I even got to meet Shelby, and I instantly liked her.

Brie Paisley

She's so friendly and down to earth. The love she and Carter share is something amazing to witness. She and I have talked a lot since she and Carter arrived, and I have a feeling we're going to be close friends. She even introduced me to Annie and William Barrett. The love they have for Shelby was so pronounced, I thought they were her grandparents. However Shelby explained they were more of family friends to everyone else, but to her, they were like family. I feel like there's a story behind it, but I didn't want to pry. I didn't feel as though it was the right time to ask, and I quickly agreed when Shelby asked me to come over one night to hangout. The only thing about today that I wish was different was how Clark still hasn't warmed up to me. I saw Caden talking to him a while ago, but I wonder what his deal is. Even if Clark is dealing with his demons and doesn't like me very much, I'm glad Caden brought me here. The Harlow family is wonderful to be around, and the love they have makes me wish my parents were here. It feels like home, and I could see myself coming over to see the Harlow family every day if possible. They're just a tight knit family that a girl like me would love to be a part of. Being away from my parents has been hard, and feeling the way I do now, it makes me realize what I had all along. I've been so consumed with finding who my mother is that I missed what was right in front of me. But if I never knew about my birth mom, I never

Caden

would've met Caden. If I hadn't made the trip to Mississippi, I would've missed out on all these wonderful and loving people.

Caden's gaze never wavers from mine, and he begins to walk toward me when he stops suddenly. Everyone's gaze snaps to Carter as he walks to the middle of the porch, and asks for everyone's attention. I smile seeing Shelby immediately go to him when he glances her way and wraps his arm around her. "I want to thank everyone for comin' over to help celebrate my baby brother's accomplishments today." Carter stops for a moment to look at Caleb, and I see the pride written all over Carter's face. "I'm so proud of you Caleb for all you've done and for graduatin' at the top of your class. You've yet again shown and proven you're the smartest Harlow brother." Smiling as everyone chuckles at Carter's joke, I'm sort of proud of Caleb too. It's an unexplainable sensation because I don't even know Caleb. However it's there. Caleb raises his beer toward Carter and gives him a firm nod. "I also wanted to ask someone special to me a very important question." Everyone, including me, gasps loudly when Carter drops to one knee in front of Shelby. The surprise is evident on her face and as her hand covers her mouth. "Shelby Ross, I've loved you since I was six years old. From the moment I laid eyes on you on that playground, I knew I would spend the rest of my life with you." My eyes begin to water with Carter's heartfelt words because anyone that isn't blind can clearly see the love he has for Shelby. "I know life hasn't been kind to us, but none of that matters now that you're here with me. Every day you show me what a strong and beautiful woman you've become, and I know if you say yes, you'll remind me for the rest of our lives how grateful I am to have you."

"Just ask her already," Caden yells, and everyone laughs loudly.

Carter shakes his head, but he has a huge grin on his face. "Since I'm bein' rushed," Carter says then turns his attention back to Shelby. "Will you do me the honor of becomin' my wife?" With Shelby's nod and her yes, we all cheer for the happy couple. Blinking the tears away as they embrace, I can't believe I got to witness this. I don't know Carter or Shelby, but their love somehow shines so brightly that I couldn't help but feel it.

As the people at the party congratulate Carter and Shelby, I feel a gaze on me. Glancing up, my eyes lock with Caden's. Sucking in a breath at the intensity of his gaze, it's as if everyone around us disappears. I wouldn't have believed it if anyone else had experienced this and was telling me about it, but just with one look, he's telling me how he feels. Those blue eyes have been hiding the truth, but a part of me has always known how he felt. There's

Caden

just no way I can miss it now. My heart drums loudly in my chest and ears, and I have to suck in a deep breath realizing how deep his feelings run.

That's a man with the look of love in his eyes.

A love so strong that it knocks me back with such a force I have to rub my chest.

Shitfire. He's in love with *me*.

eighteen
Caden

Now that the cat is out of the bag, there's no going back.

I half expect her to take off running, but when she stays rooted where she's standing, it gives me hope that maybe, just maybe, she feels the same way. I don't expect her to confess her feelings for me, not just yet anyway. But seeing Carter and Shelby finally take the next step in their relationship made my choice easier to show Savannah how I really and truly feel about her.

I do love her.

I love her more than I thought possible.

It's a little scary knowing how much I care for the one woman that isn't here to stay, but even

Caden

knowing this, I'm not giving up on her. I just know if she still leaves after all this, it'll fucking ruin me.

Which is why I don't immediately go to her. I know she needs a moment to process what I've shown her, and I give her space even though that's the last thing I want to do. The thing about loving someone else, it doesn't matter what I want. It's all about her now and putting all her needs, wants, and dreams first. I just hope she knows that I won't give her that much space. She's still mine, and one day soon, I'll be hers too.

Walking over to Carter and Shelby, I let Annie and William finish congratulating them before I say, "I'm so fuckin' happy for y'all." Slapping Carter on the back, he has a contagious grin on his face. "Seriously I didn't think Carter was ever goin' to pop the big question."

Shelby rolls her eyes as she says, "Leave him alone, Caden. He asked when he was ready."

"You mean when you were ready." It's no secret Shelby use to run as fast as she could from everything. But I have a feeling she won't be running away anymore. One can hope right?

"Caden, lay off. Don't ruin the day alright?"

"Oh come on, Carter. I was just jokin'. We all know it's CarShel for life."

"Car what?" Shelby asks.

"CarShel. Carter and Shelby put together."

Shelby turns up her nose as Carter says, "It's kind of catchy."

"Well of course, it is," I start. "I made it up, so it has to be awesome."

Shelby lightly hits my arm claiming, "You're so full of shit."

Laughing, I glance past her seeing Savannah talking to Caleb. My stomach clenches for a second hoping he remembers not to tell her what he and I talked about earlier. I just have to trust he'll keep our little secret. "You know I get that a lot. Y'all would think by now, everyone would be used to the random shit that leaves my mouth."

"I doubt any of us will get used to that," Shelby says with a laugh. Shrugging my shoulder, I start to respond when Mama calls for her.

Carter watches her leave, and when he turns back to me, I claim, "You've got it bad, bro."

His eyebrow raises as he lays a hand on my shoulder. "I'm apparently not the only one."

"You would not be wrong with that assumption."

Caden

Carter and I walk to the porch railing before he asks, "Does she know yet?"

My eyes scan around the porch until I find her again. She's still talking with Caleb, but now Clark and Cason have joined them. Hoping Clark isn't an ass again to her, I take a deep breath and glance back to Carter. "I haven't told her, but I think she knows. Kind of hard to keep my emotions in check when you're proposin' and makin' me look bad."

"My bad. It wasn't my intention to make you look like anythin'. Just tryin' to keep the woman I tend to love for the rest of my life by my side."

"I know." Looking out in the distance, it does warm my heart knowing my big brother is finally getting his happily ever after. "Hell it's about time right?"

Carter chuckles saying, "Yeah. Didn't think this day would ever come."

My tone turns serious as I ask, "You know what we have to do now right?"

"What's that?"

"We'll have to make sure she walks down the aisle and doesn't turn into a runaway bride."

Carter shakes his head because apparently I'm funny. "That's a good one."

"I wasn't jokin', man. Aren't you worried she'll put on her runnin' shoes?"

"No," he says and damn. I can't help but believe him. "She's mine, and she knows it. And if she ever did run again, I think by now we all know I'd go chasin' right after her."

"I hope you know that we'll be right behind you makin' her ass come back too."

"Now that," he says with a loud chuckle. "Couldn't be further from the truth." We're both silent for a beat, and I glance back to Savannah. I can't seem to keep my eyes off her, and I know why. It's because when she's not by my side, I have to search for her to make sure she's real and still here. There have been days when I think I've convinced myself that all this is just a fucking dream, and if it is, then I never want to wake up. Life without her would be fucking awful, and there's no way in hell I can ever go back to the way life was before her. "If I were you," Carter says pulling me out my thoughts. "I would tell her how you feel. She's goin' to keep givin' you the slip if she doesn't know how you feel."

Knowing he's right, I nod. "Trust me, I'm workin' on it."

Caden

Saying our goodbyes, Savannah and I walk toward my truck. She's quiet the whole way there, and even when we get inside. Before starting the truck, I turn to her. She's looking straight ahead, and I'm worried something is wrong. Placing my hand over hers, I ask, "Are you okay?"

She turns to gaze at me, and my breath hitches seeing the look in her eyes. They're shining back at me with happiness and dare I say, a bit of love? "I'm perfect."

"You're awfully quiet, small fry."

"I'm fine, I promise." She scoots closer to me and caresses my face. Her loving touch is unexpected, but very much wanted. "Thank you for bringing me here to meet your family."

Taking her hand back in mine, I rub circles on the back of her hand. "You're not upset I didn't warn you beforehand?"

"No. At first, I was a little surprised, but I'm not mad. Your family is amazing."

Chuckling, I say, "Yeah, they're pretty great. But then again you haven't seen their crazy side yet."

"So there's more to them than what I saw today? Because I've got to be honest here, I don't see them being anything but awesome."

"Well yeah. That's because they have me." At her confused expression, I claim, "Before me, they were pretty dull."

"Oh really?"

"Yeah. I mean not tryin' to toot my own horn or anythin', but I make them the best."

She laughs, and I'm glad she gets my joke. I'm not that cocky. "Life would be pretty boring without your smart ass comments."

Grinning, I kiss the back of her hand before saying, "You make life pretty great too, small fry." Taking my other hand, I brush her hair behind her ear and caress her cheek. She sighs deeply, and my heart warms as she leans into my touch. Not wanting this moment to end, I know it has to. We're sitting in my parent's driveway still, and the last thing I want is to be interrupted again just in case anything were to happen between us. Giving her one last rub on the cheek with my thumb, I drop my hand and start the truck. "Ready to roll?" She nods and quickly puts on the middle seatbelt. Satisfied she's safe, I start to back out of the driveway. I don't get ten feet away from my parent's house before she leans over and starts kissing my neck. Trying to keep my eyes on the road, I huskily ask, "What are you doin', small fry?"

Caden

"Kissing you. What does it look like?" Sucking in a breath as she bites my earlobe, I remind myself to stay focused on the road. That would be a really fucked up story to tell people if I crashed because she was making me crazy. Savannah continues to kiss and suck on my neck, and when she grabs onto my hardening cock, I almost pull over. "You want to go somewhere?"

"Fuck yes I do. But I don't think we're goin' to make it back to the apartment." She's driving me mad with the need to be inside of her, and there's no way in hell I can drive back into town. I want her right this very minute.

"Well then. Let's go," she says softly in my ear.

She gives me a nice squeeze on my cock, and I let out a groan. "Hold on," I warn before taking a sharp U-turn. She giggles beside me, and I'm sure she knows how crazy she makes me. Speeding toward the destination in mind, Savannah is all over me like a cat in heat. I'm not sure what's gotten into her, but fuck if I'm complaining about it. However she's making it so hard not to make it to a secluded area before I take her. "Savannah," I breathe out heavily. "You're goin' to have to ease up a bit."

"Why?" she asks sweetly then nips my earlobe again. "Don't you like this?"

"That's the problem, small fry. I like it too much."

"Well." She starts then caresses my cock. "You better hurry up and get where we're going." Thankfully we're almost there. Taking a sharp left, I turn down a gravel road. Savannah doesn't ask where we are and I know it's because she's so focused on making my dick feel like it's going to explode. Damn this need she's making me feel is almost consuming. It's hard to think of anything but her hand on me, and that hot mouth of hers on my neck. Now more than ever, I'm glad my parents bought more land when I was a kid. It's the only way I know Savannah and I won't be interrupted or get caught by my fellow cop buddies.

Quickly parking, turning off the truck, and unbuckling our seatbelts, I grab Savannah by the hips and pull her to my lap. Her butt hits the horn, and she giggles as I let out a chuckle. Her hands rest on my shoulder, and I brush her hair out of her face. "God you're so beautiful." She glances away, but I see that smile I love so much. Grateful the moon is out, I gaze at her for a few moments before caressing her face. Using my thumb to rub her bottom lip, she sucks in a breath as she glances back to me. Leaning in, she meets me halfway, and I take her mouth. The first taste of her goes straight to my cock, and I move my hand to her neck. Bringing her closer, I devour her and take everything

Caden

she's giving me. I'm like a man dying of thirst, and she's the only one that can quench it. Her hips grind on me as she moans in my mouth, and I deepen our kiss.

She kisses me back with a fervor I hadn't expected, but at the same time, it shows me just how much she wants me. Nipping at her bottom lip, I run my other hand to her exquisite breasts and take one in the palm of my hand. Kissing her neck, she pushes her chest into my hand and lets out a heavy sigh. Those hips of hers never stop grinding, which is about to drive me insane. My desire for her spikes with each of her thrusts, and I pull away from her completely to take off her shirt. Since I'm in such a rush, when I get her shirt to her head, she falls back against the horn again. She giggles as I grin, but I manage to get rid of the shirt. Tossing it to the side, I bring her back to me and run my hands up her back. She arches to my touch, and I lean forward to leave hot and wet kisses on her chest. "Caden," she calls out, and it's like music to my ears. "Not that I'm complaining," she starts, and I halt all movement. Please for the love of that's holy, don't let her say she's changed her mind. "This seatbelt buckle thingy is really starting to hurt my knee."

"Oh shit. I'm sorry."

Trying to help her, I guide her back, but she ends up hitting her head on the 'oh shit handle'.

"Okay this isn't working out so well," she says with a laugh.

Laughing along with her, I think about it for a second before I ask, "Backseat?"

"It's worth a shot." Hoping not to hurt her again, I help her climb off me, and I smack her ass when she crawls into the back. "Hey. No booty smacking."

Chuckling, I jokingly say, "You know you liked it."

"Maybe just a little. Now get your ass back here with me. I'm getting lonely."

"Well shit," I say and start moving to the back. "You don't have to tell me twice," I add. The thing about having sex in a vehicle is, it's very limited on space, and a man of my size just makes moving to the back with her more difficult. I almost make it unscathed until I hit my head on the dome light and of course, my foot gets caught on the middle console making me fall face first into the backseat. "Fuck," I muffle.

My face is pressed against it so hard, it's making it hard to breathe. Savannah laughs loudly as she asks, "Are you okay?"

Caden

"Yeah," I groan out as I get my foot unstuck from the middle console. "What's a little car sex without some bumps right?"

It's my attempt to make light of this embarrassing situation. Lord knows I get myself into these messes all the time, but shit. This crap is ruining the mojo. "Come here," Savannah huskily says, and maybe I was wrong. She moves up against the door as I hover over her, and I hope she's comfortable. The position she's in doesn't look like it is, but she doesn't complain about it. "Kiss me again," she says sweetly and how am I supposed to deny this woman anything?

Taking her lips once more, I start slow, savoring the intimate kiss, but when her hand grips my neck and the other one runs up my shirt, I get ravenous. Savannah drives me fucking crazy with her taste, her warmth, and how much she seems to want me. She urges me on with her hips hitting just where she wants, and it's taking everything in me to not ravish her until she's begging me to stop. Our tongues intertwine, and our teeth hit a few times, but that doesn't stop me or her from continuing to kiss each other with abandon. It's never been like this with any other woman before, but I already know why. Savannah isn't like them. Fuck she doesn't even compare to a single one, and my feelings for her trump all the mistakes of my past. My love for her makes everything heightened, intense as hell, and most of all the passion coming off her in waves tells me all I need to know.

These powerful feelings I have goes both ways. She's feeling what I am, and she's showing me with every caress, thrust, and how she kisses me.

It's as if she *needs* me, and this goes way beyond just lust.

Breaking away when she pulls up my shirt, I help her take it off. Letting it drop on the floorboard, I gaze down at my gorgeous girl, and I hope she knows just how beautiful she is to me. Using my hand, I caress her cheek as her eyes pull me into a trance. If I'm not careful, I could get lost in those eyes. She smiles back at me, and it's almost my undoing. Clenching my jaw, I force the words I want to tell her down. My heart pounds in my chest knowing how badly I want to utter those three words. Those three words mean everything, but they also have the power to destroy everything at the same time. Kissing her again, I focus on her lips, her taste, and push all thoughts of love out of my mind. She's not ready to hear them just yet, but one day she will be.

One day, she'll welcome me and all the love I can give her with open arms and an open heart.

Caden

Breaking away from her lips, I move to her neck, and my cock jumps hearing her throaty moans. Slowly making my way down, kissing trails down in between her breasts and to her stomach. Running my hands up her sides, she arches her back giving me the perfect opportunity to unclasp her bra. Grinning as she quickly takes it off and drops it, I kiss my way back up. Reaching her right breast, I suck and nip at her hardened nipple while caressing the left. Savannah's hips grind into mine, and I push forward giving her the needed friction she's searching for. Switching my mouth to her left breast, she calls out my name with a raspy voice. Loving the sounds she's making for me, I trace my hand down her stomach then beneath her shorts. Dipping my fingers under her panties, I jerk away from her breast and claim her mouth feeling how wet she is for me. Her hands grab me, and her nails leave a sting as she runs them up my back. Using my middle finger, I rub slow circles on her clit as I add a bit of pressure. "Caden, please." She calls out as she breaks our kiss.

A part of me loves to hear her begging for more, but the other part wants to see that look of total bliss on her face. There's nothing quite like my small fry coming apart for me. "What do you want, Savannah?" Stealing another kiss, I easily slide my middle finger inside her. "Do you want my fingers to fuck you?" She moans as I push my finger inside her deeper, and I swallow hard feeling her walls clenching around me when I add another. "Or," I huskily say and add, "Do you want my tongue?" I won't lie, knowing I was the first to taste her sweet essence was unlike anything I've ever felt before. Being her first at something so intimate made me want to claim her like a fucking cave man, and warn anyone else away. *She's mine.* "What's it goin' to be, Savannah?"

Thrusting my fingers deep inside her, she lets a loud moan escape before she finally answers me. "I want ... both. Give me both."

With her answer, something inside me snaps. Taking my fingers out of her and out of her panties, I bend to my knees and quickly take off her shorts. Her skimpy panties soon follow, and I place one of her legs on the front passenger seat. Leaning down, I slide my left hand under her thigh to hold her in place. It's a little cramped with the both of us in the back, but I don't care if I can barely move. I want to make her feel good and give her every single orgasm I can. Pride rushes through me when she doesn't try to pull away like last time, and she rotates her hips up waiting for me to make my move. "Ready, small fry?"

"God yes," she cries out, and I chuckle hearing the desperation in her voice.

Caden

Hovering over her, she grabs onto my hair, and I take it as my cue. Using my tongue, I lick her from top to bottom. "Damn, Savannah. You taste divine." I've never been the kind of guy that particularly liked going down a chick before, but with Savannah, I'll stay down here feasting on her pussy all night long if I could. It's just knowing how crazy it makes her that drives me, and knowing it's bringing her pleasure pleases me unlike anything I can explain. Alternating from dipping my tongue inside her then sucking her clit, Savannah's cries grow louder, and her grip on my hair tightens. It's almost painful, but I'm not about to say a word. Glancing up at her, the moon is giving off just enough light for me to see her. While one of her hands never leave my hair, the other is above her head. Her eyes are closed, and with each lick I give her, her breath rushes out with a moan. Groaning against her when her hips move against my face, I grip her thigh tighter with my left hand. "I wish you could see how fuckin' gorgeous you are like this," I say with a raspy voice.

Taking her swollen clit in my mouth and sucking hard, she calls out my name again before she rushes out, "Less talking. More of that."

Knowing how much she loves what I'm doing, I continue my sucking on her sensitive clit and bring my fingers right at her entrance. Slowly pushing my fingers inside her, I watch the pleasure I'm bringing across her face. Her loud cries make me eager to be inside her, and feeling how tight and wet she is for me, makes my cock harden even more. It's becoming painful being so confined in this tight space and still having my shorts on. Pushing my uncomfortableness aside, I focus on her, her cries of ecstasy, and helping her get to the point of no return. Curling my fingers inside her, I thrust and wiggle them back and forth all the while of continuing to suck her clit. Savannah's back bows as her hand above her head hits the back glass, and I can't help but grin. "Do you like this, small fry?"

"Yes. Yes, God yes," she breathes out in between moans. Feeling her walls begin to clench around my fingers, I sense she's getting close. Placing my mouth back on her hot pussy, I make my thrusts deep and quicken my pace.

And of course, my phone starts to ring.

"Don't you answer that," Savannah demands.

Knowing who it is, I say, "It's Cason's ring tone. Just let me make sure he's okay."

Savannah groans out her frustration as she claims, "I'm so close though."

Leaning up, I pull my phone out of my pocket. "I know, small fry. I promise I'll get you there again." Glancing down at my cell, I curse Cason silently for

Caden

once again interrupting us. Before I answer, I look down at Savannah. "Don't move."

"Hurry up," she responds, and I shake my head knowing how badly she wants me to make her come.

"This better be life or death," I snap at Cason when I answer his call.

"No one is dead if that's what you're askin'."

Holding my forefinger up to my lips, Savannah nods then I use my fingers to slowly slide back inside her wet pussy and ask Cason, "Then why the fuck are you callin' me?"

Cason huffs out a breath before saying, "Well fuck you too. Didn't know I needed a reason to call my own twin." Rolling my eyes, I ignore his little rant and focus back on the woman I plan on fucking real soon. She doesn't seem to mind at all that I'm on the phone and fucking her with my fingers. My guess is she's so far gone into lust she doesn't care how she gets off. Thinking of an idea, I put Cason on speakerphone, and I get back down in between Savannah's legs. I mumble out words every once in a while, so Cason at least thinks I'm listening, but I'm not. I'm so far from listening to him. Giving Savannah a squeeze on her leg to remind her to be quiet, I push two fingers inside her and use my mouth again to work her over. "Are you even listenin' to a word I've been sayin'?"

"Yeah," I say loudly, but I really haven't.

"No, you have not. What the fuck are you doin'?"

Glancing up at Savannah, both of her hands are covering her face. Knowing she's embarrassed, I know I need to end this conversation. "What do you want, Cas? I'm a little busy."

"You're busy?" He asks in a monotone voice, and I can just picture his blank face. "Whatever. Carter and Shelby want to know if we want to come chill at their place in a few."

"Do you want to go?" I ask Savannah.

"Honestly," she starts, and she's loud so I know Cason can hear her. "I really don't care as long as you hurry up and stop talking so we can finish what we started."

Trying to hold back my laugh, Cason says, "Oh my fuckin' God."

"You heard her, Cas."

"I'm fuckin' hangin' up now."

The line goes dead, and I let out a chuckle. "Nice goin', small fry. You sure shut his ass up." I won't lie, I'm proud of her. It usually takes me forever

Caden

to get Cason to shut up when he gets on his rants, but not Savannah. Maybe talking about sex is the key here.

Her hands are back over her face, and her voice is muffled as she says, "I can't believe I just said that."

Moving over her, I remove her hands from her face. "Don't be embarrassed. He should know by now to text instead of call. He's just askin' to hear shit he's not supposed to when he calls."

"Yeah, I guess so. You think he learned his lesson this time?"

Pulling her up, I help her sit on top of me. Running my hands up her sides, I shrug my shoulders. "Who knows with Cas. But I do know one thing."

Her stomach quivers as my hand grazes over her soft skin as she asks, "What's that?"

Reaching her cheeks, I caress her face for a moment before moving to the back of her neck. Pulling her to me, I whisper huskily, "No more interruptions. I don't give a fuck if the world is endin' around us. I'm goin' to have you and make you come on my cock."

"Oh," she answers, and I don't give her the chance to say anything more. Bringing her to my mouth, I push my tongue inside hers and kiss her roughly. Those hips of hers roll against me, and I push mine up meeting hers. Nothing but getting inside her tight pussy is on my mind, and I know she's feeling the same way as she quickly pulls away from me. Her hands quickly undo my shorts, and she uses the backseat's head rest to lift herself while I pull my shorts down.

I don't get a chance to take them completely off before Savannah sits back down on me. "In a rush, small fry?" I ask with a light chuckle.

"Yes," she breathes heavily. "Need you inside of me like five minutes ago."

Grinning, I suck in a breath when she grabs my cock and places it at her entrance. "Wait a second," I quickly say to stop her. Savannah's head snaps up, and I swallow hard. "I don't have a condom on me." Fucking rookie mistake but I wasn't planning on having an impromptu sex session with her. At least not until we made it back to my place. But I hadn't even remembered a condom until this very moment.

But Savannah surprises me when she slowly sinks down on my cock. "It's okay," she moans out and fuck if I can stop her now. My head falls back against the seat feeling how warm, tight, and wet she is for me. "I'm on the pill. So it's fine."

Caden

Leaning up, I pull her to me. Taking her mouth as she rides me like a fucking champ, I meet her thrust for thrust. Using my hand on her back, I bring her forward so I can feel those luscious breasts against me. Feeling her on me with no barriers between us, it makes me crazed with the need to fuck her until she begs me to stop. "Fuck, Savannah," I groan out. "You feel so fuckin' good."

Her loud moans let me know she agrees, and when her head falls back, I lean up and leave wet open mouth kisses on her neck. "Caden," she says with a raspy voice, and her walls clench tightly around me.

"Please tell me you're close." I'm barely hanging on as it is, and I know it's not going to take much more before I completely lose it. She doesn't reply, but she doesn't have to. Her walls clench around me again, and I feel the spasms happen before she cries out my name. "That's it. Let it go, Savannah." Her entire body begins to shake as her orgasm rolls through her, and I try to hold off on mine until she's done. But when she leans down to kiss me once more, I can't hold back anymore. Thrusting into her as deep as I can, I let go and groan in her mouth. Spilling inside her, I let out a few not so nice cuss words, but I never let her go.

I'm never letting her go.

Especially not after this. There's no way in hell I can watch her walk away from me, and one day soon, she'll know it too.

Trying to catch my breath, Savannah places her head on mine. Running a hand up and down her back and the other brushes her hair out of her face, I swallow hard as I hold back the words I want to say. Instead, I say, "I've never done that before."

She leans back to gaze at me as she asks, "What? Have sex? Because I'm pretty sure we've done that before."

Chuckling, I tuck her hair behind her ear. "No, not sex. I meant I've never had sex without a condom before. You're the first." *And only one* I want to say, but again I hold back.

"It's a first for me too," she quietly says.

"I like havin' first moments with you, small fry."

Savoring the taste of her lips as she gives me a peck on mine, she says, "I do too." She looks down at our combined bodies and then back to me before asking, "How are we going to separate without making a mess?"

"I hadn't gotten that far just yet," I respond with a laugh. Thinking about it for a moment, I don't think there's going to be an easy way to do this. Plus

Caden

the heat is really starting to get to me. Wiping off the sweat that's on my forehead with the back of my hand, I ask, "Can you try to find my shirt? It's somewhere on the floorboard." Holding onto her waist as she leans backward, I raise my hips as she moves around. "Easy, small fry." The last thing I want is to make an even bigger mess.

"I almost have it," she grunts out then she whips back up straight.

She hands me my shirt, and I say, "On three." Once she nods, I count to three, and when she lifts off me, I push my shirt in between her legs.

She takes my shirt from me and giggles as she sits in an awkward position next to me. "We definitely did not think this one through."

"No we didn't, but I don't regret it. Anytime I'm with you, it's worth a mess if there is one, small fry."

"You say that now, but I think you'll change your mind once you see the damage I've done to your shirt."

Shaking my head, it's just like her to try and downplay what I'm trying to tell her. Quickly removing my shorts and boxers, I use my boxers to wipe myself off as Savannah does the same with my shirt. "You owe me a new shirt and a new pair of boxers," I declare with a light tone.

She laughs saying, "Deal. As soon as you help me find my clothes and shoes. I lost my flip flops climbing on you before we made it to the back."

"Totally worth it though right?" I say as I lean over to cup her cheek.

"Yes. It's totally worth it." Taking her lips again, she caresses my face. My heart beats frantically in my chest knowing I could do this with her for the rest of my life. Pulling away, I gaze into her eyes hoping she can see how much I love her. Even if I know this isn't the right time to tell her, I still want her to know or at least consider what this is between us. "We should get dressed," she says, breaking our moment. Nodding, we do just that, but this is far from over.

I don't know how much longer I can keep putting off telling her how I feel, and I hope like hell she doesn't run away from this.

Or from me once I do tell her.

Caden

nineteen
Savannah

Sitting out on the back porch at Carter and Shelby's house, I laugh loudly listening to Caden and Cason bicker back and forth. We haven't been here but ten minutes tops and they're already down each other's throats. It all started when Caden asked to borrow Cason's shirt, and once Carter finally gave one to Caden when Cason outright refused, their fight started to escalate. Turning to Shelby, she shakes her head, and I lean over to ask, "Are they always like this?"

"God yes. I don't see how they can stand livin' with each other."

Carter and Caleb try to break them apart, and I can't help but laugh when Caden starts to make faces behind Cason's back. "Honestly," I respond back to Shelby. "I'm not sure either. I've seen them banter before, but not like this." I'm not even sure what started their little tiff other than Caden asking for a shirt, but with them, there's no telling.

"Trust me," Shelby says then takes a drink of her wine. "You'll get used to it. I've been around them most of my life, and they'll never change."

"They make good entertainment though," I pipe back with a grin.

"That they do." Finally Caden and Cason take a seat, away from each other, and Carter and Caleb sit back down. Caden huffs out a breath when he grabs his beer off the table, and Cason glares at his twin. "I've been meanin' to ask you," Shelby asks, and I turn giving her my full attention. I really didn't get a chance to talk to her much at Caleb's party, and I'm hoping to get to know her more now. She's just so friendly and easy to get along with. "What's the deal with you two," she asks as she glances at me then Caden.

"Shel, don't make her uncomfortable," Carter states.

"Oh shit. I'm sorry. Too much?" Feeling Caden's gaze on me, I ignore it and keep my eyes on Shelby. Taking a gulp of my beer, I think of something to tell her. I'm still unsure what this is between Caden and me. Seeming to realize I'm at a

Caden

loss, she says, "Forget that question. How about you tell me your favorite Disney movie."

Letting out a sigh, I smile knowing this one is easy. "The Little Mermaid."

"No shit! That's mine too."

"I got one for you," I start and set my beer on the table. "Favorite horror movie."

"Child's Play. Chuckie is my favorite. Always has been and always will be."

Grinning widely, I ask, "Why aren't we besties? That's mine too."

"Oh fuck," Caden groans beside me, and I turn to him. "Not that damn pyscho killer doll again."

With my frown, Shelby explains. "Caden hates Chuckie. He's scared to death of him."

"I am not! I just think a doll killin' people is a little creepy. Dolls are not supposed to kill people."

Laughing at Caden's lame excuse, I ask him, "So you wouldn't watch Child's Play with me?"

"He would, but then again," Carter says with a wide grin. "You might lose some of your hearin' with his screams. He does it every time we watch it."

"I do not!" Caden yells, and I let out a laugh. He stands and holds a hand out to me. "Come on,

Savannah. We don't need this kind of negativity in our lives."

Shaking my head, I take his hand and stand saying, "Don't you think you're overreacting just a little?"

"That's Caden for you," Cason pipes in.

"Hey," Caden says as he turns to his twin. "No one asked you, grumpy pants."

Before Cason can say anything back, Caleb steps in. "Alright you guys. As much as we love to sit here and listen to y'all bicker like children, I think y'all should cool it." Caden's eyes widen as if he's shocked by what Caleb said, but it does the trick. Caden and Cason glare at each other, but they seem to silently call a truce. "Anyway," Caleb starts and looks to Caden. "Do you want to check out my new golf clubs? I got them in the back of Cas's truck."

Turning to Caden, I frown. "I didn't know you played golf."

Carter snickers and Caden gives him a pointed look before he answers me. "I play, but no one said I was good at it."

"More like you're horrible at it," Shelby pipes in and I use my hand to cover my mouth to hide my grin.

Caden

Shelby, Carter, and Caleb laugh while Cason smirks at Caden's facial expression, and before I know what's happening, Caden puts me over his shoulder. "Caden! Put me down."

He smacks my ass as he says, "No can do, small fry. You're comin' with me since everyone wants to pick on little ol' me." Holding onto his waist, so I won't fall, Caden moves toward the door before stopping. "You comin', Caleb?" Seeing Caleb jump up, he follows behind Caden.

"What if I didn't want to go with you? I was talking to Shelby, and you're being very rude with manhandling me."

Caden walks through the house, and he doesn't answer me until he reaches the front door. "Trust me, you'll have all the time in the world to chat it up with Shel. She ain't goin' anywhere."

Caleb chuckles behind us, and I let out a loud huff. "This isn't very gentlemanly of you." Caden ignores me as he takes me outside and walks over by what I assume is Cason's truck. "Are you going to let me down now? I can walk you know."

Caleb chuckles as he shakes his head, and Caden grabs my ass tightly. "What if I like totin' you around?"

"Caden," I warn. "Put me down."

"Alright fine. Hold onto your panties, small fry." He slowly puts me back on my feet, and I smack him on the arm. "Ow," he yells out. "What did you do that for?"

"She told you to put her down, Caden," Caleb explains.

"See he gets it." Narrowing my eyes at Caden, he smirks then kisses me on the lips.

"I just like fuckin' with you, small fry." Rolling my eyes at his lame excuse for man handling me, he turns and lets down the tailgate to the truck. Caleb and I follow behind him as he jumps in the bed of the truck, and Caden holds out a hand to help me up. Taking a seat on the side, I watch as both brothers look at the golf clubs. I still can't imagine Caden golfing, but it would be something to watch. Especially if he's as bad as Shelby claims. Caleb helps Caden with choosing the right driver for him, and Caleb places a ball on the edge of the tailgate. "Alright, y'all," Caden says. "Watch the man hit the shit out of the ball."

"This should be interestin'," Caleb says sarcastically as he sits beside me.

Caden takes a few practice swings before he steps closer to the ball. Curiosity has me impatiently waiting for him to make his move, but it doesn't seem like he's in any hurry. He glances down at the ball,

Caden

then back up as if he's really looking for a target to hit the ball at. "Any time you're ready," I claim, and Caden turns to me with a huge grin on his face.

"Just watch and learn, small fry." He turns to his brother adding, "And you too Caleb." Shaking my head, I cross my legs waiting for Caden to hit the freaking ball. With a serious look on his face, Caden finally swings the golf club back, and right as he brings it forward, he loses his footing and takes a tumble off the truck. As I stand to check on him, he quickly jumps back up off the ground. "Who the hell pushed me?"

Caleb and I burst out laughing because he really thinks one of us pushed him. "No one pushed you, jackass," Caleb says with a shake of his head.

I can't control my laughing enough to say anything, and it earns me a hard glare from Caden, then he brushes off his shorts before climbing back up in the truck. "Okay I'm goin' to do it for real this time," he claims. Getting control over myself, Caden winks at me and repositions the ball where he wants it. Watching him closely, I wonder if he's actually going to hit the ball this time. After a few more practice swings, Caden spreads his legs and swings the club back. He does hit the ball this time, however, when he brings the club backward, it flies out of his hands. Hearing a loud crack, I whip my head toward the sound.

"Oh fuck," Caleb says with a whisper and my eyes widen.

Caleb and I turn our gaze to a wide-eyed Caden, and it seems we're all in shock. I'm not sure how Caden did it, but when he let the club go, it hit the back glass of the truck. Not only did it crack the window, but the freaking golf club is stuck inside the glass. Caden glances back to the damage he's done, then back to me before yelling, "Run!" Grabbing Caden's hand, we jump off the bed of the truck and take off running down the road. I'm not sure where Caleb went. All I know is he isn't behind us.

We don't make it very far down the road before I hear Cason's voice booming in the distance. Oh boy. He sounds pissed, but I can't say I blame him. Caden continues to run, and I start laughing at the predicament we're in. Of all the things to go wrong, this definitely isn't one I imagined happening. "Caden, slow down," I call after him and lose a flip flop. He lets my hand go, and I try to control my laughter as I walk back to get my shoe.

Out of breath, I place my hands on my knees. It's hard to get a handle on myself since I can't stop laughing. "Did that just really happen?" Caden asks, and all I can do is nod. "Cason sounded mad." Looking up, Caden is glancing back toward the

Caden

house as he says, "I don't think we should go back for a while, small fry."

Shaking my head, I suck in a deep breath before answering him. "I think that would be wise. Unless you want Cason to kick your ass."

"Psh. He can try," he starts. He places a hand on his hip as he adds, "I can't believe that just happened. What are the odds?"

Finally catching my breath, I stand and walk over to him. Wrapping my arms around his waist, I glance up at him. "It was pretty epic, but please no more running."

Caden lets out a chuckle and rubs up and down my arm. "Alright. No more runnin' it is." He steps away from me, and I wonder what he's up to now. "Why don't we just," he says and lays down on the road, "relax here?"

"In the middle of the road? Where we could possibly get run over?"

Putting his hands behind his head, I can only stare at the fine man below me. He sure is a sight to behold. "No one is goin' to run over us. Come here, small fry. Lay with me."

Letting out a deep sigh, I do as he wants. Resting my head on his now outstretched arm, I place my arm over his stomach. "If we die, I'm seriously going to be pissed at you."

Glancing up at him, he grins then says, "I promise we'll be fine. Just relax and gaze at the stars with me." Rolling over on my back, I gaze up at the stars. I'll admit, this is very sweet and romantic even though we're technically hiding out from Cason. "I used to do this all the time when I was a kid," Caden says softly.

"What? Lie in the middle of the road and wait for some lunatic to run you over?"

"No," he says with a chuckle. "I meant I would look up at the stars and wait until I could see a shootin' star, and then I would make a wish."

Admiring the stars above us, I quietly ask, "What would you wish for?"

"Well," he begins. Letting out a sigh, his arm I'm resting my head on pulls me closer. "I would wish for things little boys always want." He's silent for a bit, and I glance at him once more when he says, "When I got a little older, I wished for a love like Carter and Shelby." Frowning, I start to ask why when he begins to explain. "After what happened with Emily," he stops, and I hope I never see that woman. I hate the way she played Caden and Cason. "I wasn't sure if love would ever happen for

Caden

me. And seeing the way Carter was with Shelby, I don't know. I wanted what they had."

Understanding what he means, I lean up to gaze into those blue eyes of his. "They do have something special don't they?"

"They do. It's funny that I'd forgotten all about my wish." I feel as if he wants to say more, but instead, he caresses my face. He gazes back at me, and he swallows hard. Feeling he's about to do or say something I'm not ready for, I lean down and take his lips. He doesn't seem to mind as he kisses me back, but this kiss feels so much different than our other ones.

He's kissing me like he's in love with me.

It's so tender but holds so much passion at the same time. Even if I don't want to acknowledge what's going on between us, deep down I can feel it. My heart pounds in my chest with each caress of his tongue against mine, and my stomach dips when he sucks my bottom lip. Looking into his eyes, I feel the last brick around my heart crumble. It falls with the rest of the wall I thought I had placed securely around my fragile heart, and knowing what this means, I have to pull away from him.

He doesn't protest as I lay back down beside him, but on the inside, I'm freaking out. I wasn't looking for love when I came to Mississippi, but apparently, it found me anyway. Trying to get a hold over my emotions, I clench my jaw so the words don't come tumbling out of my mouth.

I can't be in love with him.

I'm here for one reason only, and that's to find my birth mother.

One week later …

I've been trying everything I know to put distance between Caden and I. Since that night we gazed at the stars, I've tried so hard to put my feelings aside. But no matter what I do, Caden refuses to give me space. A part of me doesn't mind that he knows what I'm doing, but that other part is freaking out. Love was never a part of my plans, but no matter what I do, it's always there threatening to surface. I fear the words are going to break free, and I just don't know if it'll be a good thing or not.

Which is why I'm waiting for Kelsey to be ready to Skype.

I need my bestie to give me advice. She's always been the one to give it to me straight, and she's the only one I trust with this. And it wouldn't hurt to have an outsider's opinion.

Caden

Sitting down on the couch, my heart continues to pound in my chest seeing Caden eating a granola bar in the kitchen. I'm not sure if he's picked up on sudden nervousness again, but it's so hard to be near him when I know I'm in love with him. He hasn't brought it up, and neither have I. Jerking my gaze away when I see him walking toward me, I remind myself to chill the fuck out. Just as he reaches me, my phone rings. Seeing Kelsey's face on my screen, I open the Skype app. "There's my favorite girl," she says with a bright smile, and I shake my head.

"I better be your only girl," I playfully say. It amazes me how Kelsey can have her black hair piled on top of her head, makeup free, and still look beautiful.

Her bright green eyes narrow at me as Caden takes a seat beside me. "You know you're my one and only."

"Am I goin' to have to share now?" Caden asks.

"Is that the handsome fella you've been hiding, Savvy?"

Rolling my eyes, I face the phone so Kelsey can see him. "You must be Kelsey," Caden says with a huge grin.

I can only sit back and watch Kelsey's eyes widen and of course, a smile forms on her face when she glances back to me. "I totally get why you've been hiding him, Savvy. He's gorgeous."

Caden chuckles at my friend's bold statement, but she's not wrong. Not by a long shot. "I haven't been hiding him," I claim.

Kelsey shrugs as she says, "Why am I just now meeting the mystery man?"

Before I get a chance to answer her, Caden leans over and kisses me on the cheek. "I've got to go to work, small fry. Be good while I'm gone."

Licking my lips, I suck in a breath as I watch him get up. It should be illegal for him to wear his police uniform so well. "I'll try my best." Chuckling, I can't help but watch as he leaves the apartment.

"Damn, Savvy. You've got it bad."

Placing a hand on my face, I groan. "I know. I can't help it." Lowering my hand, I let out a heavy sigh. "Obviously you've seen him. How in the hell am I supposed to resist that?"

Kelsey frowns and is quiet for a moment before she asks, "Why are you resisting then?" I open my mouth to explain why, but when nothing comes out, she claims, "You have absolutely no

Caden

reason to hold back. I mean you're living with the man for Christ's sake."

"I know all this, Kel."

"Then what's the problem? Seriously, Savvy. What's holding you back? Because I've got to tell you, if you don't want him, I'll gladly take him."

Glaring at my friend, she laughs, and I'm shocked by the instant jealousy that flares in the pit of my stomach. "Hands off. He does have three single brothers though."

Kelsey's eyebrows raise as she asks, "Really? Maybe a trip to Mississippi is in order then." Wondering if she's serious, I start to ask before she says, "Maybe someday." Waving her hand back and forth, she claims, "We got off track. Back to you. You were about to explain exactly why you haven't told Caden how much you love him."

"Is it that obvious?" Shit. If she can tell just by Skyping, then I'm sure Caden knows.

"Honey, it's written all over your face. Plus I know you."

Knowing she's right, I take a deep breath. "I'm in deep shit here." When Kelsey just blinks at me, I know it's time to fess up. "I wasn't expecting to fall in love with him. I didn't think I could meet someone like him."

"That still doesn't tell me why you're holding back, Savvy."

Leaning back on the couch, I pull my legs up to my chest as I hold the phone so Kelsey can still see me. Gazing off in the distance, I quietly ask, "What if he can't love me back?"

"Savannah Lynn Owens," she says sternly, and I snap my gaze to her. "That boy is so clearly in love with you. I can see it, and if you can't, then you're lying to yourself."

She does have a point, and I know it. But everything goes back to my insecurities of never being able to receive love because my own birth mother just gave me away. Not to mention, she went to such lengths to keep it hidden. "You could be right."

Kelsey lets out a long sigh before saying, "Savvy, just because your mother gave you away does not mean you can't be loved. Your parents love you more than anything in this world, and I love you like you're my own sister. You can be loved. You are loved, Savannah." Blinking back the tears that have suddenly appeared, I suck in a breath as she continues. "I know love can be scary, but you can't let the fear hold you back. Trust me. Fear rules my life, Savvy. Don't let it run yours." Wiping a tear that rolls down my face, she adds, "You need to tell him how you feel. If you don't and he slips through your fingers, I know you'll regret it."

Sniffing, I let my legs drop, and I sit up straight. "You're right. I should take the risk and hopefully it doesn't backfire."

"It will not backfire. Now why are you still talking to me? Go get your man, Savvy." Letting out a laugh, I thank her for once again help me figure my shit out.

Hanging up the phone, I place it on the coffee table feeling somewhat better about my feelings. I know what I have to do, but even with knowing, I'm still afraid. All that's left to do is to just tell Caden.

I will.

When the time is right.

twenty
Caden

It's funny how everything I've ever wanted is within my grasp, but one little thing threatens to rip it away from me.

It all started an hour into my shift. Caleb called, and I rushed over hoping the news he wanted to tell me was going to be good.

It wasn't.

It was so far from fucking good.

"You're sure this is correct?" I ask for the third time.

"Yes, Caden. I told you this already."

My thoughts are spinning with trying to process all this new information. Had I known where this road would lead me, I might have turned the fuck

Caden

around and changed directions. But now that I'm here and have all the information Savannah has ever wanted, I'm not sure how to go forward. "Can you keep this under wraps?"

Caleb frowns as he asks, "What are you askin' me, Caden? You want me to keep this a secret? Because I've got to say, I don't know if that's a good idea."

"I know, but this," I say, waving my hand in front of Caleb's computer screen. "Isn't what I was expectin'. This shit will not go down well." My instincts are screaming for me to protect Savannah at all costs. Even if I have to bury the fuck out of this information, I'm willing to do so if it doesn't hurt her.

"I get it, I do, but you have to tell her."

Knowing he's right, I glance away from the computer screen and run my hands down my face. "I know and I will. Just give me some time to figure this out. Can you do that?" As bad as I want to tell him to delete everything, and wipe the fucking evidence away, I know I can't do that. But that doesn't mean I'm going to run right to Savannah and tell her. When Caleb nods, I know he's at least given me some time to figure this shit out.

Even if I know all this could possibly blow up in my face, I have to at least consider what this means not only for Savannah but for the rest of my family too. And for the first time ever, I'm going to be lying to the ones I love. For the first time, I'll be the one holding onto a secret that could literally destroy everything I love.

Three weeks later ...

The one thing I've learned about keeping a secret is the guilt makes me do stupid things. Every day that goes by and I don't tell Savannah that I know who her birth mother is, my guilt intensifies. I want to tell her, but I'll admit I'm a selfish bastard for holding back. A part of me wants to protect her and keep her away from the fucking train wreck that's coming. But the other part of me doesn't want her to know because she won't have a reason to stay with me anymore. Granted I've had multiple opportunities to tell her the truth and come clean, but every time the words start to come out something stops me. The thing is Savannah is so happy, and she's finally showing me how she feels about me. She hasn't come out and said it, but she doesn't have to. I can see it in her eyes, feel it in her sweet caress, and above all, I see it in her actions.

Which is why I don't want to fuck what we have all up.

Caden

Every morning I wake up with her by my side and each time I swear this will be the day I tell her. Knowing she's going to wake soon, I pull her closer to my side and kiss the back of her neck. She mumbles something I don't catch, and I smile when she begins to rub her ass against me. "Mornin', small fry."

Sleeping beauty rolls over showing me that gorgeous smile, and my heart clenches in my chest knowing there's a chance I won't get to see this anymore. It's just a feeling I have in the pit of my stomach, and with the way she fought so hard against me, I know once the truth is out she'll take off running. "Good morning," she says in a raspy voice.

Pushing all the guilt aside, I brush her hair out of her face. "You still want to go over to Carter and Shelby's tonight?"

"Maybe. Ask me later okay?" Caressing her cheek, I savor this moment with her. Why do I feel as if we have an expiration date? *Probably because you're keeping a secret from her.* Swallowing hard, I know this is my chance to come clean, but just as I'm about to tell her, she asks, "Everything alright? You've been acting strange lately. Well more strange than before."

Tell her. "I'm fine. Work is just stressin' me out." God more fucking lies. I'm surely going to hell for this.

Savannah kisses me sweetly then says, "If you want to talk about it I'm always here."

"I know. It's nothin'. Just another day on the force."

She sits up in the bed then glances down to me. "You're off today right?" Once I nod, she gets out of bed and grabs some clothes. "Maybe we could do lunch later?"

Smiling, I love how she's always trying to make plans with me now. It's moments like this I think maybe she will be okay with staying with me, but then again I don't know for sure. She's never said, and although she doesn't bring up leaving as much, I worry she's still a flight risk. "Of course, small fry. I'll pick you up at the gym."

"It's a date then." There goes that bright smile again, and my heart skips a beat. "I'm going to shower before Cason uses all the hot water. Again." Chuckling as she walks out, I hear her mumble, "He's worse than any girl I've known." She couldn't be farther from the truth. I have no clue what my twin does while in the bathroom, but if you let him, he'll stay in there for hours. I don't even want to think about the nasty things he does in there. Just … ew.

Caden

Jumping out of bed, I put on a T-shirt and a pair of boxers. Once dressed I glance at the bathroom door knowing I don't have long to talk to Cason. I haven't really seen much of him since I learned the truth about Savannah's mom, and he's working a lot with adding new training equipment and a lap pool at his gym. Thankfully I find him in the kitchen. His eyes lock with mine, and he immediately sets his coffee mug down on the counter. "What did you do?" he asks, and I take a deep breath.

I'm not surprised at all by his question. Being his twin, he picks up on things more than any of my brothers. "I didn't do anythin'," I claim which is the truth and part of the problem.

"You're hidin' somethin'."

Crossing my arms, I hate this part of our bond. It would be nice to just say what I want first without all the accusations. "What makes you say that?"

Cason gives me a blank stare as he says, "I know you. What is it?"

"Alright, alright." Leaning against the counter, I glance back toward the bathroom just to make sure Savannah is still in there. "I found out who Savannah's birth mother is—"

"And you haven't told her yet?"

"Well if you would give me a minute to finish I would've told you that. Rude much?" Cason lets out a loud sigh, and I shake my head. "Anyway as I was sayin', no I haven't told her." With Cason's hard stare, I quickly add, "But I'm goin' to. I just ... I don't know how. This is big, Cas. Like life changin' big."

"You're point is what exactly? She still has a right to know."

"I know. Believe me I know, and I feel like an asshole for keepin' it from her." Cason frowns and is quiet for a while. He just stares at me and I won't lie, it's starting to get a bit awkward. "Are you just goin' to stare at me all day or give me some advice?"

"My advice," he begins as he picks up his coffee mug. "Tell her."

"Tell me what?" Jerking my head to the right, Savannah is walking toward us.

My heart races knowing this is the perfect time to tell her, but instead I chicken out. "Oh just that you're the most amazin' woman on this Earth." Cason smacks my arm, and I jump away from him. Giving him a pointed look, I opt for distraction. Grabbing Savannah by her hips, I pull her to me and give her a kiss.

"What was that for," she asks, and I smirk hearing the intake of her breath.

Caden

"Just kissin' my favorite girl."

She frowns up at me, and I swallow hoping she doesn't bring up what Cason said again. I'm not ready to tell her what I know, and as bad as it makes me seem, I want to hold off as long as I can. "Are you sure you're alright?"

Hearing Cason's grunt, I ignore him as I answer her. "Yeah, small fry. Just peachy." When she shrugs, I know I'm off the hook. At least for now. Letting out a sigh, she steps out of my reach and walks back into my room.

When she shuts the door, Cason slaps me again on my arm. "What the fuck is wrong with you?" If his gaze could kill, I would be dead. And I hate when he gets this way. "You're a fuckin' idiot. Why didn't you tell her? You know this shit is goin' to backfire on you, and you'll have no one to blame but yourself."

"I know, Cas. Jesus can you just give me the benefit of the doubt for once in your life?"

"No," he states then rubs his forehead with the back of his hand. It's clear he's frustrated with me. "I won't let you off the hook this time. You need to tell her." With a shake of his head, he leaves the kitchen without so much as a goodbye. Just like Cason to make such a dramatic exit.

"I thought you had my back," I call after him.

"I do but not with somethin' like this." My head falls back, and I let out a groan when he slams the door.

Glancing at my bedroom door, I should go in there and purge all these fucking secrets to Savannah. I hate keeping shit from her, and I absolutely hate lying about it. But I'm fucking terrified of losing her. If I tell her, there's a big chance I'll lose her. And if I keep lying to her, there's also a chance I'll lose her.

Fuck me. I'm screwed either way.

The question is how am I going to keep the one woman I love from leaving me?

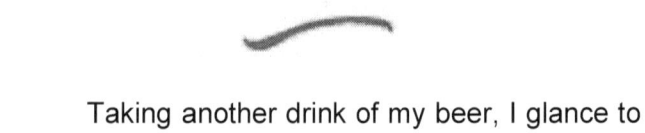

Taking another drink of my beer, I glance to Savannah loving the sound of her laugh. A grin forms seeing her so happy and free. She's changed so much since I first met her, and I hope that has a lot to do with me. I'd like to think so, but then again she's special all on her own. Not to mention, my whole family seems to be in love with her too. I knew they all would, and even Clark approached me once we arrived at Carter and Shelby's house and apologized for being a douche canoe when he first met her. I didn't ask him where he was the last time we came over because I know he's dealing with his

Caden

demons. But I'm glad he changed his tune, or I would have to change it for him. All joking aside, one would think Savannah wouldn't have any reason what-so-ever to want to leave, but I know better. Even if she's having a blast with Shelby now, and how she fits in with all of us, I know this is all temporary. Maybe I've known it all along she was never meant to stay with me, and it makes my chest constrict knowing this.

Pushing these unwanted thoughts from my mind, I try my best to act like I'm just the same ol' funny Caden. It's hard, especially when Cason keeps glaring at me from across the outdoor table, and Caleb does the same when he stops messing with his phone. Clark is sitting by Carter, and they seem to be in deep conversation. Leaning over, I place my arm around Savannah and whisper, "Are you havin' fun yet, small fry?"

When she turns to me, I suck in a breath seeing that gorgeous smile. Damn, it gets me every single time. "I am. Although," she pauses and glances down at my lips, "I could use another beer."

"You goin' to kiss me first?"

"Well," she says and turns away. Knowing she's flirting, I grab her by the chin and pull her to me. "I guess I could give you one kiss."

Forgetting that we're not alone, I huskily ask, "Just one?"

"I never thought I would see this," Carter cuts in, and I roll my eyes.

Leaning back in my chair, I ask, "See what exactly?"

"The day you were pussy whipped."

Savannah giggles beside me, and I shake my head. "I'd much rather be pussy whipped than not have any pussy."

"Here y'all go again talkin' about pussy," Cason pipes in with a monotone voice.

Smirking, I turn to him. "I happen to like pussy very much."

"Could we perhaps talk about somethin' else?" Shelby asks, and I stand.

Leaning down by Savannah, she meets me halfway for a kiss and everyone cheers. "Alright now. That's enough," I claim. Savannah blushes as I leave a peck on her cheek and grab her empty beer bottle. "Anyone else need anythin' while I'm up. I guess I'll be y'alls waiter for tonight." Everyone but Cason and Caleb hold up their empty beer bottles, and Shelby holds up her wine glass. Making my way around the table, I shake my head and declare, "Y'all are a bunch of damn alcoholics." Of course they all laugh because I am half joking. Standing by Clark, I raise an eyebrow when he holds up two fingers meaning

Caden

he wants two beers instead of one. Looks like he needs to add AA meetings to his to do list so he can get back to normal. Huffing out a breath, I snatch Clark's empty bottle out of his hand and make my way inside the house.

Summertime Sadness by Lana Del Rey & Cedric Gervais starts to play over the radio, and I bob my head to the beat as I drop the bottles in the trash. Turning around, I open the fridge then frown when I hear someone yelling outside. Shaking my head and not thinking much of it, I mumble the words to the song as I grab everyone their drinks. Just as I shut the refrigerator door, Savannah appears out of nowhere and out of breath. "Caden," she says with wide eyes.

Wondering what has her so spooked, I ask, "Are you alright there, small fry?"

She looks back outside then to me as she claims, "I need four beers and a knife."

What the fuck is she talking about? "I don't follow. I'm goin' to need you to tell me why in the hell you need four beers and a knife."

"Because." She starts as she steps closer to me. Leaning in, she whispers, "There's a donkey out there."

"Out where?"

"Outside. In the back yard."

Now I know her and I have had a couple of beers, but I hadn't realized she's apparently drunk. That's the only explanation I can come up with. "There's a donkey in the back yard?" I ask slowly because I feel like I'm missing something here.

"Yes! I told you that," she claims in an exasperated tone. Feeling confused, I start to ask her to explain why there's a donkey in the yard and why she's so freaked out when she says, "It's the neighbors apparently, and I'm terrified of donkeys."

Trying to hold back a laugh, I have to bite the inside of my cheek. She's clearly not joking around, and I never would've thought someone would be afraid of a donkey. "Why are you so afraid of donkeys? One shit on you or somethin'?"

"No, Caden. One didn't shit on me." Letting out a chuckle, I can't help myself. "This isn't funny."

"I'm sorry, small fry. Tell me why the big bad donkey freaks you out."

She glares at me then huffs out a breath. "I fell off one once, and it almost killed me by almost stomping my head. Since then, I can't be around one and not freak out."

Placing a finger on my lips, I really try and figure this out. "So you tried to ride a donkey?" With

Caden

her nod, I ask, "Why would you want to ride a donkey? That's what horses are for."

"I don't know, Caden. I was at a fair, and they had a bunch of donkeys in this ring pin, and I fell off. I don't know why I have to explain this so much. I'm afraid of them, and you should protect me from it."

"Protect you from a donkey that isn't anywhere near you?" When she rolls her eyes, I pull her to me. When she glances up at me, I ask, "What exactly would you like me to do? Stab it for you with your knife? I have to say, small fry. I'm not sure how I feel about killin' an innocent animal."

She pushes against my chest, and I let out a laugh at the look on her face. "You're an ass."

"I'm just jokin' around." She purses her lips out at me, and I wink at her. Remembering she also asked for four beers, I calmly ask, "Why did you want four beers?"

"So I can drink them. Why else would I want a beer?"

I can't deny her logic behind that one. "Alright then. I'll grab some more beers then." Turning back to the fridge, I grab a couple more beers. Thankfully Savannah helps me carry all the drinks back outside, and once I set them down, I notice Carter and Cason are out in the yard trying to round up the scary donkey. Savannah quickly grabs one of the beers off the table as Clark does the same, and she downs hers so fast I frown. "Easy there, small fry." Taking the bottle away from her, I lean over to whisper, "Don't worry. The scary donkey isn't goin' to get you."

She smacks my chest as she claims, "I shouldn't have told you that. You'll never let me live that one down."

Grinning, I take a seat and say, "I'll remember it for the rest of my life. It'll be a good story to tell the grandkids." Shelby snorts, and Savannah's eyes look like they're about to pop out of her head. "What? Was it somethin' I said?"

"It's a little scary how you claim we're going to have grandkids," Savannah retorts.

"I think y'all should at least go steady for a bit before movin' onto grandkids, Caden," Shelby adds.

"Kill all my hopes and dreams why don't you," I pipe back.

"I'm just sayin'," Shelby says as she takes a drink of her wine.

Savannah is eerily quiet during our exchange, and I hope she knows I was sort of kidding. I know it's way too soon to be talking about future grandkids, but it is something I would like to have with her. A guy can dream right? Before I get a chance to say something back, Carter and Cason return from rounding up the donkey, and I notice Savannah letting out a loud sigh. "Please tell me the donkey is back in its cage?" she asks them and I shake my head.

"I wouldn't call it a cage, but yes. The donkey is gone," Carter tells her.

"Thank God," Savannah says as she grabs another beer.

"I don't think I've ever met anyone afraid of a donkey before," Clark declares, and I take a beer for myself.

Waiting to see what Savannah will say, I lean back in my chair and cross a leg over the other. Darting my eyes to Cason, he's glaring at me again. Ignoring him, I glance to Caleb seeing he's yet again on his phone. I've never understood why people come over to hangout, but yet they're always on their phone. "Well," Savannah starts. "We all have something we're afraid of. Mine is just a bit unorthodox."

Everyone is quiet hearing Savannah's truth, and Clark clenches his jaw then turns away. I know she didn't mean to poke the bear with him, but we all know Clark is dealing with a lot of baggage. Sensing the need for a mood change, I turn to Caleb. "Oops baby, what are you doin' that's more important than spendin' time with your favorite people?"

"I've asked you to not call me that," he snaps and doesn't even bother to look at me.

I know how much he hates it when I call him that, but I can't help myself. He gets all riled up for no reason, and me being me, I push him a bit more. "I know, but it's the truth and it's your nickname."

He huffs out a breath then says, "You're the one that gave me that stupid nickname. No one else calls me that but you."

"Awe now don't be like that," I claim then snatch his phone out of his hands. Maybe now he'll actually converse with everyone.

"Give it back, Caden."

"No can do, oops baby." I don't get a chance to see what he's even doing on his phone since he jumps out of his chair and lunges for it. Moving it out of his reach, I hold him back with my hand as he struggles for it. "You really love this phone don't you?"

"Caden, give it back. I'm not playin' around."

Pushing him off me, I jump out of my chair and look down at his screen. It timed out, so it's locked now, but he doesn't know that. "Let's see what secrets you're hidin' here."

Caden

"Caden," Cason starts in a stern voice. "I would chill out if I were you."

Not understanding what he means, I shrug off his warning. "I'm just messin' around." Turning to Caleb, he's glaring at me. "Geesh, oops baby. What's the hate glare for?"

Feeling everyone's gaze on us, I frown wondering what the big deal is. "Last chance to give me back my phone, Caden."

"Or what?" I dare. When he doesn't move, I glance down at his phone and try to unlock it. I am curious to know what he's been up to since he's got here, and why he's so focused on his phone. Which is why I wasn't expecting him to tackle me. Hitting the porch hard, I lose my grip on his phone, and it goes flying across the porch as my beer shatters everywhere. Pushing him off me, I jump up and ask, "What the fuck, man?"

Caleb doesn't say a word as he walks over to pick up his phone. Where I'm standing, I can clearly see his screen is shattered and as he turns around, he snaps, "You're a fuckin' dick."

"I'm a dick? You're the one who tackled me to keep your precious secret hidden."

"You want to talk about keepin' secrets?"

Shit. I give him a warning look because I know exactly what he's talking about. "How about we talk about this in private."

Caleb shakes his head and smiles, but there's nothing funny about this. My heart drops as he says, "No, I don't want to talk in private. You're such a fuckin' hypocrite, you know that." Savannah's eyes cut to me, and I can only imagine what's going through her head. Before I get a chance to stop him, he says, "You're bustin' my balls for hidin' shit, but you're the one who's holdin' back somethin' from the girl you claim to love." He stops for a moment to glance at his phone, and I clench my jaw knowing he's just royally fucked me over. "How about you tell Savvy the truth instead of fuckin' with me."

Knowing he's right and having nothing else to say, he storms inside the house. "I'll go after him," Clark says and rushes after Caleb.

The thing is the damage is already done. Swallowing hard, I look to Savannah. She slowly stands and moves in front of me. "Caden? What did Caleb mean? What are you keeping from me?"

Feeling Carter, Shelby, and Cason's gaze on me, I know my time is up. I can't keep this from her any longer, and this is so not the way I wanted to tell her. "Savannah, just let me explain."

Caden

"Yeah, explain why the hell you've apparently been keeping something from me."

Glancing to Cason, I silently beg for help. I know I fucked up, and I know this is about to blow the fuck up in my face. Some assistance from my twin would be nice, but he only glares at me. Guess I'm on my own with this one. Taking a deep breath, I look Savannah in the eyes as I quietly confess, "I know who your birth mother is." When she steps back like I've hit her, I quickly add, "I'm so sorry I didn't tell you. I swear I was goin' to but I ... I didn't know how."

It kills me she can't even look at me when she asks, "You didn't know how to tell me what exactly?" Moving closer, I try to take her hand. She jerks out of my reach as she yells, "Tell me, Caden. Who is she? Why did you keep this from me?"

I open my mouth to explain, but honestly there's nothing I can say to make her understand. And knowing I've fucked up big time makes my stomach sink. "Your mother is Tabitha Ross."

"What did you just say?" Shelby asks.

I glance at her for a moment then turn back to Savannah. "Caleb tracked the fake identity, and it lead him to Tabitha. Then he cross referenced the hospital records, hacked into the database, and made the connection."

"But that ... that's impossible," Shelby claims.

"She did leave for a year when we were kids," Carter explains, and I can see Shelby putting everything together.

Shelby glances to Savannah as she says, "Holy fuck."

Trying once more to take Savannah's hand, she shakes her head and moves her hand out of my reach. Her eyes begin to fill with tears as she asks, "What does this all mean then?"

Seeing Cason moving toward me out of the corner of my eye, I glance to Shelby and Carter seeing their shocked expressions. Savannah is the only one that doesn't know she has a sister. A sister that's sitting in the chair right beside her. A sister that she's clicked with since the moment they met. And I'm a fucking bastard for keeping this secret from her. "It means," I say with a raspy voice. This is the hardest fucking thing I've ever had to do. Knowing I've held something like this from her for weeks and the fact she's been searching for her mother for so long, *it kills me*. My chest constricts as my stomach clenches painfully. Sucking in a breath, it's time for me to come clean. Fully. "It means that Shelby is your sister. Your half-sister to be exact."

Caden

Savannah's gaze never leaves mine, and I'd give anything to go back in time and change this. I would've never kept this fucking secret, but fuck I wanted to protect her. Tabitha is a conniving cunt, and I know every single fucked up thing she did to Shelby. Not to mention, she's the main reason Shelby left Carter for so long. So yeah, I fucked up, but dammit I wanted to save her from the pain Tabitha causes. But I know Savannah will never forgive me for this. I can see the betrayal and hurt in her eyes, and when a tear falls down her cheeks, I ache knowing I've hurt her so badly. Honestly I wouldn't blame her if she never forgave me for keeping something like from her. Even if I know Tabitha is an evil bitch, the look in Savannah's eyes tells me all I need to know. "How long?" She asks. She clears her throat then asks again. "How long have you known?"

"Three weeks. Maybe a little longer." I'm not proud of this. I feel like a shit bag for doing this to her. She sucks in a breath and places a hand over her heart as she looks away from me. "Savannah, I'm so fuckin' sorry. Please," I stop when her gaze locks with mine, and I swallow seeing the anger laced in those blue-green eyes. She doesn't say a word as she closes the distance between us, and before I can utter a single word, she slaps me across my face. She hits me so hard my head turns, and I instantly feel the sting. Slowly turning back to her, I try once more to apologize. "Savannah, I'm—"

"Don't," she says sternly. "Don't say another damn word." Her eyes close for a second as she shakes her head, and when she opens them, more tears fall down her cheeks. "I ... I can't even *look* at you," she spits out and, yeah it fucking hurts. But more than anything, her not saying a damn word hurts even more.

Then she turns around and literally runs away from me.

Not even thinking about it, I take off after her because I know if she leaves, this will be *the end*.

And I can't, *I mean absolutely cannot*, let that happen.

"Savannah!" I call after her, but she doesn't stop until I finally catch up and grab her by the arm. "Please, just let me explain," I beg.

"Don't fucking touch me!" She yells back and jerks away from me. "How could you? How could you keep this from me?"

Hearing the anguish in her voice cuts me deeper than I thought her hateful words could. But I deserve it. I deserve her anger, wrath, and everything she can give. "I ... I wanted to protect you. I swear I was goin' to tell you, but—"

Caden

"But what?" she asks cutting me off. "Why the fuck would you keep this from me knowing how much I wanted this. You fucking knew, Caden. You knew how much this meant to me, and how I've literally been looking for my mother for years."

"I know, Savannah. I know I should've told you sooner, but you have to listen to me." Taking a deep breath, she's quiet for a moment, and I take my chance. "I wanted to protect you from the truth because of your mother, the woman you claim you want to know is the worst person you could ever want to know. She nearly destroyed Shelby and Carter. So yeah. I fuckin' lied and kept this from you because I wanted to save you from goin' through the same shit Shelby did for most of her life."

"No," she says as she shakes her head. "That's not a good enough excuse."

"What do you want me to say? I know I fucked up, I know I should've told you, but I swear I didn't want to hurt you."

"Then why, Caden? Why keep it from me?"

"Because." I breathe out. Swallowing hard, I hope what I'm about to say will change her mind and let me make this up to her. "Because I love you. I love you so much that I kept something that could hurt you in the long run. I didn't want to hurt you, and I'm so sorry for that, but I knew if you found out who your mother was, you would take off to find her and leave me here without you. Savannah, I fuckin' love you, and I cannot bear it if you leave. So please, please just stay and let me fix this." This is it. I've laid all my cards out on the table. Everything I just said is the truth, and she'll ruin me if she walks away.

But I know I've lost her when she says, "You don't lie and hurt the people you love." Another tear falls down her face, and I glance away from her. Hearing someone walking up behind me, I turn to see Cason. Thinking he's here to help me convince her to stay, I suck in a breath. But he doesn't even look my way. He walks right past me, and I frown when Savannah asks him, "Can you please get me out of here?"

"Cason," I call after him when he nods and starts to walk toward his truck. "Cason, please don't fuckin' do this."

He quickly helps Savannah get inside his truck then he makes his way to me. I can feel his rage with our bond, and I square my shoulders when he stops inches away from me. "You did this, not me. I fuckin' told you this would happen, and now look what you've fuckin' done. Are you happy now? Are you glad you hurt not only Savvy but Shelby too? All because you couldn't be a fuckin' man and tell Savvy the truth." He takes a deep breath, and I can only take the verbal bashing. "I'm takin' her home so don't

Caden

fuckin' bother tryin' to talk your way out of this. I better not catch you anywhere near the apartment for a while." He starts to walk away but thinks better of it. When he turns back, I feel my entire world coming down on me just from the look he's giving me. "I hope you know I can't fix this for you either, and it's goin' to take a lot for her to forgive you."

When he turns to walk back to his truck, I curse under my breath. Everything he just said is spot on, and I can't even be pissed at him for leaving with Savannah or for him clearly taking her side. Watching them as Cason drives away, I feel my heart breaking. It literally feels as if someone is ripping the fucker out, and it's hard to breathe properly. Cason's truck speeds down the road, and I stand out in the yard even though I can't see it anymore. I don't know how long I stand here just staring off into the distance before I finally decide to move. With my head hanging in defeat, I walk to the front porch and take a seat on the steps. Running both hands down my face, I don't know why I let shit get this far. One stupid mistake has cost me *everything*, and I have no clue how to fix it. I don't know how to get Savannah to listen to me or forgive me. The last thing I ever wanted to do was hurt her, but it doesn't even fucking matter now.

I've ruined it.

I've lost the one woman I've ever loved.

Cason was right. This shit blew up right in my face, and I can't blame anyone for it. This is all on me, and I don't know what to do about it.

Hearing the front door close, I drop my hands and turn to see Shelby taking a seat beside me. She doesn't look at me, and I wonder if she's angry with me too. "So I apparently have a sister and had no idea." Not knowing what to say, I gaze in the distance. Shelby is quiet for a while, and I don't even know where to start apologizing to her. Not only did I keep this from Savannah, but I also kept it from Shelby. They both had every right to know, and I just selfishly withheld it from them both. "I know why you didn't tell her," Shelby says finally, and I jerk my gaze to her. She looks at me with understanding her eyes as she says, "I know you love her, Caden. I also know you wanted to protect her from my mother." Turning away, I let my head drop. Even if Shelby understands, it still doesn't make it right. "I hope you know even if I get why you kept this from me and Savannah, you still shouldn't have lied or kept this from either of us. But," she says with a sigh. "I do understand."

"Thank you for understanding. It's a lot more than Cas did."

"Well can you blame him?" Frowning, I glance at her as she says, "He knew what would happen, and he didn't want to see you or her hurt."

Caden

Shaking my head, I look away because I know this already. But just knowing my own twin turned his back on me, then ran off with my girl, hurts more than I thought possible. "I don't know what to do now, Shel."

"Yes you do, Caden." Snapping my gaze to her once more, she adds, "You win her back."

twenty-one
Savannah

My heart feels like it's being torn into pieces.

I've never felt so much pain in my entire life. Not when my parents told me I was adopted. Not even when I broke my arm when I was ten. This pain is so much more than I can bear, and I have no idea how I'm supposed to move forward. How am I supposed to even wrap my mind around everything that's happened? Finding out the one person I counted on lied to me and kept something from me, feels as if I'm being ripped apart from the inside out. I never once thought Caden would be the one to ultimately break my heart, but I've been proven wrong. Caden took my heart and tossed it out the fucking window then ran over it again and again.

I don't even remember getting back to the apartment. The whole way there, all I could do was

Caden

cry. Cason never spoke a word, and I was grateful. It's not like I knew what to say anyway. Plus I can't bear to look at him either. That's the thing about leaving with the twin of someone that's supposed to love you.

Love is nothing but a fucking lie.

Caden claims he loves me, but how can he even utter those words knowing what he's done? How can someone say they love someone else and hurt them so much?

I don't know what went through Caden's mind when he decided to keep this from me, and just knowing he's known for weeks makes me so damned angry at him. He's known all along who my birth mother was and that I have a sister. *A half-sister*. In hindsight, I guess it makes sense why Shelby and I connected so quickly, and why I felt as if I'd known her all my life. But even with this new information, I can't ignore how Caden has lied to me for weeks about it. If I had known, Shelby and I could've gotten closer. I could've spent time with her. Caden stole that right from me. He took away my choice to know Shelby on a different level than just a friend. The big question is what do I do now? Honestly I'm such a mess, and I have no clue where to start. A part of me wants to say fuck this stupid town and run back home. But I know I won't. Even if I'm hurting, I can't just up and leave knowing I have a sister now. I want the chance to know her, really know her, and I can't just skip out on that.

Running my hands through my hair, I will these stupid tears to stop falling. I've never cried so much in my life, and it seems I have an endless amount of tears. They refuse to stop, and I quickly wipe them away as they fall down my cheeks. Seeing Cason take a seat by me on the couch, I let out a heavy sigh. While I'm grateful that he got me away from Caden, I also feel like a terrible person for putting them in that position. I saw them arguing, and I could feel the anger rolling off Cason while he drove away. It wasn't my intention to make them fight, but I needed to get away from Caden. From the hurt, he's caused me. "I'm sorry I caused a rift between you and Caden." I can't look at him as I apologize, and I hope he knows I am sorry.

"There's no need to apologize." Cason lets out a huff before saying, "You have no reason to be sorry. Caden …" he stops for a moment, and I can hear the disappointment in his voice. "Caden is a fuckin' idiot for keepin' somethin' like this from you. I warned him, but he wouldn't listen to me."

Looking down at my hands, I swallow hard before asking, "Why did he keep this from me? I just can't understand why he would when he knew I've been searching for my mother for years."

Caden

"Honestly I think he was scared." Frowning, I glance at him for only a second before turning away. "I can't say for sure, but I have a hunch he was afraid you would leave if he told you. I know you wanted to find out who your mother is, but I do know Tabitha," his voice breaks and I can't help but wonder why. Since getting to know Cason over the past few months, he hardly ever shows emotion. But when he uttered her name, it's the most emotion I've heard from him, and I'm sure if I was looking at him I would see it too. "She's not someone you want to know, Savvy."

"Even still. He should've told me and let me decide. He took that away from me and then lied about it."

"I know. I'm not sayin' what he did was right, but in a way I do get it."

Another tear rolls down my cheek as I whisper, "It just hurts you know?"

Shockingly, Cason scoots closer and wraps an arm around me. Taking his comfort, I bury my head on his chest and begin to cry again. "It's goin' to be alright, Savvy." Hearing him say that only makes me cry harder because I don't know how I'll ever be alright again. I don't know how I'm ever going to be able to forgive Caden for this. It's one thing to lie to me and another to keep such a big secret from me, but it's knowing that *I love him* and I trusted him. I gave him the power to hurt me and destroy my trust. But knowing I have Cason here to comfort me helps some. He's like the brother I never had, and if I'm honest, I've fallen in love with the entire Harlow clan. Maybe that's another reason why I'm so upset. How am I supposed to see them again knowing Caden and I may never get back to where we were? Sucking in a deep breath, I lean back and wipe my face again. "You got to stop with the tears alright? You're makin' me feel like shit because you keep cryin'."

"I'm sorry," I say with a broken voice. Glancing at him, my stomach clenches. It's like I'm looking right at Caden even though I know it's not him. "No offense, but it's kind of hard to keep myself in check when I can't bear to look at you."

"Do you want me to put a paper bag over my head?"

Letting out a chuckle mixed with a sob, I ask, "Did you just make a joke?"

He raises an eyebrow and shrugs. "Yeah, I guess I did." He smirks then shakes his head as if he's lost in thought before saying, "For what it's worth, he does love you."

My eyes blur again with more tears, and I honestly claim, "If you love someone, you don't hurt them or lie to them."

Caden

"That's where you're wrong, Savvy." He pauses, and I wait for him to finish. "Love makes people do stupid shit, and it's usually the ones we love that hurt us the most."

Glancing away, I can't deny he's right. Love is such a fickle thing. It does make us do crazy things we never thought we would, and it also hurts that much more when the ones we love hurt us in return. Even with knowing this and agreeing with Cason, I still don't know how to move on from this. The hurt is too real, raw, and only time will tell if I'll be able to forgive Caden.

I honestly I don't know if I'll ever be able to get over this.

The next morning, I find Cason in the kitchen drinking coffee. He never utters a word as he moves to the cabinet above him and hands me a mug. Taking it from him, I make myself a strong brew. "How did you sleep?" he asks.

Pressing the start button on the Keurig, I lean against the counter as it spits out coffee. "Like shit. I tossed and turned all night." It was the worst sleep I've ever had, and I know it was from everything that went down last night. I just had so much on my mind that I couldn't turn it off long enough to rest. "Did you get any rest?"

"Not really."

Noticing my coffee is finished, I grab the cup and forgo adding anything. I need it to be as strong as possible today. Raising my mug, I say, "Thank God for coffee."

Cason huffs out in response and gazes down in his mug like it holds all the answers to the world. He's quiet for so long I almost forget he's standing in the kitchen with me. "What are you plannin' to do about this?" he asks, and I snap my gaze to him.

Not really knowing what to say, I shrug my shoulders. "I don't know. A part of me wants to go back to Florida, but then again I want to talk to Shelby first. Plus I don't want to up and leave you high and dry at the gym." I refuse to think about Caden. I just … I can't go there right now.

"Whatever you decide, you'll always have a place to work at my gym. Don't worry about that." Hearing a knock at the door, Cason slowly sets his mug down as I wonder who is here. My stomach drops thinking it's Caden, but why would he knock at his own apartment? When he glances at me, he says, "Here's your chance to talk to Shelby."

Caden

"You called her?" He only nods as he walks out of the kitchen, and I follow him toward the front door.

Holding onto my coffee mug tightly as he opens the door, Shelby walks inside and her eyes instantly find mine. I won't lie. I'm nervous as hell about this. It's one thing to think she and I are just friends, but now we both know we're sisters. This is so out of my comfort zone, and I have no clue how to act, feel, or what to even think. "I'm goin' to run some errands, but if y'all need anything just call."

"Thanks, Cas," Shelby says, and I let out a nervous sigh when he leaves. Setting my mug down on the coffee table, I turn to her wondering what to say. "So," she starts. Glancing around the room, I wonder why it's suddenly so awkward. It's not like I haven't talked to her before, and every time we've been around each other, it was easy to fall into conversation. "Am I the only one that's a bit freaked out about this?"

Letting out a small laugh, I say, "No. I'm feeling it too."

"I have to say, I'm still reelin' about all this. I had no idea I had a sister." She looks away, and I frown seeing the hurt in her eyes when she looks back up. "If I had known, I would've found you sooner."

"It's not your fault. No one knew but one person."

"My, I mean our mother," she adds. Technically Caleb and Caden knew, but if our mother hadn't made me into a dirty little secret none of this would be happening. Nodding, all my words leave me once more, and I'm surprised when she walks over and wraps her arms around me. It takes me a few seconds before I return her hug because I wasn't expecting it. "I'm sorry, Savannah. I wish I had known before."

Pulling back, I notice tears forming in her eyes. "It's okay, Shelby. I'm not mad at you or anything like that. I know you had no idea."

She wipes away a tear before it falls down her cheeks as she says, "It's just so fucked up you know?" Taking her hand, I squeeze tightly letting her know I'm here. "My mother, shit sorry. Our mother. It's goin' to take a while to get used to sayin' our." She and I chuckle because I can only imagine how strange this is for her too. "It just seems like our mother just keeps messin' with my life, and now she's added you into the mix. It's not fair, and I'm so pissed she didn't tell me about you. All this time you've been missin' from my life and I had no clue."

I completely understand where she's coming from. When I found out I was adopted, I was so consumed with finding my birth mother, and I never

Caden

dreamed of having a sister out there just living her life. I had no clue this was in the plans for me. "It's not fair, and I wish we could turn back time and get all the years that were stolen from us, but," she gazes at me as I finish. "Now we have all the time in the world to be sisters, and trust me when I say, there won't be anything stopping me from it."

She smiles then claims, "I knew I liked you for a reason." Grinning widely, I feel a rush of pride flow through me knowing I've made my sister happy. That's still weird to think, but it's the truth. "I'm glad I finally have the chance to know you, Savvy. Even though it didn't come out the way it should've, I'm still glad to finally know."

"Yeah, me too." Looking away, I know she's referring to Caden. My heart painfully clenches thinking about what he's done and how badly he's hurt me.

"Shit, I'm sorry. It's too soon to bring that up."

"It's alright," I honestly say. "I knew it was bound to come up sooner or later."

She rubs my shoulder, and I appreciate her comforting touch. It is nice to know I have not only her now, but I have Cason here if I need to lean on them. "Do you want to talk about it?"

Sucking in a breath, I shake my head as I say, "Not really. I'm still so angry about it, and I don't feel like crying anymore."

"I have an idea," she claims, and her eyes light up. "Why don't you get your things, and we'll drop them off at my house. I want to take you somewhere."

Grabbing her hand as she starts to walk toward Caden's room, I ask, "Are you sure? I don't want to impose on you and Carter."

"It's fine, I promise. Carter was the one that mentioned it before I came over. So let's get packin', sis." She winks at me, and I can't help but smile. It's like she knows just what to say to make everything better, and when she motions me to follow her, I do so without a word.

Shelby pulls into a driveway, and I sit up straighter seeing the small two-story yellow house. Wondering where we are, I glance around the yard seeing tons of bright colored flowers decorating it. Turning to Shelby as she turns off her car, I ask, "Where are we?"

She smiles brightly as she says, "You'll see. Come on. I want to introduce you to my family." Not knowing what to think, I unbuckle my seatbelt and

Caden

get out of the car. Taking a deep breath, I push down my nerves and follow her toward the house. I wonder why she brought me here. Am I going to meet more of my family too? Making it to the front door, Shelby doesn't bother to knock. Walking in behind her, she calls out, "Annie? Where are you hidin'?"

A petite woman with gray hair walks around the corner, and I know I've seen her before. Unable to place where I've met her, she smiles at Shelby and her honey brown eyes glance to me. "Well isn't this a wonderful surprise."

Shelby turns back to me and places an arm around my shoulder as she asks, "Annie, do you remember Savannah? You met her at Caleb's welcome home party."

My gaze locks with Annie as it clicks into place. I do remember meeting the sweet and very motherly Annie a couple weeks ago. It seems like so much time has passed since then. "I do remember," Annie says. "I could never forget such a beautiful girl."

My face warms at her compliment. "Thank you."

"No need to thank me, honey. Y'all hungry? I'm about to make some lunch."

Annie turns around to walk into the kitchen, but she stops when Shelby says, "Annie, I need to tell you somethin'."

Annie immediately turns around with wide eyes. "Oh goodness. No one is hurt are they?"

I smile as Shelby lets out a laugh. "No, Annie. Everyone is fine. In fact," Shelby stops and turns her gaze to me. Wondering what she's up to, I glance between her and Annie. "I just wanted to drop by and introduce you to my sister."

With wide eyes, I look at a very shocked Annie. She's holding a hand to her chest as she says, "Well I'll be." Annie doesn't ask how we're sisters or anything of the sort. She walks right up to me and Shelby steps away from me as Annie wraps her small arms around me. Hugging her back, I'm a little surprised at her reaction. When she pulls back, she has tears in her eyes. "Welcome to the family, sweetie. Oh we have to tell William," she exclaims proudly and turns to go find him.

"I hope you're ready for a lot of huggin'," Shelby says quietly.

Watching Annie rush out of the house, I ask her, "Are they my family too?"

Shelby shrugs and explains. "Technically no. But just because they aren't blood-related doesn't mean they aren't family. Annie and William took care

Caden

of me pretty much half my life, and I consider them my parents." Waving her hand back and forth, she adds, "It's a long story."

Before I can ask what she means or to explain more since I know a bit about the situation, Annie comes back inside with William right on her heels. I recall talking with William some at Caleb's party, and I smile noticing the height difference between him and Annie. She sort of looks like a midget compared to him. "What's all the commotion about?" He asks.

"Just hold onto your horses," Annie says as she looks to me then Shelby.

William waits for someone to tell him why I'm here and why Annie is so excited. "I'm not gettin' any younger," he declares when no one speaks up.

Shelby glances to me, and I take it she wants me to tell him. Feeling a bit nervous, I suck in a breath before saying, "I'm Shelby's sister."

"No kiddin'?" His expression is the same as Annie's was. Nothing but pure shock and surprise. William glances to Shelby then to me before he says, "I thought y'all looked alike when I met you before." He smiles at me, and I can't explain why but I feel as if they are my family too. Maybe it's the way Annie and William are looking at me with nothing but love in their eyes. Maybe it's because I know Shelby says they're her family. Either way, my heart warms when he says, "Well get over here and give me a hug."

Grinning widely, I don't hesitate to do just that. He embraces me tightly and all the hurt I felt before coming here, eases just a bit. It's still there, but having Shelby's family welcome me with open arms makes everything seem just a bit better than before. When William lets me go, Annie hugs me once more. Squeezing her tightly, she whispers so low that only I can hear her. "I'm so happy you and Shelby found each other." Not knowing what to say when she pulls away, I give her a smile and nod letting her know I heard her. "How about some food?"

"Why are you always tryin' to fatten us up?" Shelby asks, and I let out a laugh.

"Food is the cure for everythin', and I happen to like feedin' y'all," Annie says back.

"I know I'm not complainin'," William says to them as he rubs his belly.

"Well," Annie starts. "Y'all take a seat, and I'll whip us up somethin'."

Shelby nods her head toward the table, and I follow her. She and I sit next to each other as William sits on the other side by Shelby. Annie busies herself with making lunch, and a calmness washes over me when I hear her humming. "I have

Caden

to ask you, Savannah," William starts, and I glance over to him. "Are you still with that heathen Caden?"

My stomach drops hearing his name and thankfully Shelby cuts in. "We aren't talkin' about him, William."

"What did he do now? Do I need to get my shotgun out?"

"William," Annie warns.

I hold back a laugh hearing the seriousness in his tone, but it is nice to know he's willing to risk jail time for me. Even if he doesn't know me, he's already showing me he takes care of his own. "How about we don't kill my fiancé's brother just yet," Shelby states.

"I won't kill him. Just want to scare him a bit."

Shelby gives William a pointed look before saying, "I think we should let them figure things out before any of us interfere."

William looks to me when he declares, "If you need me to ruff him up a bit, I will. My offer will never expire."

"I appreciate that. And I might take you up on that offer," I say with a wink.

Shelby leans over, and I hold back a laugh when she says, "Don't encourage him. He's dead serious."

For the next hour, I find I really enjoy being around Annie and William. I can totally see why Shelby considers them family. They have no idea who I am, but yet they've opened up their home and their arms to me. They've made me feel as if I am a part of their family within moments of being here, and I can see myself wanting to stay here. I can see and feel the love they have for one another, and I hope one day they give me the same love.

For so long I've felt like an outsider, even with my own family. But being here with Shelby, my sister, and her family makes me finally feel complete. The only thing that's missing is the one person I don't know if I can ever face again.

Caden Harlow.

After helping Annie clean up the kitchen, Shelby wanted to show me her favorite hangout. Following her out to the backyard, I squint when the sun shines in my eyes. "You're goin' to love this," Shelby says as she looks back to me.

Taking her word for it, I tag along with her until we reach a treehouse. "Wow," I exclaim. "How old is this thing?"

Shelby looks up with her hands on her hips as she answers. "It's pretty old. William built it for me

Caden

and the Harlow boys. We use to play up there all the time when we were kids." Glancing away from her, I look up and wonder if she wants to climb up there. "Come on. I want to show you the inside."

"Uh ... Shel?" She turns back to me as I ask, "Are you sure it's safe?" It doesn't look very safe to climb, and I'm not sure how I feel about sitting inside a very old treehouse.

She laughs and shakes her head then says, "I know you don't want me to mention Caden, but he once said the same thing." Trying to act like it doesn't bother me hearing his name, I take a deep breath. "I promise it's safe. Carter and I still come up here sometimes."

"Ew ... Shel. I do not want to know that."

"We don't do that up there," she claims with a huge grin.

"I don't know. With the look on your face, it tells me all I need to know."

She shakes her head but doesn't say anything. Watching her as she starts to climb the makeshift ladder, she turns back to me. "Are you comin'?"

Pushing out a breath, I say a little prayer hoping I don't fall to my death. "I'm right behind you." Shelby grins widely then begins to climb again. I follow behind her, but I'm much slower. I take the wooden ladder carefully because I don't want to slip and fall. Not to mention, I'm a little worried the wood will somehow come out of the tree, and I'd rather not die at twenty-two. Looking up, I notice Shelby is gazing down at me through an opening in the floor above me, and once I reach the hole she helps me up. Taking a look around, my heart pounds seeing how high up we are. Seeing the neighbor's yard, my hand shakes as I move to grab the railing. "Shit. I didn't realize how high up this was."

"I know," Shelby says, and I glance to her seeing her bright smile. "It's great isn't it?"

Raising my eyebrows, I claim, "I guess so. Unless you're afraid of falling to your death that is."

She lets out a laugh before saying, "I used to love coming here. I felt as if I could escape all the worries and problems of my life when I was up this high." I frown seeing her smile fade, and I wonder what she's thinking about. Whatever it is, it seems it still haunts her. "Let's go inside," she says, and I don't say anything as I follow her once more. We both have to duck as we walk inside, but once we're clear of the door frame, we both stand tall. Glancing around the room, I smile seeing the knickknacks of her childhood. A few bean bags sit in the corner behind some old horror posters, and I pick up to look at the mixtapes sitting on a shelf. There are even some old army men toys lined up by the tapes. "This was my safe place," Shelby says as she sits on one of the beanbags and looks around the room. "It's like comin' home every time I come up here."

Setting the tapes back down, I take a seat next to her. "I have to say, I'm impressed. Not only because we haven't fallen to our deaths yet, but because I can see why you love this place too much. It's cool."

We both let out a chuckle then she says, "It's too bad you couldn't be here when William built it. It's a little worn out now, but this place holds so many memories."

I can't help but think Shelby is holding something back. She keeps looking off into the distance as if she remembers things from her past, and I can't decide if they're good things or not. "Will you tell me about them?"

She turns to me with a wide smile as she nods. "Well there's so many. I don't know where to begin."

"What's the first one that comes to mind?" I want to know more about her and her life. I have so much to catch up on, and this seems like the way to go about it.

"Let's see," she starts and looks up at the ceiling. "Oh I know." When she glances back to me, she says, "Carter and I lost our virginity up here."

"You're lying," I say in disbelief.

"I'm not." She giggles. "It happened right over there," she says as she points toward the only window in the room. "It was awful. We had no clue what we were doin', and it hurt so bad."

Unable to hold back a laugh, I glance away from the spot she's looking at and try to put the picture of her and Carter out of my mind. "Yeah, my first time wasn't that great either. Why didn't anyone warn us how bad it would be?"

"I honestly have no idea." Laughing with her once more, her laughter slowly stops. "Can I ask you somethin'?"

"Of course."

"How was your childhood?"

Her question catches me off guard for a moment, but I quickly recover. "It was wonderful. My mom and dad were the best. They used to take me to the beach, and they were very loving. To be honest, I feel like an asshole for how I've been acting toward them since they told me I was adopted." Shelby doesn't say anything as I continue, and it feels good to be able to talk about my family again. I

Caden

miss them like crazy, and even if I found my blood family with Shelby, I wish my parents were here to meet her too. "I was sixteen when they told me, and I didn't react to the news very well. I thought they had lied to me for so long, and some part of me thought since I was adopted, that meant I didn't belong with them."

"I understand not feelin' as if you belong. I've dealt with that all my life."

"It's not a good feeling. I hated that I felt that way, which is why I fought so hard to find our mother."

She nods in understanding, and she's quiet for a while before she finally says, "I'm glad you had such loving parents, Savvy. Trust me, you do not want to change who your parents are."

Frowning, I wonder what she means. "Can you tell me what you mean by that?"

She sighs deeply as she looks away and I suddenly wish I hadn't asked. "Let's just say our mother won't ever be winnin' mother of year awards. I'm sure Caden and Cason have told you our mother isn't someone you want to be around, and they're right. She wasn't lovin', not in the slightest. Our mother is who she is, and she'll never change. She's a very selfish woman, Savvy. Which is why I've clung to Annie, William, and the entire Harlow family. They were there when our mother starved me, let me go days without a bath, and was downright hateful." Reaching over, I grab her hand and squeeze tightly. I had no idea how different our childhoods were, and it makes my heart hurt knowing that our mother was so different than I thought. "Anyway I'm still tryin' to keep all that in the past, but I want you to know that Caden was tryin' to keep you away from that." Glancing away, I don't know what to say. "I'm not sayin' what he did was right by any means," she says and lets out a small sigh as she continues. "I understand why he did what he did because I've lived through that kind of hurt. He loves you, Savannah."

"I don't know if I can believe that."

"Why not? Isn't it obvious?"

"To a point yes," I pause as I try to get my emotions under control. I suddenly feel all the hurt he's caused blubbing up, and it threatens to take over. "I've just been looking for so long for our mother, and now I know who she is and that I have a sister. It wasn't right or fair to either one of us that he decided to keep all this a secret."

"I know. I really do get it from both sides. And I wish Caden hadn't lied to either one of us." She lets out a sigh before saying, "The only way I think you'll understand is if you meet her."

Caden

"What?" She can't mean what I think she does.

"I think," she says with a heavy sigh. "I think it'll be good for you to see for yourself how our mother is, and maybe then you'll understand why Caden did what he did."

Staring at her, I wonder if this is a good idea. But knowing how badly I want to meet her, I don't really give myself a chance to think it over even knowing Caden, Cason, and Shelby is clearly warning me away. "You would do that for me?"

"Yes. Because you're my sister, and in this family, you'll also see we'll do anythin' we can to protect you and give you everythin' you need."

"Thank you."

Shelby shakes her head and lets my hand go as she stands. "Don't thank me just yet, Savvy." Ignoring her warning once again, I nod. I can't deny I'm excited to finally meet my birth mother, and I'll finally get the answers I want.

The thing is I hope the answers I desperately crave are the ones I want to hear.

twenty-two
Caden

A week goes by without a single word from Savannah, and I feel myself falling deeper into despair. I can't focus on work. I can't think straight, and I don't even want to think about how I can't get a good night's rest since everything went to shit. It's probably because I've been crashing with Clark, and with his one bedroom apartment, I've had to sleep on his hard ass couch. I can't complain too much, but I miss my own bed. The thing is I can't go home since Savannah left. The one time I did go back, I couldn't handle seeing all her stuff missing, and all that was left was the memories her and I made. I know she moved in with Shelby and Carter, and I know it's for the best. She needs to be around family, and I know Shelby isn't going to let Savannah out of her sight. One good thing is Cason finally started speaking to me again and caught me up on what's

Caden

been going on, but he refuses to let me know how Savannah is doing with everything.

Huffing out a breath, I rearrange the hard pillow behind my head. Clark left earlier to go talk to his therapist, and with me taking some leave from work, I have nothing left to do with myself. Yeah, I'm feeling sorry for myself, but I don't know what else to do. Mindlessly flipping through the channels, nothing catches my attention until I see Supernatural on TNT. Clenching my jaw, I shut off the TV hating I can't even enjoy my favorite show anymore without thinking of her. I guess I should be happy she didn't run back home like I thought she would, but then again it sucks knowing she's so close but so fucking far away. If she would just talk to me, maybe I wouldn't feel like such an ass. But no matter how many times I call or text, she won't answer me. I've all but given up because what else can I do? Apparently Savannah doesn't care to hear my side or why I did what I did, and even if I know I really fucked things up with us, I want to explain why I didn't tell her about her mother.

I doubt I'll ever get the chance now.

Hearing the door open, I snap my head to see every single one of my brothers walking in. Groaning out, I yell, "I'm not in the mood for playtime. Come back later."

"Shut up and get dressed," Carter demands, and I roll my eyes.

"Who died and made you boss?"

"No one, but I am the oldest so get your ass up and put some clothes on." Groaning again, I glare at him as I get up and walk over to my bag on the other side of the couch. Being the ass I am, I only put on a shirt. Honestly I don't care what I look like. It's only my brothers. Carter shakes his head when he sees me, and I flop back down on the couch.

Placing my feet on the coffee table, Clark doesn't say a word when he knocks my feet off. "What's with y'all? First, y'all interrupt my me time, and now Clark is beatin' me."

Am I being a tad bit over dramatic? Yes, but I don't care. I'm hurting, and I don't want any more lectures from anyone. I've had to swallow my pride already when I apologized to Caleb, but I don't want to hear what they have to say. "Can you for once in your life stop thinkin' about you and listen to what we have to say?" Cason says with a stern tone, and I swear I want to punch him in the face. To be frank, I'm still hurt for what he did that night Savannah left. I know he was angry with me, but I've never felt so alone when he turned his back on me.

Caden

Sitting up on the couch, I grab the pillow and wrap my arms around it. "What's with the whole gang? I must have really fucked up this time."

"Always with the smart ass comments," Caleb retorts.

"We all knew this wouldn't be easy," Clark adds.

Watching closely as they all surround me, I won't lie and say it doesn't put me on edge. "Why do I get the feelin' y'all are up to somethin'? Preferably somethin' not good."

"Caden," Carter starts as he sits down beside me. Clark takes a seat on the coffee table in front of me, Caleb stands by Carter, and Cason moves to the other side close to me. "I think you know why we're all here," Carter finishes.

"Honestly I feel like y'all are about to give me the shittest news ever."

"No," Caleb says. "We're here to help you get Savannah back."

"Yeah well good luck with that. The last I checked, she won't even text me back, so I don't think this little plan y'all have cookin' is goin' to work." Clark just stares at me while Cason glares. Carter lets out a heavy sigh, and Caleb just looks uncomfortable. But they know I'm right. You can't fix anything if the other person isn't willing to even communicate. "Look," I huff out. "I appreciate all this," I say waving my hand around. "But we all know this shit can't be fixed. And I hate knowin' that, but it's what I deserve for what I did. So y'all can all see yourselves out the door." Frowning, I quickly add, "Well not you Clark since you live here."

"So that's it? You're just givin' up?" Cason asks.

Turning to him, I hold up my hands then drop them. "What else am I supposed to do?"

"You fight for her," Carter cuts in. "If you love her as you claim, then you'll do whatever it takes to get her back."

"Y'all make it sound so fuckin' easy," I interrupt.

"I didn't take you for a quitter," Clark pipes back.

Running a hand down my face, Caleb asks, "Can you live with yourself knowin' you didn't do everythin' possible to get her back? Because I know you, Caden. If you don't try harder, and she slips through your fingers, you'll regret it."

I know they're all right, but I still have my doubts. "What do y'all suggest I do then?"

Caden

"Shelby and Savannah are leavin' tomorrow to go on a road trip." With my confused gaze, Carter adds, "Shelby thinks it'll be a good idea for Savvy to meet their mother. She told me she thinks Savvy will understand why you did what you did once she meets Tabitha."

"It shouldn't take much," Cason claims, and I can't argue with him.

Looking to Carter, I ask, "Is that really a good idea? I mean I know Savannah wants to meet her, but wouldn't it be better to keep her away from her?" I'm not saying Savannah shouldn't meet her mother, I just don't want her to be hurt more than she already is. No thanks to me.

"Shelby said she could handle it, so I have to believe Savvy will be fine." I don't know about that, but I keep that tidbit to myself. It's just I know how devastated Savannah was when she learned Tabitha had a fake identity to keep her birth a secret, and I don't want her to go through any more pain. "I know you want to make this right, Caden. I also know you still love her. You still tryin' to protect her, tells me all I need to know."

"Which is why we're not leavin' this apartment until you get your shit together and we come up with a plan to win her back," Cason says with a firm tone letting me know not to argue.

Glancing around to each of my brothers, my heart warms knowing even at my worst, they're still here for me. "Y'all sure do know how to give a good pep talk. I think I might cry." Even if I'm joking around, it means the world to me knowing I can still count on them. Our bond is strong, and no matter how bad I fuck shit up, they'll always have my back.

"And he's back," Clark claims with a smirk.

"Are we goin' to hug now?" I ask them.

"Fuck no," Cason answers, and I can't help but laugh.

Turning to him, I say, "Awe, Cas. You know you love me." He rolls his eyes at me, but I see the corner of his mouth twitch. "Alright ladies." That earns me a smack from Carter and another glare from Cason. Clark and Caleb shake their heads, and I grin widely. "Seriously guys. Can we stop with the jokes and get down to business?"

"I'll grab some beers," Clark says, and I'm not surprised.

Caleb moves to grab two chairs from the kitchen table and hands one to Cason. "I'm guessin' we're goin' to be here for a while."

Carter slaps my shoulder as he says, "That we are. We're not leavin' until we get this perfect." Nodding, I hope they all know how much I appreciate

Caden

this. I might not say it because I am a dude and we're not good with feelings, but I have a sense they know. Carter nods back, and I know he gets it. I remember not that long ago he was where I am, and Cason and I did everything we could to get him and Shelby back together.

This is the best thing about having brothers. They're always there when you need them and no matter what, I know without a doubt, I'll never have to go through life alone. I most certainly won't have to figure out how I'm going to win Savannah back alone.

I just hope she's ready because between the five of us, there's no way she can run away from me again.

twenty-three
Savannah

Putting the last bag of mine in the trunk of Shelby's car, I step back and shut it. Wiping the sweat off my forehead, I glance to the front porch seeing Carter and Shelby walking toward the car. I can't help but smile seeing them together. It's clear they are so in love with one another, and I'm happy my big sister has someone like Carter. Even if it's only been a week since I found out Shelby was my sister, I've come to care for her deeply. It's as if we were never apart, and I know with this road trip, our bond will continue to grow. Letting out a sigh when I see them share a sweet moment, my heart clenches wishing I had that. I thought Caden and I had something special like Carter and Shelby, but I'm not so sure about that anymore. I'm usually okay until I'm alone at night. That's when the pain hits me the most, and I'm still unsure what to do about him. He's

Caden

tried over and over to reach out, but I'm not ready to talk to him just yet.

But I do miss him.

I miss his goofy laugh, his smart mouth, and especially the way he made me forget about everything that's going on around me.

The thing that stops me from answering his texts or calls is how he broke my trust. I don't trust easily, and I'm still so hurt by what he did. The worst thing about all this is my feelings for him haven't changed. I might be hurt, but the love I feel for him hasn't stopped growing. Lord knows I've tried to stop thinking about him and all the moments we shared, but it seems no matter what I do, he's always on my mind. Kelsey thinks I'm being too hard on him, but I don't think so. I also think she's a bit biased about the entire situation since she knows how happy Caden made me. I know she just wants me to be happy, but I'm still unsure. I feel like I'm stuck in limbo.

"Are you ready to go?" Shelby asks pulling me out of my thoughts.

"Yeah. Just waiting on you."

"Sorry," she says with a smile when Carter wraps his arms around her waist from behind. Shaking my head, I lean against the car as they show off some serious PDA. "Carter, we have to go."

"I know, but I wish you would let me go with y'all."

"Oh no." I cut in. "This is a girl's only trip. No boys allowed."

Shelby nods agreeing with me, and Carter huffs out a breath in annoyance. When Shelby told him about us going to South Carolina to see our mom, he immediately protested saying he wanted to go. He didn't really explain why he wanted to go so badly, but Shelby seemed to understand. "I know this is a girl's only trip," he sarcastically says. "I just want to make sure y'all get there safely."

"I know how to drive, Carter," Shelby sasses.

"Fine." He lets her go, and I move to get in the car. Shutting the door behind me, Shelby gets in and rolls the window down. "Please be careful."

"We will. You have nothin' to worry about."

"I love you, Shel." I have to look away seeing the look in Carter's eyes. I can't lie and say it doesn't hurt hearing and seeing them so in love when I'm mending a broken heart.

Trying not to be bitter, I gaze out the window as Shelby says, "I love you, too. I'll call you later." Moments later, Shelby starts to pull out of the driveway. "Sorry about that," she says to me, and I shake my head when I notice Carter waving so big

Caden

the entire neighborhood will see him. "He's such a worry wart."

Shelby told me a bit about what happened between them this past week so I can understand why he would worry. Seems Shelby and I both have the runner's gene. "Well I hope he knows I'll bring you back kicking and screaming if I have to."

Shelby laughs as she says, "I don't think you have anything to worry about either, sis." Leaning my head back against the headrest, I roll my window down as Shelby turns up the radio. Smiling, I glance over to Shelby as she sings along, and I can't believe this is my life right now.

I never in my wildest dreams thought I would be heading to meet my birth mother with my sister driving. It feels like everything is finally coming together, and for some reason, I have a good feeling about this trip. Maybe it's because I'm finally going to get the answers I've wanted since finding out I was adopted. Maybe it's because I found my sister.

Or maybe it's a combination of both of them.

My stomach begins to clench painfully with nerves as Shelby parks the car in front a three story house. We arrived in Charleston, South Carolina a few hours ago after driving for four days. Shelby and

I weren't in a hurry to get here, and I enjoyed every second of our trip. Our bond is becoming stronger with each passing day, and now we're actually sitting in front of our mother's home, I start to feel queasy. "Are you okay?" She asks.

Pushing out a breath, I say, "I think so. Why am I so nervous?"

"Do you think it's because you're about to meet our mom?"

"Maybe." Turning to Shelby, I quietly ask, "What do I do if she hates me?" All my fears about my mom never loving me come to the surface, and I don't know how I'll react if she tells me I was just a mistake.

"Can I be brutally honest with you?"

"Of course, Shel."

She looks away and gazes at the house for a few moments before turning back to me. "I just want you to be prepared when we go in there." With my frown, she adds, "Our mother is not what you're expectin'. She's goin' to say a lot of hateful and downright mean things, and I just want you to know whatever she says, it's not true." She takes a deep breath before saying, "I know it sounds like I'm tryin' to change your mind about meetin' her, but I just know how she can be. Trust me, Savvy."

Caden

I don't know everything about what our mother did to Shelby, but I know she wouldn't be warning me without good reason. Shelby isn't the type of person to just lie about things like this, and even if our sisterly bond is still forming, I trust her. "You'll be right there with me?"

"Bet your ass I will," she says with a wide grin. "There's no way I'm lettin' you do this alone."

Giving her a smile back, I hope she realizes how much this means to me. Not only because I'm about to meet our mother, but because she's going to be right beside me. "Okay," I rush out with a nod. "I think I'm ready now." Opening the car door, I step out and quickly make my way over to Shelby as she does the same. We glance at each other for a moment before she starts to walk toward the house.

My nerves are at an all-time high as we make our way to the front door. I'm a little overwhelmed seeing all the high-end houses in the neighborhood, and this entire subdivision screams money. I'm yet again out of my comfort zone, but I can't complain. I've been waiting for this moment for so long and in the back of mind, I know this visit could go terribly wrong. Even knowing with everything Shelby has told me about our mother, I still want to meet her. I still have to know why she gave me away, and why she covered it up. It just seems strange she would go to such great lengths to keep me a secret.

Brie Paisley

Once we make it to the door, I swallow hard and suck in a breath. Shelby turns to me with worried eyes, and I give her a small smile letting her know I'm ready. She nods then squares her shoulders before ringing the doorbell. My heart won't stop pounding in my chest, and my stomach feels like it's in knots. "Remember what I told you," Shelby says right before the door opens. "Hello, Mother," Shelby says, and I hold my breath as I finally see the woman that gave birth to me.

Shelby was so right. She's nothing like I expected. The only way I could describe how she looks is she's had way too much plastic surgery or Botox. Her skin is so tight over her cheekbones, and I inwardly cringe thinking they might cut open her skin. I would have to guess she's in her fifties, and it shows. Her hair has been dyed blonde so many times it looks like it's all about to fall out, and I instantly know I made a mistake coming here. It's the way her eyes cut to me then Shelby that sends a chill down my spine. "I can't say I'm surprised to see you, Shelby. I always knew you would come home." Seeing Shelby visibly take in a breath, I want to grab her and take her away from this woman. "Who's the fat one?" Tabitha asks, and I open my mouth in shock.

Is she fucking serious? "Excuse me?"

Caden

Her hard gaze lands on me, and I clench my jaw when she asks, "Are you deaf?"

"Can you just for one second pretend to be nice and invite us inside?" Shelby cuts in, and I know it's her way of trying to defuse the situation.

Tabitha huffs out a breath as if she's annoyed with our visit. "If you must." My eyes dart to Shelby, and she gives me a concerned look. Even with my instincts going off that this isn't a great idea, I walk in behind Shelby. We don't go very far in the house, and I'm glad for it. It's comforting to know the door is right behind us if we need to make a quick getaway. "Is there a reason for this visit because unless you're ready to remarry Easton, you aren't welcome here."

Shelby must feel my eyes on her because I had no idea she was married before. I would've never guessed it. "Easton is my ex-husband," she says to me. Turning to our mother, she says with a hard tone, "And he will always be my ex and a mistake." Shocked doesn't cover what I'm feeling in this moment. I wonder why Shelby never told me, but then again it's going to take more than a week to learn all of my sister's past.

"I suggest you tell me what you want then because I don't have time for this, Shelby."

Brie Paisley

Shelby's face turns red, and I see her jaw clenching. I can feel her anger coming off in waves, and I decide to step in and give her a moment to cool down. "I'm the reason we're here." Tabitha's gaze turns on me, and before I chicken out, I blurt, "I'm your daughter."

One would think a mother that gave her child away would be shocked or possibly happy to be meeting them but not Tabitha. She looks annoyed and bit angry, and I cannot believe I wanted to meet this woman. It's clear I've made a grave mistake coming here. "You've got to be kidding me. Didn't I get rid of you?" Her words cut deep, but I hold my own. Remembering what Shelby told me, I try to act like her hateful words and tone don't affect me. "I can't believe this. All that trouble I went through to make sure you stayed out of my life, and now here you are with my other mistake."

Feeling tears beginning to burn in my eyes, I blink them away and suck in a breath. "So I was a mistake, and you never wanted me." I sense Shelby's gaze on me, but I refuse to look away from Tabitha. I'll lose all my bravado if I see Shelby's worried expression.

"Of course you were a mistake," Tabitha spits out. "Just like Shelby. You both are nothing but huge mistakes, and I never wanted either of you."

Caden

"Then why have either of us then?" I ask. It makes no sense why she would even have us if we were nothing but a fucking burden.

"I had no choice," she sneers.

"Oh my God," Shelby exclaims, and I glance at her wondering what she's figured out. "You got pregnant while Dad was still alive. Which means I saw you cheatin', and you left him. Did he know? Is that why he basically killed himself?"

Tabitha doesn't seem surprised at Shelby's accusation. She just huffs out a breath as if she's just annoyed and crosses her arms. "Yes. He knew, and I left to make sure it," she says to me as if I'm good enough to even acknowledge. "Was out of the picture for good, but apparently all my efforts were wasted."

Feeling confused, all I can do is glance between Tabitha and Shelby. "I can't believe you. It wasn't enough to ruin my life, but you kept my sister away from me because you wanted to what? Keep up with appearances? But yet, you're the reason Dad was drinkin' the night of his wreck. That's why he's six feet in the ground because you couldn't keep your legs closed."

"You will not talk to me like that in my house," Tabitha snaps.

"Shelby," I say, and grab her hand. "Come on. We don't need this shit." Shelby looks to me, and I know she's on the verge of crying. I see the tears in her eyes, and I feel awful for putting her through this. All this time I've wanted to know who my mother was but instead, I found a horrible person and hurt Shelby in the process.

"That's right," Tabitha starts with a hateful tone. "Run away just like you always have, Shelby."

"Why don't you just go to hell," I pipe back. "Come on, Shel. Let's go." Thankfully Shelby nods and follows behind me. Hearing Tabitha say something behind us, I ignore her knowing whatever she has to say isn't worth listening to. Shelby and I don't speak to each other as we quickly walk back to her car, and once we get inside, I feel like I might vomit. I can't believe I put Shelby through all that. I should've listened to her when she tried to warn me, but I just had to see for myself. I've been so dead set on meeting our mother for so long, and now I feel as if it's all been one big ass mistake. "I'm so sorry, Shel. I should've listened to you, and now I feel like an asshole for putting you through that."

Keeping my gaze straight ahead, I don't know if I can face Shelby knowing I'm the reason I put her through Tabitha's verbal bashing. I'm not sure what I'm feeling with finding out my own mother never wanted me and thinks I'm a mistake. Honestly

Caden

seeing her and knowing how awful she was toward Shelby and me, I don't know how I should react. For so long I've wanted this, but then again I'm not as hurt as I thought I would be. If anything, I'm glad I know Shelby and I won't ever be coming back here or see her again. Feeling her hand on mine, I glance down at it as she says, "There's no reason for you to be sorry, Savvy." Taking a chance, I look up and see a tear rolling down her cheek. "I know how much you needed to meet her, and it's not your fault she's such an evil person."

"But you're hurting because of me," I quietly say. It feels like a lump is forming in my throat, and seeing her so upset makes me feel like shit.

"No, I'm not hurtin' because of you." Her tone is firm, and I do want to believe her, but I can't. If I never wanted to come here, she wouldn't have gone through what she just had. "I'm hurtin' because just when I thought our mother was done messin' with my life, I find out somethin' new." She wipes a tear from her face with her free hand as she says, "It's not that comin' back here brought back my past with my ex, and seein' our mother again wasn't as bad as I thought it would be. It's just knowin' she went through such great lengths to keep you hidden, and she was the catalyst that ended my father's life." Tears fill my eyes as I listen to her and it's apparent in her voice that she cared very much for her dad. "I've always blamed her for what happened with my dad, and now I know my blame was accurately placed." She squeezes my hand and places her other hand on mine before she declares, "None of this is your fault. Our mother is the one who was selfish and didn't care about us. She's always put her needs before anyone else, and don't for one second think this is on you, Savvy."

Letting out a sob, my tears come, and I don't try to stop them. "All this has been for nothing. You were right about her, and I'm sorry I didn't listen to you." If I could go back, I would've listened to her warnings. I hate knowing I put her through this.

Shelby pulls me into her arms, and I willingly go to her. Wrapping my arms around her, I'm grateful to have her here with me. I know I couldn't have done this without her, and knowing she doesn't blame me for what we've learned makes me feel a bit better. Pulling back, I sniff loudly and use my shirt to clean my face. "I promise you have no reason to be sorry. I know you had to meet her for yourself and now that you have, I hope you can put this behind you and see what you have right in front of you."

"You're right, and I'm glad I know this part of my life is finally over." I am glad I finally know the truth about my mother. Even though she was nothing like I imagined, I know I can finally put this chapter of my life behind me and move forward. I hate Shelby and I had to find out the hard way, but I can't

Caden

regret it. This trip brought Shelby and me closer, and I have a feeling we'll both be alright.

"How about we get the hell out of this shit town?"

Smiling, I nod. Shelby takes in a deep breath then starts the car. She begins to drive down the road, and an idea hits me. "What do you think about taking a trip to Florida?"

"As long as we can lay on a beach, I'm so down for that." With our new destination in mind, Shelby smiles and turns up the radio. Relaxing back in my seat, I have a feeling she's going to love what I have planned.

With Shelby standing by me, I wait anxiously for my mom or dad to answer the door. Normally, I would've just walked in, but I wanted to make sure they were surprised. Shelby still hasn't put it together she's about to meet my parents, and I know this stop will be a lot better than our last one was. I'll admit, I was very wrong about Tabitha, and I'm surprised I'm not more hurt by finding out I was a mistake. I guess a part of me always knew it, and the other part is finally okay with knowing for sure. I can't regret the path I've taken because if I hadn't, I probably would've never met Shelby, the Harlow family, or

Brie Paisley

Annie and William. I don't regret a single thing because I've finally found my family.

My real family. Which is all I've ever wanted.

"Are you goin' to tell me where we are?" Shelby asks.

"Nope. You'll just have to wait and see." Chuckling at her apparent impatience, I say, "Trust me. You're going to love this."

"We're still goin' to the beach later right?"

"Yes. That's a must before we go back home."

"Home huh? So you're comin' back to stay?"

Ringing the doorbell once more, I guess my parents are out back. Turning to Shelby, I grin widely as I honestly say, "Yeah. I think I'll stick with my sister if she's alright with that."

Her face lights up, and she pulls me in for a tight hug. "Of course I'm alright with that. If it were up to me, you'd never leave my sight again."

Pulling away, I smile loving how she wants me by her side. Even if my own mother didn't want me, it's a wonderful feeling knowing Shelby wants me in her life. Before I get the chance to respond, the front door opens. "Hey, Mom," I say with a grin when I see it's her.

Caden

Mom's warm brown eyes fill with tears as she pulls me to her. Embracing her tightly, she whispers, "I'm so glad you're here."

Letting her go, I ask, "Is Dad here?" Once she nods, I steal a glance to Shelby seeing her bright smile. Following Mom inside, I can't help but feel at ease being back home. It feels different now that I know everything I do, and I won't ever take it for granted again. I shouldn't have left the way I had or thought for one second my parents didn't love me because I wasn't actually theirs. The only thing I regret is thinking otherwise. But now I'm determined to show my parents how grateful I am they adopted me and gave me this wonderful life.

While Mom goes to tell Dad we're here, Shelby stands beside me and asks, "So this is your parent's house?"

"I thought you would like to meet them."

"I do. Thank you, Savvy."

Grabbing her hand, I hold it tightly. "Now you'll have my family to add to yours." I know I made the right choice when she nods and squeezes my hand.

There's not a chance I can regret anything knowing all the pain and hurt brought me here. I have my sister by my side, and I'm about to have my loving parents in my life again.

Brie Paisley

Two weeks later...

A lot has changed in the past two weeks. Not only did my parents and I mend our relationship, but they also welcomed Shelby with open arms. Mom and Dad were shocked to find out I had a sister, but that still didn't stop them from treating her like she was already a part of our family. Shelby and I spent a few days with my parents while also hitting the beach, and I learned so much about Shelby and her past. Not to mention mine as well. It was hard to hear how bad Shelby's childhood was, and what all our mother did to her over the years. Shelby also opened up about her first marriage, and I wanted to drive back to South Carolina just to punch Tabitha in the face for having a hand in Shelby's abusive marriage. I've never been more grateful or proud that my sister got out of that situation and found her way back to Carter.

The most shocking thing I learned was who my father was. Shelby was the one that connected the dots, and once she remembered seeing Tabitha cheating, she knew exactly who he was. His name is Maxwell Howell and was Shelby's history teacher, when she was in high school. I'll admit, after everything that happened with Tabitha, I wasn't so quick to find him. Plus after she and I did a Google

Caden

search on him, we found out he's in prison for statutory rape. Needless to say, I thought it would be best to leave my biological parents alone and forget they ever existed.

After our trip to the beach, we finally decided it was time to come back to Mississippi. Since being back, Shelby, Carter, and I have fallen into a regular routine. Every morning we have coffee before they leave to have breakfast with Carter's family, and every morning they ask me to go with them. I wish I could because I miss the rest of the Harlow family, but I know Caden will be there. Even if I miss him more and more with each passing day, I'm still not ready to see him just yet. Shelby tries so hard to get me to talk to him, but I don't know. He hurt me deeply by lying, and as much as I want to forgive him, I'm not ready. Even if I understand now why Caden kept such a secret from me, I still feel betrayed and cheated out of time with Shelby.

Taking a deep breath, my heart feels heavy thinking about Caden. He's never far from my mind, and he's making it harder by texting me all hours of the day. It's as if he wants me to know he's still here and still wants me in his life. Running a hand through my hair, I grab three coffee mugs and place mine under the Keurig. My coffee brews as I wait for Carter and Shelby to make their appearance, and I frown when I hear the doorbell ring. Glancing around the corner, I don't see Carter or Shelby coming to answer it. Deciding I should at least see who it is, I make my way to the front door. Once I open it, I frown as I look around. Seeing no one in sight, I start to shut the door thinking someone is playing ding-dong ditch when I see something out of the corner of my eye. Looking down, my stomach drops seeing the bouquet of white lilies. Taking another look around, I still don't see anyone. Picking up the flowers, I notice a white card attached with my name on the front. I shut the door behind me and pull the card off the flowers. Walking back to the kitchen, I lay the beautiful flowers down on the counter and look at the card.

Flipping it over, I look to see if anyone signed it on the outside. I have a hunch it's from Caden because he's the only one that knows white lilies are my favorite, and I don't know anyone else that would send me flowers. "Who was at the door?" Shelby asks as she walks in the kitchen.

"No one apparently." Turning around, I hold the card in my hand as I glance at her. "They left flowers though."

"Huh," she says like she's not that surprised. "Who are they from?"

"I don't know. I haven't opened the card." Narrowing my eyes when she starts to grin, I ask, "Do you know who they're from?"

Caden

"Why would I know?" She says with a high-pitched tone.

"Why would you know what?" Carter asks as he walks toward Shelby.

"Savvy thinks I know somethin' about her gettin' those beautiful lilies."

They share a knowing glance, and I feel like I'm out of the loop. "Okay guys. What's this about?"

"I have no clue what you're talkin' about," Carter claims, but I see the smirk he's trying to hold back.

"I'm with Carter," Shelby adds. "We have no idea what's goin' on. You should check the card though." Watching her turn to open a cabinet, she pulls out a vase and hands it to me. "You should keep the flowers too. They're too pretty to just sit out on the counter."

Still feeling as if they're in on something that I'm not privy to, I shrug my shoulders and take the vase from Shelby. Placing the flowers in the vase and filling it with water, I set them aside as I look at the card again. "What if they're from Caden?" I ask them both.

Shelby places my coffee mug by me as she quietly says, "Then you read the card. It doesn't hurt to see what he has to say if it is from him."

"Plus," Carter starts. "You read every one of his texts and listen to his voice messages, so this isn't any different."

Letting out a sigh, I guess they're right. Taking my mug, I walk to the kitchen table and sit down. Setting my coffee by me, I wish my heart would stop beating so fast. Deep down I know Caden sent the flowers. It's just a hunch I have. Deciding to find out for sure, I open the card. Seeing the messy handwriting, I swallow hard as I pull out the note and read it what it says.

Sassy Savannah,

I saw these lilies the other day, and I instantly thought of you. I couldn't pass by them without grabbing some for you because I know they're your favorite. They remind me of you because they're beautiful just like you. They're also delicate and should be treated with the utmost care.

I didn't do that, and I hope you know how sorry I am for what I've done. I hope one day you can forgive me and give me a second chance to make it up to you.

I love you, small fry.

C.

Caden

Closing my eyes, I clench my jaw willing the tears that threaten to fall away. Caden knew just what to say to make me think about my choice to stay away from him, and it seems he has a knack for it. A part of me wants to drop everything and go to him. That same part is screaming for me to forgive him, and welcome him back with open arms. But this other part of me is silently saying to be careful, and it reminds me how much he hurt me by lying.

My heart wants Caden.

My mind warns me to stay away.

And yet again, I'm right back where I started when I first met Caden Harlow.

Each day I get a new surprise.

It's gotten to the point where I look forward to seeing what Caden has left for me, and I know Carter and Shelby know what's going on. It's a bit strange how every morning they're conveniently nowhere to be found and how they act once I tell them what I got. They don't seem the least bit surprised by any of this.

The day after Caden sent me flowers, I got a nice backpack with small fry in hot pink embroidery on the front. Inside there were maps, tour packets of

London, England, and a bunch of my favorite snacks. On the third day, I was shocked to find a brand new Canon camera. Shelby and I had a little disagreement about me returning it because I thought it was too much. In the end, Shelby's point won me over.

Today is day four, and I won't lie and say I'm not looking forward to seeing what Caden gives me today. I also won't deny that with each day that he gives me something that I told him about when we had our first date isn't wearing me down because it is. It's not the gifts that are making me listen to my heart more, it's the fact he cares enough to give them to me. Caden actually listened and remembers what I said. Plus with each gift, he leaves a note telling me how much he loves me still and wants another chance. I still haven't fully made up my mind, but I don't think I can go much longer without going back to him.

Standing close by the door, I hear someone walking up behind me. Turning around, I see Shelby with a huge grin on her face. "Waitin' for somethin'?"

"Maybe," I vaguely say.

"What do you think he'll send today?"

"I'm not sure," I say. Glancing at the door, I suck in a breath when I hear the doorbell.

"I think this one is goin' to be the best one yet."

"Why do I get the feeling you knew all about this the entire time?" Looking back, Shelby makes a motion like she's zipping her lips closed. "You're not going to tell me are you?"

"Nope. Now answer the door, Savvy."

Shaking my head, I grin knowing she's acting sassy. "Yes, ma'am." Glancing back once more before I open the door, I frown when I realize Shelby is nowhere in sight. Well that's strange.

Not thinking anything of it, I reach down and twist the doorknob. Pulling the door open, my breath catches in my throat when I see him standing right in front of me. "Hey, small fry." He grins widely, and I realize how much I've missed him. It takes every ounce of willpower not to wrap my arms around him, and kiss him until we both are left panting. "Surprise." He says like he's unsure if he made the right move.

Stepping out outside, I shut the door behind me. "What are you doing here?"

"I wanted to give you your last gift in person," he huskily says. "And I wanted to see you, small fry. I've missed you like crazy."

It takes me a few moments to respond. I'm having a hard time breathing properly. "I've missed you too."

"Really?" It's hard to contain my grin with hearing the shock in his voice. Nodding, he drops his head and when he looks back at me, my heart skips a beat. That's the look of pure love. That's the look Carter gives Shelby, and knowing how much Caden loves me without even saying those words, makes my heart beat rapidly in my chest. "I'm so glad to hear that, Savannah." My face warms hearing him say my name because no matter how many times I hear it, it still sends a tingle throughout my entire body. "Before you say anythin' else, I have a speech prepared."

Shaking my head, I let out a small laugh. "You prepared a speech for me?"

"Well yeah. I thought since I'm here in person, I would just tell you what my note would've said." He seems nervous when I don't say anything in return, and I wait patiently for him to start. "I had everythin' I wanted to say perfectly in my mind, but now that I'm seein' you, I can't remember a damn thing." He pauses for a moment before adding, "You make me forget everythin' but you, Savannah." Watching him with wide eyes, he takes a deep breath before brushing my hair behind my ear. When he drops his hand, I will him to bring it back. I've

Caden

missed his sweet and tender touch. "There's so much I need to say to you, but the first thing I want to say is how sorry I am for what I did. It wasn't right or fair of me to keep somethin' that meant so much to you from you." Caden looks away, and I know he's sorry. It's hard not to believe him with the look of regret on his face. He glances back then says, "I don't expect you to forgive me easily, but I want you to know I don't care how long it takes, I'll be right here fightin' for your forgiveness. I won't stop until you're mine again. Meetin' you has been the best thing that's ever happened to me, and I can't make it another day without you by my side. You're everythin' to me, Savannah. Your beauty, wit, and everythin' about you makes you special. It makes you perfect for me." Swallowing down the lump in my throat, he steps closer to me. My eyes land on his lips when he licks them, and my gaze finds his as he caresses my face with both hands. "If you give me another chance, I swear I'll never hurt you again. I promise to love you with all that I am, make you feel like a fuckin' princess, and give you everythin' you've ever wanted. I can't promise there won't be bumps in the road because I'm me, but I know you'll be right there to put me back in line. I need you, Savannah." When he pulls back, I frown wondering what he's doing. My eyes widen when he pulls out plane tickets from his back pocket, and my heart races as I wait for him to explain. "I bought this ticket for you. It's a one-way ticket to London, England."

My eyes fill with tears as I say, "You bought me a plane ticket to go with the backpack and camera."

"I did, small fry. I want to be the one to give you all your hopes and dreams. I want to be the one to give you that gorgeous fuckin' smile knowin' I gave you everythin' you've wanted. But most of all," he says and pauses as he grabs my hand. "I want to be there to see you spread those wings and be free. I've never seen anythin' quite like it when you let yourself go, Savannah. It's a sight to see, and I hope you'll give me the chance to witness it every single time." A tear rolls down my face, but it isn't because I'm sad. No, it's because he's giving me everything I've ever wanted. Traveling and capturing it on camera has been my dream since I was a child, and I know he's offering me this because he loves me. Gazing into his bright blue eyes, he wipes the tear away and asks, "What do you say, small fry? Will you give me another chance to make it up to you?"

Thinking about it for only a second, I claim, "I have one condition."

"Of course. I'll do anythin' you want, small fry."

Caden

Smiling, I sweetly say, "You have to come with me, and you have to stay with me."

He lets out a sigh, and his shoulders sag. It's as if what I said lifted a weight off him. "I plan on bein' with you forever, small fry." He pulls me to him, and I instantly wrap my arms around his neck. "Plus I bought two tickets, so I'm goin' wherever you go."

Laughing loudly, I ask, "Cocky much?"

His eyes never leave mine as he says, "No. I just was hopin' you'd want me to go with you, so I came prepared."

"Good because I don't want to go anywhere without you."

"I promise you're never leavin' me again. I'll chain your fine ass to me if I have to." Letting out another laugh, I close the distance between us and take his lips. It's a sweet and gentle kiss, but I feel every emotion he's trying to show me. One of his hands caresses my face tenderly as the other pulls me closer even though I can't. It's almost as if he's trying to merge our souls into one, but he doesn't need to even try.

Our souls have been intertwined since the first day we met.

"It's about damn time," Shelby loudly states, and I pull away from Caden.

Standing by him, I take his hand as I ask her, "Have you been listening this whole time?"

"I told her not to," Carter says as he walks up behind Shelby.

"Well I had to make sure she said yes. I mean come on, even I was swoonin' just listenin' in."

Shaking my head, I can't even think about being mad she was eavesdropping. "Thanks for the support I guess," Caden says.

"I got your back," she declares with a wink.

Grinning as Carter pulls Shelby back in the house, I turn back to Caden. My heart swells with so much love seeing him smiling back at me, and I have to suck in a breath when he caresses my cheek. Leaning into his touch, I gaze into his blue eyes. "What is it, small fry?"

"I just realized I never told you something very important."

His eyebrow raises as he asks, "Really? What's on your mind?"

"Oh nothing much. Just that I love you."

I wish I had my new camera to capture the look on his face. It's absolutely priceless. Shock, surprise, and then happiness shine in his eyes as he asks, "You love me?"

Caden

Wrapping my arms around his waist, I look up at him. "I do. I've loved you for a long time now."

"Why didn't you tell me before?"

"Honestly," I start. Taking a deep breath, I confess, "I was scared. The way you make me feel isn't like anything I've felt before. It's powerful, consuming, and utterly breathtaking. But now, I realize I can't be afraid to love you. I can't be afraid to give you my heart."

"You have no idea how good it feels to hear to finally say that."

"I think I have an idea." And I do. Knowing he loves me in return, well it's unlike anything I can explain.

He places a finger on my lips as he huskily says, "I love you too, Savannah. And I'm never lettin' you go ever again."

I know he won't either. I see it in his eyes, hear it in his voice, and most of all I know without a doubt, I can finally let him in. He's always been here for me, even when I didn't want to admit it. He's always had a place in my fragile heart, even when I fought against it. But now I realize there's no fighting what we have. I never had a chance really. Caden Harlow had my heart before I knew he did, and I know he'll protect it.

Brie Paisley

He'll keep it safe and give me all the love I've ever wanted.

Caden

epilogue
Caden

Sitting on the couch across from Savannah's dad, I feel a bit out of place. It's mainly because I've never met the parents before, and because Phillip is glaring at me. Savannah thought it would be a good idea to make a pit stop to see her parents before we head to London, but now I'm not so sure. Miranda was just a peach when Savannah introduced us, Phillip on the other hand, not so much.

Glancing over my shoulder, I smile seeing my small fry in the kitchen with her mom. They're making pies or something. Whatever it is, it smells amazing. Feeling his eyes on me, I slowly turn back around and take a glance at Savannah's dad. God this is so awkward. Not to mention, Phillip is very intimidating. He's a bulky man, and I'm sure he could take me if he tried. It's kind of scary to think about.

He leans forward, and I just know he's about to say something that'll make me shit my pants. "I'm only going to say this once," he starts, and I hold my breath. "If you hurt my little girl, I promise you no one will find your body."

I can tell he's going to be a tough cookie to crack. Which is why I do what I do best. Put my foot in my mouth. "With all due respect, sir. You do know I'm a cop right?"

"You think that'll stop me?"

Pushing out a breath, I glance back to the kitchen. Seeing Savannah laughing with her mom makes me smile, and knowing she's out of earshot, I turn back to her dad. "No. I think you love Savannah just as much as I do." Phillip doesn't even blink as I add, "But I also think you know I would never hurt her." I want to say again, but I keep that part to myself. "One day, I intend on marryin' her and tyin' her to me forever."

"Is that so?" He asks with a serious tone.

"Yes, sir. She's my world, and I'd be stupid not to marry her."

He nods, and I relax some. "That's good to hear. I'm glad we're on the same page then."

He leans back in his recliner, and before I can respond, Savannah walks over by him. "Dad, are you giving Caden a hard time?" She sits on the arm of the chair, and he wraps his arm around her. "Don't let him scare you, Caden. He's all talk."

"I don't know about that, small fry. He kind of scares me."

She laughs, and to my surprise, Phillip grins. "See, pumpkin," he says to Savannah. "I knew this one was smart."

"Phil, I told you to be nice," Miranda scolds.

"I'm being nice." He turns to me and asks, "Isn't that right, Caden?"

Feeling everyone's gaze on me, I quickly say, "Oh yeah. We're like besties now."

Savannah shakes her head as Miranda laughs and says, "I like this one. He's funny." I'm glad I at least have Savannah's mom's approval. I can tell Phillip is going to take a bit more work, but I decide that's alright.

The day I won Savannah back, I was prepared to do anything to keep her. I know Phillip is just looking out for his little girl, and I can respect that. It means he cares about her and loves her. The thing is I hope he realizes that I love her just as much, if not more, and there isn't anything I wouldn't do for Savannah.

Not one thing.

Brie Paisley

Walking hand in hand with Savannah inside the airport, we take our time as we look for our gate. I can't help but smile seeing how her eyes are lit up like a kid at Christmas. Those blue-green eyes take in everything around her, and knowing I'm the reason she's so excited sends a rush of pride through me. Finally finding our gate, I lead Savannah toward the seats by the counter. She sits down beside me, and I notice her legs won't stop bouncing. "Are you nervous, small fry?"

Her head whips to mine as she says, "Not really. I'm more excited than anything."

"And a bit impatient?"

She rolls her eyes, but I see that smile. "Maybe just a little."

"You do realize this flight is goin' to be long right?"

"I know, Caden. I'm just ready to get there and see everything there is to see."

Letting out a chuckle, I have to admire her spunk. "I promise we'll see everythin' there. Did you bring your camera?"

She gives me a look like I'm crazy as she states, "Of course I did. It was the first thing I

Caden

packed." Grinning, I should've known. Since I bought her that camera, she takes it everywhere with her. I mean everywhere. I'm surprised she hasn't tried to capture me on the toilet or something really embarrassing. "You know," she says as she turns toward me. "I never thanked you for doing this for me."

"Doin' what exactly?" I ask.

"You know? Buying our tickets to go visit London, for fighting for me, and for you just being you."

Taking her hand, I place a kiss on the back of her hand. "There's no need to thank me, small fry. I told you I would give you everythin' you've ever wanted, and I make good on my promises."

"I'm beginning to see that."

"Good. Because trust me when I say, this won't be our last trip abroad. I'm goin' to show you the world, small fry."

She smiles brightly at me, and my chest warms seeing it and knowing I'm the reason for it. "I'd like that very much."

"You keep smilin' at me like that, and I might think you love me." Now I'm just messing with her.

She shakes her head before leaning in closer. "You know I love you very much."

Brie Paisley

God I wish she could feel what I do when she says those words. It makes me that happiest man on the planet knowing how she finally feels about me. Every time she utters those three words, my heart beats rapidly in my chest, and I swear there's nothing better than hearing them. Brushing a strand of hair out of her face, I cup her cheek. "I love you too, small fry. I just love hearin' you say it."

She leans into my touch, and I grin knowing how much she loves it. "I know you do. Which is why I tell you all the time."

"I know. And you better keep tellin' me. You know? Just in case I forget." She smiles, and I don't care that we're in an airport full of people. Leaning over the arm rest, I take her lips. Giving her a tender kiss, I savor this moment. I commit every single bit of it to memory because these precious moments cannot be taken for granted.

When she pulls away, she's the only one I see. I know there are a lot of people around us, but it's her I see. It's almost like tunnel vision, except without the light headiness. Gazing into her eyes, I feel like I've just won the most beautiful thing in this world. It's a powerful feeling knowing she's mine again. I won't lie, I was worried I'd lost her forever and I didn't think she would give me another chance.

But she did.

Caden

And knowing she's giving me all of her, every single piece, makes me the luckiest man alive. She's my everything, my soulmate, and my other half.

I'll spend the rest of my life making sure she knows it, and just how much I love her.

the end

about the author
Brie Paisley

Brie Paisley is a small town gal from Mississippi. She always wanted to write at a young age and was always filling journals with her thoughts and short stories. Brie started with the idea of Worshipped a year ago and with the encouragement of her husband and sister in law, she was able to write her first book. When she is not writing, you can find her reading a good book, painting, scrapbooking, or watching a good movie with her husband and her boxer.

Caden

Facebook:
https://www.facebook.com/authorbriepaisley

Twitter: @author_brie

Instagram:@authorbrie_paisley

Made in the USA
Columbia, SC
09 September 2017